X

50690011124184   2017-04-25 7.01 AM

Branard, Lynne

Traveling light

9/27/17

Traveling Light

Center Point
Large Print

Also by Lynne Branard and available from Center Point Large Print:

The Art of Arranging Flowers

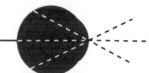

This Large Print Book carries the Seal of Approval of N.A.V.H.

Traveling Light

Lynne Branard

CENTER POINT LARGE PRINT
THORNDIKE, MAINE

This Center Point Large Print edition is published
in the year 2017 by arrangement with
The Berkley Publishing Group, an imprint of
Penguin Publishing Group, a division of
Penguin Random House Company LLC.

The text of this Large Print edition is unabridged.
In other aspects, this book may vary
from the original edition.
Printed in the United States of America
on permanent paper.
Set in 16-point Times New Roman type.

ISBN: 978-1-68324-378-6

Library of Congress Cataloging-in-Publication Data

Names: Branard, Lynne, author.
Title: Traveling light / Lynne Branard.
Description: Center Point Large Print edition. | Thorndike, Maine :
Center Point Large Print, 2017.
Identifiers: LCCN 2017003208 | ISBN 9781683243786
    (hardcover : alk. paper)
Subjects: LCSH: Large type books | BISAC: FICTION / Romance /
Contemporary. | FICTION / Contemporary Women. | FICTION /
Family Life.
Classification: LCC PS3602.R34485 T73 2017b | DDC 813/.6—dc23
LC record available at https://lccn.loc.gov/2017003208

I dedicate this story of what it means
to travel light to the many terminally ill patients
who served as my teachers when I worked
as a chaplain with hospice.
You taught me how to let go of
the many burdens I tend to carry.
You taught me that this journey
on earth is swift and full, and that
I must learn where to pay attention
and where not to linger.
Thank you for the lessons.
I hope you have found that
final journey that we will all take
to be easy and light.

The open heart is not heavy
And love's hold is never tight
To get to where you want to go
You must travel light.

Acknowledgments

On this journey of publication, I travel light because I am surrounded by such smart and capable people who, for whatever reason, have agreed to pilgrim with me. Thank you to Sally McMillan, the agent who transitioned a long time ago to being my friend. You have never said no to me. Thank you to Jackie Cantor, the editor every writer dreams about. Thank you for thinking my stories should move to the printed page and for making sure they get there. Thank you to Sheila Moody, the copy editor, who takes so very seriously the work of fact-checking and smoothing out every bumpy sentence. Thank you to all the staff at Berkley, Bethany and Lauren and all the others; your belief in this book, your support of the story, has carried it to this moment of fullness. Thank you also to Alissa Searby for first bringing the story of "finding a box of ashes" to my attention and for being such a rock star.

On this journey of life, I travel light only because I am surrounded by kindness and love. Thank you to my family and friends who graciously haven't gotten sick of me and chosen a different path, pace, or partner. I am not easy, I realize, so the persistence and care, the delight and support I receive on a daily basis, sustain and energize me. I can be my best self because of this love. You bear witness to the Divine for me, and I am eternally grateful.

And finally, to my husband, Bob, this journey would mean nothing without you beside me every step of the way. I love you. You and Carmella are my favorite traveling companions on the interstate as well as on the highways and byways of life.

Chapter One

The only thing I remember about Mama was how she was always moving. Years before the small tumor grew, the mania finally linked to the cancer in her brain, Mama never stopped moving. I think it wore Daddy out, but I loved it. I loved her. The way she danced while she cooked our breakfast, pancakes delivered to the table as if she were a rock star shimmying to the final notes of the Rolling Stones' "Beast of Burden," the way she lifted my sister from the crib, twirling her the whole time with me straddling her foot, clinging to her leg. She would sweep and sing, stopping just long enough to clutch the broom like a diva with her microphone. She'd change the furniture in the living room, giving us new hiding places for another round of hide-and-seek, and she would strap both of us in the backseat of that old station wagon and drive to the ocean or south to White Lake or even all the way to Asheville and the cold, foggy Blue Ridge Mountains and their twisting, curvy roads. She could not stay still.

Of course, I never knew she was sick or exhausted. I never knew that the dancing and the spinning and the driving and the darting from one place to another were symptoms of illness. I thought she was immortal. I thought I was the luckiest child alive to have a mother always buying new paint sets and giving us long rolls of white paper to decorate, a mother who seemed to know the most beautiful spots for girls-only picnics, a mother who was able to balance on her toes while she hung the sheets on the line in the backyard, calling us to come and smell the sunshine caught in the wide stretch of fabric. I thought the movement and the action were simply a part of the great adventure of life, of childhood; and I woke up every morning wondering what she had planned for that day and how she would dance my sister and me through every minute of it.

And then, one day in the spring of my fifth year, she simply stopped moving. She stopped dancing and spinning and changing the pictures on the walls and cleaning the house from ceiling to floor, finding coins and sliding them into our palms, telling us they were gifts from angels; and suddenly everything I knew about being a child —every step, every movement, every lift and twirl—came to an abrupt and unexpected halt. Everything just stopped. The music, the dancing, the laughter, the games, the unlimited extravaganza of our imaginations, all of it seemed to freeze in time, all of us standing in the wake of her death, paralyzed by our loss.

And now, thirty years after she died, I realize I haven't moved an inch since then. At the age of five I sat down in my life; I took my mother's place in raising my sister and caring for my father and keeping the house neat and clean with only scant movements and no flair and I never stepped away. Until now. Until I pulled open the big overhead door on that storage unit in Wilmington and pilfered through the cartons of driftwood and the bins of tools and the baskets of rope and the stacks of boating magazines, blankets, and camping equipment, all the way to the back, and found the box. The box I see now placed in the passenger's seat of Faramond, my old Volkswagen Bug that Daddy bought for me at my high school graduation, giving me the permission to leave which I did not take. The box of ashes with a business card and a receipt from the Serenity Mortuary in Grants, New Mexico, taped on top. This box of ashes that is now sending me away from my home. This box of ashes that is finally making me move.

Exactly nine weeks ago I entered my name and random bid in the storage war meant to be a promotion for a television station in Raleigh. I had seen the reality show that was being imitated by WRAL. I had watched the winners strutting behind the chain-link fences, over to their newly claimed vaults, opening the doors and finding all kinds of meaningless junk and often wonderfully unexpected treasures. I watched as they found buyers for their eighteenth-century antique tables, their glass trinkets, and their refurbished wooden trunks and highboy chests. I saw their eyes light up as the cash register tallied their sales and the money changed hands; and so without too much thought I turned on my computer, found the registration site, stuffed a cookie in my mouth, and typed in my name, Alissa Kate Wells. I gave my phone number and address and casually put in a bid of one month's salary, gross, not net, from my job at the *Clayton Times and News*, where my father is my boss. I hit send on the top of the Web page and in a few days forgot I had even done such a thing.

When the e-mail arrived saying I had won the contents of a storage unit at the Affordable Storage Facility in Wilmington, North Carolina, I thought it was spam, unwanted advertising. I was just about to hit delete when I remembered the contest. Suddenly I recalled the evening I'd heard about the promotion and how I had just gotten off the phone with my sister, Sandra, and how I walked over to the pantry, opened another box of Girl Scout cookies, the snickerdoodles, the ones Daddy buys but doesn't like, went back to my computer, and entered the WRAL storage unit bidding war.

Once I arrived in Wilmington to claim my prize, it was an hour before I found the box of ashes. Later I called the funeral home located in the small mining town west of Albuquerque, trying to find the family that belonged to the person whose remains had been placed in a small wooden box with a butterfly carved on top, and ultimately abandoned in a storage building in North Carolina. And it was two weeks later that I packed my hatchback Faramond with bottles of water and my last box of snickerdoodles; called Millie to watch Old Joe, my blind cat, and water the boxes of pansies that I had just planted around my grandmother's house, now mine, on Tree Street; and helped Casserole get in the back, holding his hip and pushing him in so that his three legs didn't tangle on the suitcase or the bags of groceries I'd stowed there.

I called Daddy last night to tell him I was taking my vacation, the days I hadn't used now accumulated to over four months. We talked about the early rains and whether the Democrats were going to lose control of the House and then I told him.

"Dad, I'd like to take a trip."

"Yeah, to Paris? Idaho? You want to go fly-fishing with me?"

"I need to go to New Mexico."

"Not much fly-fishing there."

"I need to return something I found."

"What?" he asked, and I told him about winning the contest, about all the stuff I'd found in the storage unit and carried back to the house, how I'd crammed it all in my garage with plans to do something with it later.

Then I answered the question. I told him what I'm taking back to New Mexico.

"Ashes," I said. "A box of someone's remains. I found them and I want to take them back to where he lived."

"You need me to go?" he asked.

"Nope, it's just for me," I confessed.

And then, there were just a few moments of silence until he asked me if I had trained Dixie on how to set the copy, reminded James William when to call for the advertising, and showed Ben how to size and crop the photographs. After I answered yes to his questions about the state of the newspaper, he just told me to have a good time. And that was it. No seasoned reporter's questions of when, where, how, and why. No employer's diatribe about the mess I was leaving him with. No interest in what the ashes meant to me. He just poured out a long breath the way he always did when he was stumped about a story and told me to call when I got to where I meant to go, keep a quart of oil in the car, watch the engine light, and have a good time.

And just like that, I am heading west to a place most people in my hometown don't even know is a state in our fine union to deliver the remains of a man that no one has claimed. I have along with me my trusty companion, Casserole, a little-bit-of-everything mutt that showed up at my door nine years ago; a box of motor oil; a hundred dollars' worth of drinks and snacks; a map, even though James William showed me the new MotionX GPS Drive app that I could purchase on my phone; and these ashes. I loaded up and I'm ready to go. I am driving away from the only place I have ever lived, listening to Mick Jagger, tapping my fingers on the steering wheel. I am alive and moving.

As I pull out of my driveway and down to the corner where I make a turn to get onto Interstate 40, I imagine my mother dancing, smiling down from wherever she is, watching me. For some reason, I think she must be proud.

Chapter Two

"You use regular for that, right?"

He is beside me before I even turn off the engine. Tall, skinny, his thin black hair slicked back into a ponytail, he leans in, his face just above the top of the window I rolled down for the late-morning breeze after the sun came up. The name *Buster* is sewn on a patch pinned to the top left pocket of his long-sleeved denim shirt, and I can see the edge of a tattoo trailing beneath the collar. He is smiling and his eyes never leave my face. He does not take note of anything else in my car and it's easy to see that he is used to minding his own business.

"Credit?"

I nod. "Yes to both questions," I answer. "And use the low octane."

I glance around. It's surprising in this day and age to have someone show up to pump my gas, and at first I think maybe I have mistakenly stopped at a full-service venue and will be paying more for the assistance.

"There's no charge for the service," he explains, clearly used to the surprise of his customers.

I smile and hand him my card.

"No knocking?" he asks, stepping back and turning to the pumps.

"No knocking," I reply, demonstrating my understanding of the language of a car mechanic. Low octane means the engine is running smoothly and a higher grade of gasoline isn't necessary.

Buster inserts my credit card, punches in a code, and pulls down the handle. He returns to my open window and hands me back my card.

My daddy taught me the basics of automobiles when I was twelve. After Mama died there were few places where he was comfortable around his two daughters. One was anywhere outside he considered wild, including the patch of woods at the far end of town and down along the banks of the murky Neuse River. Another was in his office at the newspaper, where we would often play under his desk when he was researching a story or putting the final touches on a late edition.

The place where he seemed the most relaxed, however—a man standing between two little motherless girls—was in front of one of his cars, the hood open, his hands and arms greasy from his work, leaning forward, stretching out across the radiator and filters, explaining to the both of us where to check the oil, why it was important for a person to know that the pistons were firing correctly, and how to stop an engine from rattling.

Sandra never stood alongside him for more than ten minutes before she would head back inside the house to play with her paper dolls or, when she got older, to flip through the pages of a fashion magazine; but I stayed as long as he did, trying to take in anything he could teach me, soaking in every second of what it was to feel him at ease, comfortable in his skin and at home, happy to have me near him.

I watch Buster move to the rear of my car and open the gas tank cover. He screws off the cap and starts pumping. I can hear him whistle softly as he leaves the gas tank and moves around to the front of the car to clean the windshield.

I look in the rearview mirror. Casserole is sitting up and I know he needs to take a walk. I leave my place, open the door, push up the seat, attach the leash to his collar, and lead him out. Even though this isn't a spot we have been before, he seems to know right where he needs to go so I simply follow, holding the leash loosely in my hand.

The sun is out of the eastern sky, high and uncovered by the clouds of the night before. It is a southern summer, early but already in its fullness; the air is thick and humid, the wild daylilies are stretching to reach light above the ditch banks, and the gnats and mosquitoes, already out for the morning, are buzzing around my head. It is a good day to leave.

"Hurry up, Cass," I say as I slap at my neck, missing the flying insect that has already drawn blood. "I'll need bug repellent if we stay out here much longer."

Casserole sniffs around the narrow stretch of grass planted next to the gas station, finally finding a clump of bottlebrush where he's able to steady himself on his three legs and do his business. I watch only for a second and then glance away, knowing that even years after he came to live with me, it still bothers him to have an audience. He quickly moves on, retreating to the car, where Buster is topping off the gas and replacing the pump handle back into its holder.

"There's a bowl of water by the door," Buster says, wiping his hands on a rag that must have been in his back pocket.

"Oh, that's okay, I have some in the car." I help Casserole back into his place in the backseat, unhook his leash, and get the gallon bottle of water that I have prepared for him.

He waits until I have finished pouring it and

placed the bowl on the seat beside him. He looks at me, his way of saying thanks, and then drinks, careful not to spill.

"You want me to check your oil, tire pressure, anything else?" Buster asks, and it suddenly dawns on me that I should probably tip him. I step back to the front seat and reach for my purse.

"I don't take tips."

I begin to wonder if he can read minds.

"The women's room is around back," he says then, and now I'm sure he must be a little psychic since that was going to be my very next question.

"Do I need to move the car?" I ask, speaking quickly, glad that he hasn't answered that one, too.

"Nah." He shakes his head slowly. "It's usually slow this time of day. Next customer won't be here for another hour or so." He glances out toward the highway as if he knows the direction of the anticipated car.

I follow his eyes and we stand there together in a moment of silence.

"I'm going to New Mexico," I tell him.

He nods like he knew my plans and puts his hands on his belt, sticking his thumbs in the loops. He appears to be thinking, and he doesn't take his eyes off the interstate.

I peer where he is looking, but I can't seem to see whatever has captured his attention.

"It's a nice drive out there," he finally says. "Road is good."

A long truck speeds past. And then a moving van, and then a sports car.

"I've never been beyond Tennessee," I confess. "I don't know what to expect."

He turns to me and I don't know why I'm suddenly sharing such private information with this stranger. I rarely give out such details of my life; I have always been the one to gather the data, reluctant to share any of my own personal details.

And just like that, I realize that I learned more from my father than simply how to clean a carburetor and replace spark plugs. I also learned the paper business. Oscar Wells, the publisher and editor in chief of the *Clayton Times and News*, taught his elder daughter how to get the news, how to write it in five hundred words or less, and how to fit it into six vertical columns with margins on four sides. I learned how to measure out the gutters and raise the cost of advertising when customers demanded a double truck. I learned how to ask the questions and not to bury the lead. I even learned how to size the photographs and decide where to make a jump.

And I learned something else, something even more profound. My father taught me how to keep from talking about myself, how to navigate the conversation away from what I thought or how I felt. He taught me how to steer clear of the details of my own life story, how to turn diversion into an art form.

"Everything changes just outside of Little Rock," Buster says, pulling me away from my thoughts, making me wonder about the great state of Arkansas and what I might find there.

I turn to hear more, but, just like a good reporter, Buster isn't giving much away. "The sky just seems to stretch out in front of you, deep and long and blue." He shakes his head. "You'll see," he adds and then turns to walk back into the station. And I am left staring at the road that lies before me, feeling like I have just received some blessing.

Chapter Three

"They're in the top drawer of Dixie's desk," I tell James.

I am three hours into the trip, still in North Carolina; and the story of my departure is just now settling upon the staff at the paper. This is the second call I've had since watching the flatlands of eastern North Carolina rise to foothills. The first one came just as I weaved through Winston-Salem, choosing to take the business route because I like the way the road seems to go right through the middle of Baptist Hospital. It's more interesting to me than the interstate.

Ben called first to congratulate me on winning the storage war and seemed to think this trip was somehow a part of the spoils of victory. He assumed I was gone just for a day and simply wanted to know where I had filed the photographs he e-mailed to me over the weekend.

Ben fancies himself a professional photographer, an artist, and keeps his digital cameras locked up in an aluminum case. He does often find interesting shots, but the idea of his pictures of car wrecks and construction sites being art is more than just a stretch. Still, he's a decent guy, taught high school business classes until he retired and came to work at the paper. He's got a comb-over that starts just above his right ear and he wears the same outfit he wore when I took his class as a sophomore—black trousers and a white button-down short-sleeved shirt, three ballpoint pens in the front breast pocket. He's only altered his wardrobe once that I know of and that was when James William told him he looked like a Mormon. The next day he changed to a light blue shirt, the same pants, and the same three ballpoint pens sticking up from the front left pocket. He went back to white when the weather changed and the missionaries returned to college.

Ben hung up and ended our conversation before I could explain that I was going to be gone for longer than just one weekly edition of the paper. A man of few words, he never will stay on the phone for very long.

This call is from James William, the man who

motivated Ben to modify his wardrobe. James is our other full-time employee. He covers sports and crime. He runs around with all the policemen and sheriff's deputies and likes to think he can still play ball. He called because he can't find stamps.

"It's tight," he says, and I know he means that this week's edition is crammed with ads and that my story about the possible closing of the post office in Wendell won't make the cut. "Leslie Peele bought an ad to celebrate Lucy's graduation and apparently the word got out. We have a full page completely dedicated to members of the Class of 2016. The Senior Wildcats are running rampant."

"You didn't use that as the streamer, did you?" I asked. James sometimes gets a little carried away with his sports headlines.

"Nah, you know the old man wouldn't let that happen."

Right and thank God, I think but do not say. Daddy is a great editor and never lets a paper be printed that he hasn't gone through story by story, line by line.

"Anyway, we'll hold your P.O. story and my baseball forecasts for next week's news hole. There isn't too much going on over at the court-house so there's just farming reports and another story about the bypass scandal."

I signal, merge over to the left lane to pass a

semi struggling to get up the hill. James William has been covering the story of the North Carolina highway expansion projects and the state legislators cited for passing the contracts to their buddies.

"When you coming back?" he asks.

I hit the gas pedal and watch to see if the engine light comes on, since it sometimes does that in the summer. "I don't know exactly," I tell him. "A couple of weeks, maybe more. I'm not sure."

"But you *are* coming back, right? You ain't having one of those midlife crisis and left for good?"

I'm not sure which bothers me the most about this sentence, the bad grammar or the fact that James William thinks I'm having a midlife crisis.

"I'm thirty-five years old, James."

Well, now I guess I know what bothers me most.

"And I'm not having a crisis."

There is a pause and I wait. The sportswriter is doing math.

"You're only eleven years older than me?"

"Than I."

"Than I what?"

"Eleven years older than I. Not me, I. Never mind; that correction remains debatable."

"Right, okay." He breathes into the phone. He never hides his frustration at grammar lessons. At least I don't have to see him roll his eyes.

"Yes, I am only eleven years older than you."

"Jeez, you seem more like you're my mom's age. She had a midlife crisis a couple of years ago, but she didn't leave town like you—she bought a tanning bed."

I glance in the rearview mirror just to get Casserole's reaction. He has heard this kind of conversation more than a few times. He stands up on the seat and circles around his blanket, pointing his backside in my direction, his way of letting me know what he thinks of James William.

"She sold it after she got stuck in it that time."

Now I'm hooked on this conversation. I haven't heard this story, and besides, I've never really liked James's mother. Kimmie Johnson sings soprano and thinks I should cover it when she's giving a solo at church or singing the national anthem at a soccer match. She likes to make the news.

"She was yelling and screaming. Finally, Coach Brown's wife heard her, thought she was being molested or something, called the cops; and Reggie had to get her out. I guess she wasn't wearing much 'cause they both still act really weird when they see each other. He quit singing in the choir and she drives way out of her way not to have to pass by the police station. Neither one of them will talk about it and she won't go out anymore without slathering on the sunscreen; so I don't know what happened."

I hear what sounds like a desk drawer closing.

"Anyway, I found them. Dixie had 'em way stuffed in the back. How come we can't never keep no scissors around here?"

I'm not even going to attempt to work with that one.

"All right, thanks, Al. We'll see you." And he hangs up the phone without waiting for a reply.

"Yep," I say to no one.

James William has been with the paper for four years. He was the star quarterback of the high school football team, had a scholarship to play at State but blew out his knee trying to do some street dance at the senior prom. He started his freshman year in Raleigh, but from the stories I've heard, he drank and smoked a lot of pot, and got thrown out of school. He was heading down the wrong path when my dad saw him at a high school game a year or so later and struck up a conversation. The next thing I knew I was teaching the town jock how to tell the difference between a sidebar and a shirttail and editing everything he wrote.

Four years later, he still doesn't know when he dangles his participles, but he certainly knows how to run down scores and even make football sound interesting. And he loves to hang out at the courthouse and find out who got arrested or sued. Most of the stories we can't print, because it's the local business advertising that keeps us afloat. If we mentioned the names of everybody who spent a night or two in jail, we'd end up with only church and anniversary ads. We'd be shut down in a week.

"Midlife crisis," I say to myself and to my dog. "I have just turned thirty-five and as far as I know from writing obituaries, most everybody lives past seventy. I'm not even close to the middle of my life."

But the truth is I don't know how much time I have left. Maybe I *have* lived almost half of the span of my life. Maybe I will just make it to seven decades. In fact, if I had only my mother's genes, her unexpected inclination toward brain tumors, her unchecked cerebral cells growing and mutating, I'd already be dead. I'd have been gone for as many years as James William has been reporting sports for the *Times and News*.

Apparently my stem cells are stronger than any irregular ones and I sidetracked an early demise. And so I've simply gone along like every other person, pretending I have plenty of years left to do whatever it is I think I'm supposed to do, offended at the very thought that I might be running out of time.

I look at myself in the rearview mirror and I see the beginnings of the crow's-feet at the corners of my eyes, the tiny lines at the edges of my smile. And I turn back to face the road. If I am having a midlife crisis and I will be dead before I'm seventy, then at least I'll die before I'm old and wrinkled and unable to read the news and correct the mistakes I find there; and, unlike Kimmie Johnson, I'll still be able to look the local police officers in the eye.

Chapter Four

Roger Hart is the name of the man whose remains I believe to be resting in the small wooden box now strapped in the passenger's seat beside me. I glance over at it once again, something I have been doing fairly regularly since I left Clayton, to remind myself why I'm doing what I'm doing.

The butterfly carved on top is in profile. It is the complete outline of only one wing, one side, the other one hidden from the wood-carver's view. The insect seems to be perched upon some unseen branch or stem, awaiting something before taking off. Like me.

The waiting, the inability to move on and transition, the sitting in space unable to take the next step because of not having the next step to take, these were the thoughts that kept me up night after night once I'd found the ashes. The soul of some man named Roger Hart has been stuck in a box in the back of a storage building in Wilmington, North Carolina, two thousand miles away from the last place he was, two thousand miles away from the mortuary that cremated him, two thousand miles away from where he made his home, lived his life, and died.

I feel responsible for getting him back to Grants, New Mexico, his last known address, so that he can get on to the next step. I feel somehow charged with the duty to return him so that the butterfly can spread both wings, lift itself upon the gentle breeze, and fly away, free. A spirit stuck and lost and forgotten will finally be released. It seems like the least I can do now that the box is mine.

"Are you going to stop by and see your sister?" That's what Millie asked me when I explained where I was going.

When I called and told her my plans she was happy to feed Old Joe and watch the house because she hasn't forgotten how I took care of things for her when she had that stay at the rehab center in Southern Pines. She knows I know she wasn't hospitalized because she mixed up her medicines while staying with her cousin and attending a family reunion like she told everybody else in town. In fact, she showed me the discharge papers documenting her suicide attempt and providing the name and number of a psychologist in Goldsboro she was given and was planning to see. She trusted me with the truth, but she never talked about it, only said how grateful she was to be away from the sorrowful memories of Pinehurst, their hold on her still vast and far-reaching, and how appreciative she was that I'd watered her peonies and picked up her mail and aired out her house.

There's a story there, of course, but I never pushed. Some things, I have learned since working at the paper, aren't meant to be reported.

"I doubt it," I said, feigning indecisiveness even though I knew with great certainty I wasn't going to stop in Asheville and see Sandra. "I think she's at her beach house now anyway," I added, trying to sound like my sister and I had actually discussed the location of where she might be when I drove through.

"Well, that's a shame," Millie replied and then let it go after that.

I know she thinks Sandra and I are still close. She watched us grow up, watched how I took care of my little sister, how I learned to cook the family meals and looked out for her when we walked to school, how I set her on the handlebars of my bike and rode to Martha Day's dance studio on Main Street until I could drive and then took Daddy's car three days a week to Raleigh to get her to dance classes so that she could compete in contests and win all those pageants.

My neighbor thinks having a sister must be the best thing in the world because she only had brothers; and for some reason the image of Sandra and me standing side by side in front of Daddy, dressed in new Easter dresses, holding hands, smiling even though our mother was dead and gone, is the picture she likes to keep in her mind.

Millie doesn't know that Sandra learned how to fill up a room and take over a place by the time she was eight years old, how she charmed her way into getting things from people—money, lessons, clothes, grades, engagements—how she thought I actually enjoyed doing everything for her, and how, even though she claims differently, she really doesn't remember our mother. My elderly neighbor, wrestling with her own demons of depression and despair, doesn't know about the fight we had when Sandra was a freshman and I was a senior. She doesn't know how my sister stole away the only boy I ever loved, how rotten she is to Daddy, how she shrugs away my requests and never even realized how broken was my heart. Millie likes to think I'm happy, and why should I take that away?

I glance over again at the box, at the remains of Mr. Roger Hart, the stilled butterfly carved on top, and wonder if he had siblings. I wonder if there's some sister in New Mexico who doesn't know what happened to the ashes of her loved one and who will weep at the sight of the box, who will clutch the remains to her chest and tell me a story of some break-in after the funeral or some crazy mishap of boxes and belongings and how she lost the ashes and thought they would never be found. She will say again and again how much it means that I found them and that I returned her beloved family member to her and promise her eternal gratitude and we will exchange phone numbers and e-mail addresses, promising to stay in touch.

Or maybe there's a brother who will open the door, firmly plant his feet, pull back his shoulders, and tilt his chin, keep his hands loosely at his sides, smile the perfect smile, asking first if there is some compensation that will be given along with the ashes or if there were other items recovered from the storage building. Once these issues are cleared up and it's explained that there is nothing else to hand over, he'll exchange a warm and confident handshake with me and tell me that as much as he'd like to become involved, this is really not the best time for him and it is actually better handled by someone else. There will be the most sincere expression provided with the apology; but in the end, since there is no benefit, there will be no assistance offered.

This thought crosses my mind and I realize that I am still slightly bitter regarding my sister. Even though what happened between Sandra and me occurred a very long time ago, I have not let it go.

I pass the second exit into the town of Asheville, the one I'd normally take to get to my sister's house. I would then drive along the state highway north for six or eight miles to the gated tree-lined driveway that winds up the side of a hill. There the grand estate sits, overlooking the city where she still thinks she reigns as queen, married to her king. There I'm sure I would find her eating her chef-prepared dinner with her perfect husband and her perfect children. She'd be drinking her second glass of wine and watching herself in the gilded mirror she hung next to the table, so approving of how it all turned out, so sure it was all by her own doing.

I hit the gas without even looking north.

"I hope it's a brother," I say to the box as I drive west, chasing the setting sun. "I imagine we'll do better if there are just men involved."

I think about Daddy and the things he has told me about his family, especially about his twin brother and how hard they fought as children. How they gave each other black eyes, knocked out teeth, and pummeled each other all the way through their childhood and adolescence, but managed to build a genuinely good relationship later. I think about how he came to love his sibling, how he still calls Uncle Mack every Sunday evening to talk about sports and cars and anything else that happens to come up, how he seems happy and relaxed after making that contact every week.

I glance in the rearview mirror, watch the cars taking the exit and heading in the direction of Sandra's fancy house.

"If I find a female sibling and if she's got something against you," I mutter out loud, "well, I'm afraid I can't help you with her. Girls got their own ways to pummel."

I reach over and tap the top of the box.

"You're on your own if we find a sister."

Chapter Five

First stop is Newport, Tennessee, just across the state border from North Carolina, west of the Great Smoky Mountains, east of Knoxville. It's a town defined more by the east-to-west interstate traversing through the middle of town than it is by the Pigeon River that first brought the European settlers to the area in the early 1800s. And it's big enough to have hotels that are pet friendly but small enough that I won't be stuck in some horrible commuter traffic when I leave in the morning. Newport is situated along the banks of that river and near the confluence of the French Broad, the Pigeon, and the Nolichucky in an area once known as the Forks of the River but now simply referred to as Douglas Lake, created in the 1940s. There's a railroad station, a county courthouse, and a very rich history of moonshiners and shady lawmen. There is also a nice diner near the Holiday Inn that serves sweet iced tea and fried pickles and has just been designated

"Cobbler Capital of the Smokies," according to the write-up added to the menus at all the tables.

I decide on the blueberry cobbler, since it's too early for peaches and a little late for strawberries; and with a scoop of vanilla ice cream, I am happy to give them my vote to keep their cobbler capital title. The waitress, however, informs me the ballots have already been collected for this year's contest. The next one doesn't start until blackberry season, sometime in the fall.

"What comes after that?" I ask.

"Nothing until the cherries," she replies, looking a little gloomy. "There's a cobbler lull in the winter," she adds. "We sometimes freeze the fruit and make a mixed berry one in December; but nobody is really interested. We're all about the pies after Halloween."

She's a young girl, not yet twenty, I'd say, and her name tag reads *Blossom,* which I find a little dehumanizing. As a salesperson, she seems to know her product better than most; and as a member of the food service industry, she is quick and professional. If I were a food writer or a restaurant critic, I'd give her four out of five stars just for not calling me honey when she took my order and for the way she can carry four plates on both arms without any apparent effort. Blossom is no lightweight.

Daddy used to have a restaurant review in the paper. He rated places with little fork icons instead of stars and for a few months we got to eat for free at every place in Clayton and Smithfield. We'd go to the downtown Denny's for breakfast, Dizzy's Hot Dogs for lunch, and sometimes even dress up a little and hit the steak house for dinner on the weekends. It wasn't long, however, before he ran out of local places to appraise. And when he contacted restaurants in one of the other towns—Raleigh or Durham, for example— no one really cared about how many forks they got in the *Clayton Times and News*, and it got to be too expensive to run the reviews. Besides, we both gained ten pounds and knew we needed to eat more meals at home.

After a while Daddy ditched the restaurants for movies. And we still get to go to the cinema for free. He prides himself on giving good critiques, although some of the Baptists have complained that he sees too many R-rated movies and they want a more "family-friendly" column. But Daddy refuses to waste his time watching "cartoons," as he likes to call the G-rated films. I think he's about to hand it all off to Dixie, who has been practicing how to write quick and informative reviews and who happens to have a two- and a six-year-old. It would be one more writing assignment he's given away this year. I know something is going on with him; I just don't know what and I haven't asked. I guess I'm afraid to hear what he'd have to say.

"You want some more tea?" Blossom is standing behind the counter but close enough to my table that I know she is talking to me. She's pretty in a bohemian kind of way, long hair, no makeup; she's the kind of girl I always wanted to be.

I shake my head. "The caffeine will keep me up," I reply. "I'm hoping to get a good night's sleep, since I always have trouble when I'm away from home."

"Where's that?"

"East of here, North Carolina."

She nods. "You're not that far from home, then," she says.

"Not yet," I reply, thinking she will probe a little more.

"Warm milk?" she asks, not probing at all.

"You serve warm milk?" The suggestion surprises me.

She shrugs. "Some of the truckers say it works after driving all day. They're all trying the melatonin and the tryptophan, green tea, warm milk—anything natural, since there's a lot more random drug testing now. After that famous comedian got messed up when his limousine was hit by a booted Walmart trucker, the drivers say they get cupped in every state."

I assume "cupped" means giving a urine specimen, but I don't ask. There are other diners sitting near me and I doubt they want to hear the word "urine" while they're eating their fried pickles.

"You serve a lot of truckers?"

"That's our bread-and-butter," she answers.

"Or cobbler?" I reply, smiling.

"You're funny." She cocks her head when she says this and I get the sense that she really thinks I am.

"No, not really," I say, wondering why I'm disclosing a truth of my personality to a young waitress named Blossom, wondering if being on the road has already loosened me somehow.

She heads around the counter and is now standing next to my table.

"Where you heading on your trip?"

"West to New Mexico," I answer.

She nods slowly, like a woman with more years of life experience than I had first imagined. I notice a tattoo on the inside of her arm. It looks like a stem with small green leaves wrapping around her biceps.

"I've been there. Went with a vanload of hippies last spring. Rainbow Family," she adds.

"I've heard of them," I respond.

Jasper, a crusty old journalist from New York who moved to North Carolina and settled in Clayton about ten years ago, covered them in the seventies. I've heard about them for years. Mostly young, mostly harmless, traipsing about the country spreading goodwill. Blossom looks like she would have fit right in.

Jasper won a Hillman Prize for the reporting.

I read the piece and I thought he was fair and that the writing was decent although not exactly what I would call "award winning." He sometimes handles the features for the paper when Daddy and I are swamped with some national news story that everybody expects will be covered.

Jasper said he lived with the Rainbow Family for six months, which I guess is investigative reporting at its finest. Truthfully, I always thought Jasper stayed with the hippies more for the "free love" than he did for the writing; but that's just my prejudice showing. Jasper just never struck me as a committed journalist and he seems to talk about sex a lot.

"We camped along a river up near Colorado. In fact, it looked a lot like it does here." She smiles. "But it wasn't here," Blossom notes as| she buses my table.

"How long were you gone?" I move my arms so she can pick up my plate and the napkins I balled up and placed near my knife.

"Just a few weeks," she replies, taking away my glass and utensils.

She holds the dirty dishes in her hands, peering out the window facing the highway, reminiscing, I suppose.

"It was fun in the beginning," she tells me. "We'd drive awhile and then camp out under the stars. We cooked everything on a campfire, told stories, sang all these old folk songs, smoked some good weed," she says, nodding, looking like she doesn't care at all that she's confessing to a crime.

"But in the end, you missed Newport. You missed your home," I say, thinking I know how this chapter ends, thinking that she's standing next to me because her hippie trip didn't work out and that the moral of her story is that there is no place like home.

"Nah, it wasn't that," she answers. "I was pregnant when I left Tennessee. Didn't know it until I was halfway up to Washington State."

The change of direction surprises me.

"Not really fair for a baby to be born in a van. Figured I'd get a little more help here than I would living with people who don't own anything more than sleeping bags and Grateful Dead CDs."

"And your baby?" I ask, thinking she's probably going to pull out her phone and show me photographs.

"Never happened," she says with no real emotion. "Lost him the first night I got back."

I glance away. I have always been unnerved by loss.

"Best thing, really," she adds and I'm not sure if she's telling the truth or just trying to ease the awkwardness that has now edged between us. "I figure I'm much better at pushing cobbler than I am at being a mother right now."

I turn to her and smile. I like Blossom. There

is more to her than I have given her credit for.

"I'll have the milk," I tell her, happy to take her suggestion.

"It'll help," she says as a final assurance and walks away.

Chapter Six

It is Casserole who wakes me up just as the sun is rising in the east over the Smokies. He is sitting next to me, his hot breath blowing on my face. I blink and yawn and suddenly remember that I was dreaming of a book of pictures, a photo album of sorts, the pages flipped and turning too fast for me to discern them. I was asking questions even as I dreamed. *Are these pictures of people I know? Are they from the archives of the paper?*

I merely watched as the pages turned, detached from the book, detached from what the book represented, harboring very little concern or emotion regarding the faces or events I did not recognize. In my dream, I could tell that the album clearly represented a well-documented life but not an especially interesting one.

"Well, I told you to get me up before seven," I say to my companion as I sit up and glance over at the clock on the bedside table. It's just after six. "But I think you might be taking your job just a bit too seriously."

Casserole turns and looks toward the door and then looks back at me. He has waited long enough and needs to go outside.

My old dog was already three-legged when he showed up at my back door. He was skinny and weary, but still retained a certain amount of confidence that he was actually where he was supposed to be. I sat with him for a few minutes, rubbing his head, talking to him while assessing his physical condition. He wasn't bloody and didn't seem to be hurt; and after giving him some water and a little something to eat, I drove him over to the vet's office.

After a thorough examination, Clifford Hill, Clayton's only veterinarian, seemed to think Cass was born this way, that the smooth tiny stump that should be a right front leg was not the result of an injury or fight. He thought then and still thinks that the dog is way too adept at movement and survival, that this handicap is clearly too much a part of his canine identity to have been a recent occurrence. He said Casserole just seems naturally accustomed to an unsteady life and that his knack of achieving balance is a true lesson for us all.

I figure our veterinarian talks this way because of his background in ministry. Clifford went to seminary and was planning to be a priest, when he realized he wasn't so comfortable serving in a religious setting. He said he had always believed that the church provided a sanctuary for authentic relationships and a place for people to be their true selves, but then he came to the realization that this was not the case at all. Concerned and bewildered, he tried to talk to his mentors and to the other seminarians about this, but they all dismissed him as taking things too seriously; some even suggested that he was just plain crazy; and he eventually dropped out of seminary and went to veterinary school.

He says his vocation is better fleshed out now that he cares for animals; and I've learned from the town gossip mill that even though he no longer claims to report to a higher authority, he decided to keep a vow of poverty, living in the back of his office, giving most of the money he makes to animal shelters, and providing free care to those who can't pay. And apparently he maintains his vow of chastity, too, since it's well reported that he's resisted more than a few advances from the single female pet owners in town who seem terribly concerned about their recently acquired kittens and puppies, apparently needing to take them to the vet weekly for an expert consultation or some kind of examination.

"You don't have to guess about animals," he told me once, after Old Joe had come home from the fight with a rooster that left him blind and I had rushed him to Clifford's office. "They're loyal. They don't hold grudges; and they understand the notion of kindness."

I watched as he held my cat in his arms to place the IV into his leg, so masterful with his tenderness.

"Al, you can learn a lot from Old Joe," he said as he laid him on the table to attend to his injured eyes.

"Well, I've certainly learned that a chicken can whip a cat," I said, trying unsuccessfully to make a joke. I was attempting to hide the fact that I was desperately afraid I was going to lose my pet. I could feel the red splotches forming on my neck and face and knew that I was nervously shifting my weight from side to side as I tried to catch my breath.

Clifford walked over to where I stood and then led me closer to the examination table. He took one of my hands and placed it on Joe's chest and held it there.

When I felt the beating of his heart I looked up and saw Clifford had closed his eyes, praying, I suppose; and I was flooded with a sense of relief or peace or hope, which at that moment were all one and the same. And for that glorious moment I felt as if I had landed right smack in the presence of the divine and I was grateful, so grateful, that Father Clifford had turned away from the church and obeyed his call.

"Let me put on some clothes," I say now to Casserole, who has hobbled over to the door to wait. And I'm hurrying because I know that my pet is considerate and has waited until the very last minute before waking me. I also know that even though he is very smart about understanding exactly how much time he has before he loses control, he hasn't been in Tennessee long enough to take certain things into consideration, like how many steps he has to negotiate before making it to the grassy area or how many other dogs may be sharing the space with him.

"Okay, okay." I scoop him up and run down the stairs, because we have both learned to accept that sometimes speed just makes more sense than independence. I get him to the designated pet area, glad to find that we are all alone. We sigh our relief together.

A box of plastic bags is stationed at the gate and I walk over to get one. I yank it out and glance around, taking in my surroundings now that the sun is bright and shining, remembering that our arrival to this Tennessee mountain town happened in the dark and I had not really seen how close we were to the highway and how many cars were coming and going near us.

I clean up behind Casserole and watch as he walks around the small containment, taking in the smells of the others who have been here, accumulating important information that I do not understand, more than likely the sizes, ages, and home habitats of all the dogs that have walked along the perimeter.

"You don't really need to keep notes about this place," I tell him, heading back over to throw the bag in the trash. "I doubt we'll be coming here again," I add.

And he looks over at me, acknowledging my remark but clearly disagreeing with my opinion, as he continues to check every blade of grass for some significant detail I surely cannot comprehend.

"You're up earlier than I thought," comes a familiar voice from behind us.

Casserole glances up, wags his tail as if he was expecting this slight intrusion, and turns around to survey the part of the containment he has not examined.

"You brought your dog," she says without judgment. "You should have told me last night and I'd have given you a few scraps to bring him."

I look back and feel my surprise turn to a vague kind of interest.

"I always keep a box of leftovers in the kitchen for the truckers who have dogs. It's a violation of the health codes, but I hide it pretty good, so I don't think the inspectors will find it."

She is standing near the gate and I cannot imagine how she got there without me seeing her.

"Hey," I say.

"Hey," she replies and comes in through the gate and closes it behind her.

"What are you doing here?"

"Just hanging out," she answers.

"Okay," I say, thinking that it seems quite odd to find my waitress from last night greeting me so early this morning.

"You sleep good?"

"Fine," I reply. "You?" This is such an odd conversation.

She nods and pauses, drops the bag she has hanging on her arm. "So, here's the thing," Blossom says, and I wait. "I like you; I feel like maybe we might have known each other in another time, maybe, another life."

I realize that she's saying she feels connected to me, but I don't quite know what to say; so I just smile and nod.

"I thought I might ride with you to Texas if you don't mind." And she drops to her haunches. "I can drive and I'll even help pay for gas."

I open my mouth and then close it. I cannot find the words to respond.

"I'm not crazy, in case you're worried."

And I do it again. I open my mouth and then close it. Even Casserole seems confused at my response.

"I thought it would be fun. I'm not bad company."

Open. Close.

And she holds out her hands and my dog walks over. He's immediately smitten and Blossom scratches him behind his ears and she turns to

47

me and smiles as if she's saying that since my dog approves I will as well.

And I must admit I'm shaken. Sharing the trip with some waitress from a Tennessee diner was the farthest thing from my mind.

Chapter Seven

"Wow . . . okay . . . good morning," I say, stuttering my way through a greeting. I walk over in her direction.

"What's your pal's name?" she asks and she's really giving him a good scratch.

I glance over. "Casserole," I say and then wait for the usual comment of surprise. *Oh, what a weird name,* or *How did you come up with something like that?*

And just as I'm getting ready to explain, she interrupts.

"Cool," she answers—not at all the reply I expected. She holds his snout with both hands and gives him a kiss on the nose.

I don't know what to say.

"Cass," she calls, using the nickname I gave him; and my dog rolls over on his back.

I watch as she scratches his belly, exactly the way Casserole likes it. He raises his chin, asking for more, and then closes his eyes, clearly enjoying the unwarranted attention. Blossom feels around his body, lightly, carefully, gently touching the stump, and then, apparently satisfied and finished, stands back up and wipes off the front and then the back of her legs.

She is wearing jean shorts and a flimsy T-shirt, old sneakers, and quite a lot of turquoise jewelry —bracelets, earrings, a choker, and even a thin chain made from blue stones wrapped around her ankle. Her hair is long and brown. It was in a ponytail last night, but this morning it's down and pushed behind her ears.

"I need a change," she tells me. "And after last night, after meeting you, I felt, I don't know, connected or like it was meant to be or something, and I thought, what the hey, you're going west, you're alone." She pauses and glances back down at Casserole. "Well, I mean alone as in without people company."

She grins, but it doesn't matter because clearly my dog is not offended.

"And so I just decided to show up this morning to see if I could catch you before you headed out."

I look around the parking lot. Maybe I'll recognize something that will help to explain this young woman's arrival. But I see nothing that offers any explanation. "How did you get here?" I ask.

"Walked," she answers, motioning in the direction behind the hotel. "I do that anyway when I come to work. It's about six miles to my grandma's."

"Did you walk last night?" And for some reason I suddenly feel very concerned for her safety.

She shakes her head. "Booker T, the cook, he drove me home."

I bite my lip. I'm still looking for a clue that will help me to understand this strange twist in my plans to get to New Mexico.

"I don't smoke or anything," she says, as if this might be my biggest concern, as if she's applying for a job and understands my hesitation, can see my need for proof that she will be a good hire.

"Why do you want to go to Texas?" I ask finally, trying to organize the facts and figure out this story. I'm a journalist, after all.

She shrugs. "My dad."

I wait because I don't know what this means.

"He lives in Amarillo. He's a carpenter, builds houses and things. Last year he got his electrician's license, so he does some of that. He helps out on ranches, too."

I nod, thinking for some reason that I ought to be writing this down.

"He moved out there when I was twelve, but we're still close." She smooths down her hair and sticks her hands in her back pockets. "My mom took off when I was four and he raised me for a while, but then let his mama take care of me while he tried to get a job. Turns out he can make more money in Texas."

"Why didn't you go with him?"

"Grandma was sick for about a year after he left, and I had this boyfriend." She lifts her shoulders and then lets them drop. "You know how that can be."

I raise my eyebrows, although my expression doesn't really give anything away. I recall the pregnancy she mentioned and wonder if it's the same relationship, but I decide not to pry; besides, I'm still trying to figure out what I'm going to do with Blossom and her request to join me on my road trip.

"Anyway, she's better—even got married six months ago to this trucker I introduced her to." She shakes her head. "Did not see that coming," she says, and she laughs. "So, I feel a little like a third wheel, and since Dillon and I broke up after the miscarriage . . . I don't know." She takes her hands out of her pockets and raises them up as if she is going to catch something thrown her way. "So I figure now's as good a time as any to make my break. I've been thinking about it for a few weeks and then last night I met you and it just felt right."

I continue to nod, without quite realizing that I'm doing it. And it's not my *I agree with you* nod; it's my *I am trying to take all this in* nod. Except that Blossom certainly doesn't know the difference. As far as she's concerned, my acknowledgment of what she's telling me is a clear sign that this is going to work out great.

"So, I'll go get us some breakfast if you want, something to eat on the way." She pauses for a second. "Or would you rather go in and sit down?" She's peering over at the diner. "I need to pop over and tell Donny I'm quitting."

I'm still nodding away.

"The French toast is always good, but so are the egg sandwiches if you just want me to get you something to go."

By now I've crossed my arms over my chest. Even Casserole seems a little put off by my mixed signals.

"You want me to grab him some bacon?"

He stares at me now like he suddenly approves of what's going on.

"No bacon," I finally answer and I give Cass my best disciplinarian look. "Pork makes you gassy," I tell him.

"A little steak, then?" The young waitress shrugs, trying not to cause trouble. "You drink coffee?"

It's past time for me to assert a little authority.

"How old are you, Blossom?" I ask.

I rely upon facts. I live my life based upon facts. I don't feel like we're meant to be together. I feel like I need some facts.

"Seventeen," she says, surprising me even

more than I am already surprised by this entire morning's encounter.

"Seventeen!" Now my nod is a turning from side to side. "Does your grandmother even know you're leaving? Shouldn't you be in school or planning to take classes somewhere?"

Blossom stifles a laugh. "I graduated from high school three weeks ago," she reports. "I started school early, when I was five; and I finished on time even though I missed a lot of classes when I left with the hippies last year and then after the miscarriage when I went and stayed awhile with Dad in Amarillo. I've thought about nursing school or even going through the management training that Donny offered me."

I wait.

"But Grandma is fine; Dillon and I are still not together. I don't really like blood. And I don't want to spend my life closing up the restaurant. So I feel limited by my job options. It just seems like it's the right time to go," she says in conclusion. "I turn eighteen in a month."

I nod again. Only this time it's not quite so ambivalent. Still, I can't say for sure exactly what it means. Or how I feel about things. At least I know I'm hungry.

"Okay, yes to the coffee and the egg sandwich." I glance over at Casserole, who has started panting a little.

"And the steak?" Blossom asks.

"And the steak," I answer; and my dog closes his eyes and raises his chin. No ambivalence there. He is suddenly and most certainly pleased with the way this trip is going.

Chapter Eight

Along with a box of ashes of a man I know nothing about, I'm now driving to New Mexico with a teenager who has seen a lot more of the world than I have and clearly loves the art of conversation.

That's a nice way of saying she talks a lot.

I've told her about Roger Hart and the funeral home in the small town of Grants, how I happened upon his remains, and how I feel destined to return him to his western home. I've shared information about my job at the paper, my mother's cancer, and why I don't like my food touching on a plate. I wouldn't have delved into that part, but she called attention to it at lunch when I asked for the stewed apples to be in a separate bowl from the hamburger and after I placed the fries on a napkin. She, on the other hand, stirred her green beans into her black-eyed peas, cut up her country-fried steak into little pieces and threw them in, and then spooned the whole mess onto a biscuit, adding salt, pepper, and hot sauce.

If Blossom's life is anything like her lunch,

she leans more naturally in the direction of chaos.

"So, Al, what's up with that name?"

And this from a girl named Blossom. The question doesn't throw me, though. I'm used to it.

We took our time getting to Knoxville and now have a couple of hours before we get to Nashville. We both agreed it was better not to use the air conditioner and have all the windows rolled down.

Casserole has his nose in the air, taking in the mountain aromas from his spot in the backseat.

I have to yell so that she can hear me. "It's Alissa, actually. Alissa Kate. Al came from my dad."

"And Alissa Kate?"

"A friend of my mother," I tell her.

"First and middle?"

"Just middle," I reply. I lean my head against the seat and think about the woman with the long red hair who visited us so often before my mother was sick. They had been childhood friends, grew up together, and I knew her as Aunt Kate, while she took to calling me Katydid, what we named the bush crickets in North Carolina. Daddy always seemed angry when she was staying with us, acted jealous or put out, something I never quite understood; and after Mama died, I never saw her again. She wrote me cards for a while, ones she made with pictures of butterflies and streams of water. She promised that she would always love me, that I was a special girl; but I never heard from her again.

"And Alissa?" Blossom apparently thinks our names define us or at least open some door to understanding who we are. I suppose she's just trying to get to know me.

I shake my head as I merge into the left lane to pass a motor home. It's a big bus, shiny and new, pulling a Hummer behind it. Somebody obviously spent a lot of money to take their house with them.

"Don't know," I answer. "Guess my parents just liked it. Mama called me Alley Cat. Now it's just Al."

I remember my mother's voice, the way she would softly sing my name in the mornings to wake me, or yell it from the kitchen window when I was playing in the backyard, calling me in for supper.

She was the only person in the world who could make Alley Cat out of Alissa Kate; but she always had a way of pulling something unexpected from what everyone else would have considered mundane. A song, a dance, a name, she could make magic out of anything. And talking to my passenger reminds me that I haven't been called Alley Cat since my mother died. I doubt anyone even knows that was how I started every day.

"My mama named me, too," Blossom explains.

"My grandmother says she told her that when I was born I looked just like a flower, bright and red faced." She slides her feet out of her shoes. "I didn't really like it when I was little; but I guess it could have been worse."

I wait, wondering what she thinks is worse than what she got.

This girl is a mind reader. "Poppy," she says with a grin.

Not what I was thinking of; but I have to agree. It seems to me that would have been a lot worse.

"She could have gone with Rose," I say. "That's not bad for a red flower."

Blossom shrugs and places her feet on the dashboard. "I was never that refined," she responds. "Roses are too cultivated, high maintenance. Even though it seems Mama wasn't really cut out for the whole domestic life, she knew enough about her baby to see that I was too wild to be named for a garden flower."

"So she called you Blossom."

"That's what's written on the birth certificate." She folds her arms across her waist and lifts her chin up, just like Casserole. I wonder if she's sniffing the air, too.

"When I was little I used to think it was because of me that she left. You know, because I was bad or a lot of trouble. I used to think she hated me, hated being my mother, even hated the thought that I had been born."

57

I don't look over. I keep my eyes right straight ahead as I signal and pull back into the right lane.

"But Grandma told me once that she called me Blossom out of her love for me and that she had to have been thinking about me and hoping for me or she wouldn't have given me such a beautiful name."

Now I turn to glance at her. She has her eyes closed, but she seems peaceful. And she doesn't add anything else.

I think about a mother leaving her daughter when she's not even yet five, how that departure must be wrestled with and misunderstood and calculated, analyzed over and over, year after year. I think about my own loss and how my mama left, too, even though it was because she died; it wasn't her fault. And I remember how I try not to blame myself every day I have lived without her.

It never seemed to matter to me that it was cancer that left me motherless. There was no comfort in that. I was still ashamed of it, still somehow defined not by my grief but by her abandonment, as if she had made the same choice as Blossom's mother, only took off not with a packed suitcase to hitchhike on the interstate but rather by getting sick and not overcoming her terrible illness. It had always seemed like a choice to me, her choice, and I have always felt somehow responsible.

"Wells," Blossom says, pulling me away from those old thoughts that I imagined I had put away but which still manage to haunt me.

"What?" I ask.

"Wells," she repeats. "Your last name."

I nod.

"Alissa Kate Wells." She calls it out all together.

"That's me," I answer.

"Deep," she adds. "Deep and remembered like a friend," she says. I guess she thinks she's summed up the essence of my name.

"What's your last name?" I ask, thinking it's only fair that she gives as good as she gets.

"Winters," she answers.

"Snowmen and hot chocolate."

"That works," she replies, nodding, as if she's measuring how our names balance each other. "Wells and Winters," she notes. "Sounds like something on the Nature Channel."

This makes me smile. "*Whales in Winter.* Yeah, it kind of does." And then I hit the gas.

Chapter Nine

"I know a place," Blossom tells me as we exit off the interstate and head into Nashville.

She started driving after we stopped for gas outside of Knoxville. I was standing by the pump and writing down the mileage and adding the receipt to my zippered pouch when she jumped behind the wheel. I have to admit I was nervous about a seventeen-year-old taking over, and I was about to tell her I would drive for the rest of the day; but then I figured it was best to know as soon as possible whether or not she could manage the highway.

It turns out that Blossom is a very good driver and I make a mental note to ask her when she was behind the wheel last, since she talked about walking to work in recent months.

She slows down as we make our way off the ramp and stop at a light.

"When have you been in Nashville?"

"I came at Christmas," she replies. "Grandma and Tony brought me along when they took their honeymoon."

I raise my eyebrows.

"I know, it sounds weird," she admits, "but he'd been living with us anyway and it wasn't like this was some young virgin with her lover. Besides, Grandma said she wanted to do something nice for me since I lost the baby and still managed to get back into school."

Makes sense, I think.

"Grandma thought Tony was taking us to the Opryland hotel, but he said it wasn't the best place for country music anymore and we ended up getting rooms at this little boutique hotel that used to be a train station. From there we could walk to the bars and to Ryman and to the restaurants. It was cool. And I met a guy who plays guitar, trying to make it big, I suppose."

Blossom makes a turn, slows down, looks in both directions, and heads down a street. Next thing I know we're in downtown. There are bars and restaurants and lots of people standing on the sidewalks.

"He wrote a song for me," she adds, but I am so interested in the sites we're passing I have forgotten what she was talking about. I've even forgotten that I had planned to drive to Memphis tonight.

"How long were you here?" I ask, partly because she seems to know where she's going and because it just dawned on me that a boy wrote her a song.

She shrugs as she checks the rearview mirror. "A week."

"You met a boy and he wrote you a song in one week?" I shake my head. "I've never had a boy write me a song," I confess.

"It wasn't so great," she says. "He kept rhyming Blossom with awesome."

"That doesn't really rhyme," I note, stating the obvious.

"Right?" she responds, still driving as if she knows exactly where she's going.

I sit back and enjoy the ride. I figure I don't know any better; and besides, staying in Nashville seems like it will be fun. Of course, I've read lots of reviews of Music City. We've posted stories for the travel section and Jasper spent a weekend here a couple of years ago, wrote a few columns about the Country Music Awards show. He's always trying to get Daddy to spring for him to travel.

He's been scheming all year to go to California and I've read all the proposals he's made, including a wine country trip and driving the coastal highway. I heard Daddy tell him that in Clayton there'd be more interest in the bluegrass festival held every year in Roxboro than there would be in some California trip and suggest he buy a tent and a banjo if he really wanted to reach the readers.

I somehow don't think that reaching the readers is really Jasper's intent; but I'm pretty sure Daddy has enough sense to know that too. For a brief moment, as we're driving down Broadway, I think about calling Daddy, see if he got the futures calendar done for the summer and if he hired that college kid who came around last week wanting to do an internship. I want to tell him where I am and ask if he wants a souvenir or a copy of the Nashville paper; but then I decide I'll just wait until I'm ready for bed, make it a late-night call. I check the clock on the dashboard and realize he's probably still at the office, putting the finishing touches on the final edition.

"You hungry?" Blossom asks and I pull my attention back to the things at hand.

I think about it. "Sure," I answer, wondering if

she was planning a stop when she took the exit from the interstate.

"You like ribs?"

I shrug. "I guess."

"As long as they're not touching your cole slaw, right?" And she grins.

She whips down one street, makes a right, then a left. I'm shocked that she's so comfortable driving in a city she's only been in once. She signals, pulls into a parking lot, and stops, turns off the engine.

It's a saloon, just a few streets over from what looks like the main drag.

"How did you remember how to find this place?" I ask, unbuckling my seat belt. I pull down the visor and check my face and hair. With the windows down for the past three hours, I'm pretty much a mess.

"Tyrone," she says, like I'll know who she's talking about.

I wait. I don't know a Tyrone.

"The boy who plays the guitar. I came here every day after we met to see him."

"You think he's still here?" And I'm beginning to think Blossom had this planned the whole time. And as soon as I have that thought I feel that old feeling I had for much of my adolescence, the familiar one of being used, of being taken advantage of by my sister. I can't believe I let myself fall for this again.

Sandra used to do this kind of thing to me all the time when we were teenagers. She'd say she wanted to go somewhere and then pretend she was surprised when we happened to be at the same spot as some boy she was interested in. She'd flirt and then head off with him, a different guy every time, leaving me to drive home by myself and lie to Daddy about where she was.

I check my face in the mirror and see the red splotches starting to form on my neck and cheeks. This is not what I want from my trip. Bringing this seventeen-year-old along was a terrible idea.

I'm just about to say something to Blossom, just about to tell her this is not going to work and we need to get back on the interstate and go to Memphis like I had planned; but she's already out of the car and stretching beside the door. Her arms are raised above her head and she's leaning from side to side.

"You want me to walk Casserole while you go get us a table?"

I take in a deep breath. I'd rather just get this over with now. I look in the back. Casserole is waiting to be let out. He doesn't care about Tyrone or why we've stopped; he would just like to be released.

"Is he still here?" I ask, my eyes facing the front door of the restaurant.

"Who?"

Oh, she's good, all right, I think. But not to worry, I have been with the best.

"The boy," I answer, since I don't even want to say his name.

"What boy?"

I wait. Blossom's smart enough to figure that one out and she's also about to figure out this is not going to play well with me. I put my hands on my hips. Why did I say yes to this girl?

"Oh, Tyrone," she finally answers. She shakes her head. "I doubt it." She places her hands on the bottom of her spine and leans back, exposing her belly. I see a long scar running beneath her navel and for some reason it makes me look away.

"He wrote me after I left, said he had moved to Hollywood, going to try and make it as an actor." And she laughs like it's true. She laughs this easy, wholesome, pure laugh. "Maybe he's better at that than writing songs. Besides, I didn't come here every night to see him." She smooths down her hair on both sides, tightens the rubber band around her long, full ponytail. "They've got killer ribs."

And she walks around to the passenger's side where I am standing, opens the door, puts the leash on my dog, and lets him out. I watch as the two of them head to a grassy area beside the parking lot. I shake my head, glance around at the restaurant, and still have a hard time believing she's not got something else planned besides dinner.

Chapter Ten

"So, why did you turn so red back there?" She slides into the booth across from me.

I look behind me through the glass door at the car. I see Casserole's face from the backseat staring in our direction. I notice that Blossom has left the car windows rolled down. It's not too hot since the sun has set and I take in a breath and turn back around.

I shake my head. I'm ashamed to answer her question. "Just the heat," I say, and I turn my attention to the menu that a waitress, not a boy named Tyrone, gave me before Blossom came in.

She doesn't reply and I glance up. She has apparently taken me at my word. She's reading her menu and the server appears.

"Something to drink?" she asks Blossom as she places the tall glass of iced tea I have ordered in front of me.

"Can I get a Mountain Dew?"

"Small or large?"

"Large," Blossom answers, as if that's the only way soda should be served. The waitress walks away.

"So the ribs come with two sides and if I remember correctly the baked beans and the sweet potato fries are the best."

I have already decided on a Cobb salad. I did not plan to take a road trip in order to gain ten pounds. I'm still trying to work off the extra weight I put on when Daddy and I went crazy with the free food during the restaurant reviews.

"It's not hot," Blossom says and I'm wondering if she's talking about the ribs or one of the side dishes.

"What?"

"Outside."

I'm confused.

"You said that you turned red because of the heat; but it's not hot out there. Even Casserole wasn't panting. It's cool."

"Here's your soda." The waitress has arrived and saves me. "What'll it be?"

"Cobb salad," I say, closing the menu and sliding it over.

"Ribs, baked beans, and corn," Blossom responds.

"Muffins or corn bread?"

Blossom turns to me as if I get to make the decision.

I shrug.

"How about one of both?" She certainly knows how to work her way in a restaurant.

"Sure," the waitress answers, swiping up both menus from the table. She smiles and heads off.

I hope Blossom has forgotten the question she just asked, the point she just made.

"So?"

She has not.

"So, I don't know," I reply.

"Okay." And she drops it just like that. She removes the paper from her straw and places the straw in her drink. She takes a sip and raises her eyebrows at me while she smiles. In this light she looks like a child.

"I'm not usually surprised by people," I tell her. I'm trying to answer her question without really answering it. It's something I've learned how to do since I started interviewing politicians.

"Well, that's where we're different because people surprise me all the time," she responds. "You think you know how much a person is going to tip, and the one you think will leave you a five will be the very one who stiffs you, and the one you think may not even have enough money to cover the bill will sometimes leave you thirty percent." She slides down in her seat. "I quit trying to figure folks out a long time ago. Now I just try to enjoy them."

This makes me smile. It's a fine way to live.

"Who surprised you?" comes the question.

"You," is the truth.

"Yeah?"

"Yeah."

And she doesn't even push for more. Blossom would make a terrible reporter, but probably a very good friend. But I don't have many of those so I'm not sure even what that means.

"I think it's nice, by the way," she says.

"You think what's nice?"

"That you're taking that man's ashes back to his hometown."

Before I can even open my mouth to respond to this, our food arrives and is placed in front of us. We both agree there's nothing more we need and the waitress leaves again.

That's when I try to respond to her comment. "I don't know if it's nice or not," I say, spreading the vinaigrette dressing around my salad and poking at the lettuce with my fork. I glance over at Blossom's plate of ribs and the beans and I wish I had just ordered what I want.

"Yeah, it is. Not many people would do what you're doing. The most some folks would do is put the box in a mailer and send it to the funeral home. You're taking this all the way."

I stab at my salad. I suppose Blossom is right. And hearing her talk makes me realize that I'm not sure why I'm doing this. I have no idea what I'm going to do with the ashes when I get to New Mexico.

"How do you think they ended up in North Carolina?"

I shrug as I chew. "Some family member, I guess, took them with plans for a burial or spreading and then just forgot about them. I tried to find out the name of the person who rented the unit, but I couldn't get any answers from anyone."

"That's cold, right?"

"That's something," I say, not sure how I feel about the ashes being left in a storage building, not sure why I feel responsible for somebody else's remains.

"It's one of those surprising human things," she says.

I poke around my salad a little more, trying to find something other than the long pieces of lettuce.

"See, folks are weird." Blossom is working on her ribs. She sucks the meat off the bone. Her face is a mess and it makes me laugh.

"What?" She grins. I think she knows. She picks up the napkin from her lap and wipes off the sauce. "How's the salad?" she asks, taking another bite of a rib.

"It's a salad," I answer.

Blossom takes the bread off the plate and places half of her dinner on it. She spoons on beans, corn, and at least two ribs and she slides the plate over to me. "Eat a meal," she says and takes a drink from her Mountain Dew.

And I push aside my bowl of lettuce and dig into the gift she's given me. Like everything today, it is a pleasant surprise.

Chapter Eleven

"I want to buy a nightshirt. I left my Willie Nelson one at home. Actually, I think it's time to end that relationship and sleep with someone else."

Blossom has convinced me to stay the night in Nashville. She says I really need to see Printers Alley and the bars on Broadway; so we found a pet-friendly hotel near the interstate and checked in. I suspect Casserole is already making himself at home, lying on the bed watching doggie porn and ordering room service. We're in a souvenir shop nearby, browsing through the offerings on a rack.

"Keith Urban?" I ask as she holds up a long pink T-shirt and grins.

"Australian country dude. I believe this demonstrates I'm moving on, exploring my options." She tucks the hanger under her arm and keeps searching the racks.

"You and Willie breaking up, are you?"

"He's never around anymore, chose Texas over Tennessee. Plus I think he has a drug problem."

"Well, that and he is eighty years old," I say.

She pulls out another shirt, Blake Shelton, holds it up and wrinkles her nose, puts it back. "His age never bothered me," she says, in all serious-ness. "Willie is timeless."

This girl makes me laugh.

I step away from the nightshirts to investigate what else this store has to offer. There are bandannas and cowboy hats, jewelry for boots, rhinestone-studded plastic purses, and big shiny belt buckles: Nashville at its finest. Even though I'm usually not snooty about souvenirs—I have, after all, an entire collection of shot glasses from around the country, all given to me, since I have never gone anywhere—there is nothing that interests me in this store, so I walk outside to hear the music coming from next door.

The street is filled with folks walking in and out of the bars and shops—couples, families, groups of young people. I can see why tourists like this town. It's teeming with life, music everywhere you turn, people celebrating the art of guitar picking and all the stories people tell in songs.

"Welcome to Music City," a voice behind me calls out and I turn to find a guy handing out playbills. "It's the lineup at Tootsie's," he tells me and hands me a paper. "No cover tonight."

I nod and glance down at the list of bands appearing at the bar two blocks up. It's a different music group every hour.

"You from Tennessee?" he asks, and I shake my head.

"Lineup at Tootsie's," he announces again and hands out a few more papers to a group of boys walking past. He turns to me again, waiting for something else. "That's usually the setup for you to tell me where you are from."

"Oh," I reply, obviously unfamiliar with the cues for conversations on the street.

"North Carolina," I tell him.

He nods.

"Not too far away," he responds and passes out the remaining bills left in his hand. He's wearing a backpack so I figure he has more with him.

"You waiting on your husband?" he asks, motioning with his thumb to the store I just walked out of. "He buying you matching hats?"

I smile and shake my head. "A friend buying pajamas," I tell him, taking a closer look at this guy who works for Tootsie's and for some odd reason is chatting me up.

He's maybe twenty-five, thirty; and he's attractive. Tall, sturdy build, with long arms and a goatee, sandy colored, that matches his hair. He's got brown eyes, is wearing a diamond earring in his left lobe, and hasn't stopped smiling since he started talking. I'm not sure if that's a clue to a naturally sunny personality or if he's just learned how to be charming while passing out Tootsie's show bills.

"My band plays at nine," he announces.

"You play in a band?" I ask.

"Darling, you're in Nashville. Everybody plays in a band."

I nod. "Good to know." I glance down. "That

73

means you must be in the Alabama Alligators."
I read from the piece of paper he gave me.

He nods while I continue to read the drink specials. Draft beer is three dollars from seven to nine.

"What do you think about that name?" he asks.

I glance up and shake my head, uncommitted, and then I look back down at the list of bands appearing at Tootsie's. "Well, it's slightly better than the Rocky Mountain High Notes," I say.

"Slightly better," he repeats, clearly unimpressed by my reaction. He nods and slides the back-pack off his shoulders and unzips it. He takes out a bottle of water and takes a long swallow. "We started out as the Alabama Rockers; but that just made us sound old." He returns the water, takes out another handful of papers, and slips the pack onto his back.

"How long do you do this?" I ask. I'm not wearing my watch, but it must be close to nine by now.

"We show up about fifteen minutes before we go on. I work out here for as long as I want before or after a gig."

"You get paid by Tootsie's?"

He shakes his head. "No, it has to do with the crowd I attract. If folks show up the night we play and especially if they're in the house when we're on, we have a better shot at making more money, getting more prime slots. It's just a way to demonstrate to the management that you're creating a following."

I nod. I never realized all the intricacies involved in trying to make a living playing music in Nashville. I glance up and down the street and see there's somebody on every corner passing out pieces of paper.

"You like country music?"

It's certainly a fair question. I think about it.

"I like the old standards—Patsy Cline, George Jones, Tammy Wynette." I'm not even sure why I said that. I really haven't listened to Tammy in years.

"That's the roots, for sure," he says approvingly. "Anybody actually living you listen to?" He's still smiling.

"Is Tammy dead?" I ask. Clearly I haven't been keeping up with the obituaries of the stars of country music.

"Nineteen ninety-eight," he answers. "Blood clot. Patsy Cline in 1963, George Jones in 2013."

His wealth of information impresses me. "Well, aren't you the Wikipedia for dead singers?"

"Sorry, it's what I do."

I nod. I actually do the same thing with journalists. Martha Gellhorn, 1998; Dorothy Thompson, 1961; Murrow, 1965. It is true what my neighbor Millie says, "We do not let go of the details of those who shape our lives."

"Can't think of anybody?"

His question jolts me back to Broadway. "Oh, sorry. Contemporary country music stars . . ." I'm thinking.

He laughs and shakes his head. "Shania, Little Big Town, Rascal Flatts?"

I bite my lip.

"I like some of their Christmas music," I say.

"Well, that's something," he responds.

I blow out a long breath; I didn't really want to confess, but it appears an explanation is necessary.

"I'm just not really a fan of country music," I say and watch his face fall. "The truth is I don't listen to a lot of music of any kind. I like podcasts, speeches, TED Talks—that kind of thing."

He nods. I can see he's trying to understand; but it must be difficult for a musician to hear this sobering commentary. "So, words are okay, just not melodies. No instruments to accompany these great speeches?"

"I sound like a snob, don't I?"

"Well, no, because even snobs like music."

I shrug. I didn't come here to justify why I don't have playlists, why I don't listen to music, download some catchy tune, why I don't listen to the radio and get all sentimental when some cowboy goes on and on about having his heart broken. I like talks; I like to hear a well-thought-out argument and I like to be swayed by words, spoken not yodeled.

I'm about to make an effort to change the subject when the door opens and out comes Blossom.

Chapter Twelve

"So, I settled on Alan Jackson. Did you know he wears a hat to cover a scar on his forehead?" She's holding a bag and has practically run right into me.

I move a little to get out of her way.

"Oh, you're right here." She pauses. "With a man."

She's suddenly watching me and the guy who's been giving out playbills, the one clearly offended by my lack of enthusiasm for his passion. I watch as this light sort of goes on in her eyes.

She pulls away. "I'm so sorry; I didn't mean to bust up a meet-and-greet." And she starts to back up like she's retracing her steps through the door behind me.

I step aside to give her more room and for some reason this comment from her makes me blush. "Hey," I say to her and then falter a bit. "You finish shopping?" I ask.

She nods slowly. I catch on. She's waiting to be

either introduced or given a sign of what to do.

"Um, oh, this is . . ." Awkward, that's what this is. I turn to the man with the playbills. "I'm sorry, I realize I don't know your name, just your band's."

And just like that, Blossom has this big goofy grin on her face. She looks exactly her age, exactly seventeen, and it dawns on me that this guy probably thinks she's my daughter.

He holds out his hand to me, not Blossom. "James Hicks," he says as a way of introduction.

I smile.

"Well, that's a good country singer's name right there," I say, taking his hand, shaking it, and then dropping mine clumsily at my side. "Maybe you should just go with that." I hope this provides some measure of redemption after the last dumb thing I've said.

He smiles and slides a strand of hair away from his cheek, places it behind his ear. "I'm not so sure the rest of the band would agree."

"Right, those other guys."

He laughs and I hear a clearing of the throat.

"And this is Blossom," I say quickly, having almost forgotten that she was there.

He nods at her and smiles. "Hello," he says and then turns back to me. "And you, Miss Carolina Book on Tape, you are?"

I feel them both watching me closely.

"Al," I say.

"Wells," Blossom adds.

"Nice to meet you, Blossom, and Al Wells." He winks. It seems that he hasn't taken great offense at how our conversation ended before we were interrupted, and truthfully, I'm relieved we had an interruption. Maybe he won't push for more.

"So, an Alan Jackson fan?" he says, addressing Blossom and her most recent purchase.

" 'Hard Hat and a Hammer.' 'Mercury Blues.' " I'm guessing these are song titles.

"Can't forget 'It's Five O'Clock Somewhere,' " the Alabama Alligator James Hicks chimes in.

"And, oh, Lord, I cry every time I hear 'Remember When.' " Blossom clutches her bag to her chest.

Unlike me, Blossom apparently knows her country music genre, and I am now the silent bystander to this dialogue on the street.

" 'Old ones died and new were born.' " Well, of course he can quote lyrics.

"Yeah, love that. 'Life was changed, disassembled, rearranged.' "

And clearly Blossom is no slouch, either.

"What do you like about Alan Jackson music?" he asks her. And I'm certain this is for my benefit.

"He's classic, that's for sure. His choices, musical and lyrical, they're what's great about country music. They speak of the things we feel but often cannot express." Blossom suddenly sounds older than her seventeen years. I have to admit I'm impressed.

"These songs can make grown men cry like little girls. I know because I have seen it happen."

"Somewhat more evocative than just a speech, wouldn't you say?" And he peers at me once the question has been asked.

Blossom looks at him and then at me. She raises her shoulders and her hands come up in a kind of *well, duh* gesture.

"I didn't say music isn't evocative," I say.

"You just don't listen to it," he adds.

"You don't listen to music?" Blossom has now taken a side. "Who doesn't listen to music?"

He shrugs.

"I listen to music," I try to explain.

"You have a Rolling Stones cassette tape," Blossom says. "And I saw some soundtracks to old movies under the seat," she adds.

So that's where my *Dirty Dancing* CD went. I knew I had it when I started this trip. I'll have to remember to pull it out before we head to Memphis in the morning.

I nod. "See?"

"Well, now, that is something. I have to say, you had me worried there, Ms. Al Wells from Carolina. I thought I was going to have to kidnap you off the street and make you listen to Garth Brooks until I made a believer out of you."

"Who's Garth Brooks?"

He actually appears astonished.

"You know, maybe I should have gotten a Garth shirt." Blossom opens her bag and takes a peek.

He stares at me a bit longer and then shakes his head.

"No, I think you made a wise choice," he says and then returns the playbills to his backpack. I guess he's done drumming up business for the night. "You cannot go wrong sleeping with Alan Jackson." There's that million-dollar smile. "Or so I've heard."

He pulls out a cell phone and reads the time. "Well, as stimulating as this conversation is, I probably need to be heading over." He returns his phone to his pocket. "My band is on at nine," he tells Blossom.

"Do we know the location?" she asks me.

"Tootsie's," he and I answer at the same time and then face each other.

"The Alabama Alligators," I add.

"Nice name," she responds, nodding her approval.

He turns to me and I do a kind of applause motion with my hands.

"Well, we will just have to hop over there and see you," Blossom responds. "Are you the lead singer?" she wants to know.

"My brother and I both sing," he answers.

"A brother?" Blossom responds, raising her eyebrows.

I have absolutely no idea what this is supposed to mean.

"Then we are heading right to Tootsie's and find ourselves a seat," she adds.

"Great," James responds. "Well, I will see you over there. And I will try to put one song on the list that has talking in it." He pulls at the straps of his backpack and walks across the street.

"Okay," I say.

"Okay," Blossom says, too. And she pulls me by the arm down the sidewalk while I still feel the flushing sensation spread from my face down my neck.

Chapter Thirteen

"You should call him." Blossom is sitting on her bed. Her hair is wet and she has it twisted in a towel on top of her head. She's wearing her new purple nightshirt, which goes down to her knees.

Casserole is asleep on the floor between the beds and Roger Hart is on the dresser. I have just walked out of the bathroom and I head over to my suitcase and put my dirty clothes in the top zippered compartment. I check the front door to make sure it's locked and then pull the covers down on my bed and jump in. I realize how tired I am, and this prone position feels very good. I close my eyes and breathe out a long, contented breath. I can't recall the last time I have been out after midnight.

"I'm not calling James Hicks," I say, knowing that she saw him give me his number when we were leaving Tootsie's.

The Alabama Alligators turned out to be a decent cover band, but the truth is that even though I don't know anything about country music I can't imagine that they're going to break out into some big national sensation.

"He's got to be ten years younger than me," I add. I'm pretty sure my first impression wasn't trustworthy. He seemed like a college student once I saw him onstage.

"Age doesn't matter," she responds. "But I'm not talking about the guitar player anyway."

"Age does matter," I reply. "And I'm not calling him, either."

I know that Blossom is still talking about Phillip Blake, the boy I had a crush on from sixth grade until we graduated from high school. I told her about him at the last bar we went in.

When the Alligators had finished and were packing up their instruments, we left and walked a block or two. There was a little dive on a side street where a duo was playing guitar and mandolin, two girls that Blossom claimed sounded like Maddie and Tae, singers I don't know, so we stayed longer than we had at Tootsie's. I even had a piña colada, something I rarely do, and I'm still feeling the effect of the rum.

When we could talk, in between sets, she asked

me about boyfriends, and after denying I'd ever had a boyfriend or a teenage crush, I gave her some of the Phillip Blake story, how he got braces in seventh grade, how he grew a foot taller over the summer when we matriculated to high school, how we shared books in American history. I told her a lot—well, not the Sandra part—sipping on my fancy coconut drink.

Apparently, she found him on Facebook while I paid the bar bill and used the restroom and now she's obviously even dug a little deeper using the Internet white pages.

"I have his number," she says, waving a piece of paper in front of her face. She's written it down.

"I am not going to call Phillip Blake," I tell her, throwing the sheet over my head, hoping she will stop talking.

"Because of a bad breakup?"

I sigh and roll over, the sheet still covering my face.

"It says he's not in a relationship." She is clearly not as sleepy as I.

"It doesn't say he's *not* in a relationship; it just doesn't say that he's in one." I know there's no category for "not in a relationship" on Facebook.

I may not know anything about Snapchat, but I know my way around most of the grown-up social media sites.

"Same thing."

"Not the same thing," I answer.

To be honest, I'm pretty sure Phillip is still married; but I actually can't say for sure. It's been years since I engaged in my cyberstalking.

"He lives in North Carolina." She is quiet for a moment. "High Point, I think. Is that a town? Sounds more like an achievement."

"It is—and I know," I tell her and there is a pause and I roll back over, pull the sheet down, and glance in her direction to see if the silence means she's letting this go.

Her eyebrows are raised and she's staring at me. "So, you *have* kept up with him."

She is not letting this go.

I roll my eyes and shake my head, punch at the pillows behind me. "I know he stayed around Winston-Salem after he finished college, was still there when he got married. His mother never left Clayton. She subscribes to the paper. She and my father are friends. The real kind," I add.

"Did she tell you he's still married?"

"She told me when he got married. That was nine or ten years ago. I haven't asked her about him since."

"He's divorced," she says and I can see her scrolling down her iPad, her finger sliding along the side.

"It doesn't say that," I tell her. "And even if he is, I am not calling him."

"It says it on his timeline."

I raise my head. This surprises me. "He wrote on his timeline when he got a divorce?"

"No, there's just postings from a few months ago from friends celebrating his 'newly found freedom.'" And she makes air quotation marks with her fingers when she says "freedom" as she rests the tablet against her legs.

I close my eyes and think about the wedding picture his mother brought to the paper. I hadn't seen Phillip since we'd both finished our senior year but just to see him in the glossy five-by-seven stirred up all the old feelings I recalled from high school.

He was marrying a girl from Greensboro, Hillary something. She was pretty, with long blond hair, big brown eyes. Perfect, of course. They met at college, Wake Forest. She had just finished her degree and was going to graduate school to become a pharmacist at the time they got engaged. He runs an insurance company; or he did. Like I said, I didn't keep up with him after posting the wedding announcement.

The bride was wearing a white satin gown with a ruched empire bodice and crystal detail. The bridesmaids were all in matching short teal V-neck halter dresses. The groom and groomsmen wore Vera Wang two-button gray tuxedos. After the honeymoon in Costa Rica, the couple will be residing in Winston-Salem.

I remember typing the piece, Daddy eyeing me from across the room.

Suddenly I sit up.

"How are you able to read his timeline postings?"

She slides her teeth over her top lip and glances away. These are telltale signs that Blossom is guilty of something.

"He friended you? He doesn't even know you."

I am surprised that Phillip would just confirm a request from a girl named Blossom from Tennessee; but what do I know about men and Facebook?

"Actually, he friended you," she says.

"What? When?" I have thrown my legs over the bed and am now facing her. "That's not possible."

Chapter Fourteen

"How can you not be on Facebook?" she asks. "Aren't you, like, a newspaper journalist? Aren't you supposed to be all savvy about the computer and these social media sites?"

"I don't want to be on Facebook," I answer her.

I set up a site for the paper a couple of years ago; it's good for business. But I never created a personal account for myself. I always thought the amount of time that people devote to those sites is ridiculous. James William spends more time posting his workout accomplishments and photos of plates of food he's ordered at some restaurant than he does promoting sports stories for the paper.

"Blossom," I ask now, "what have you done?"

She won't look at me.

"Your profile picture is a really good one," she says sheepishly.

"From tonight? You posted a picture you took tonight?" I can't believe this girl. I close my eyes and try to remember when she took a photograph of me.

There was one with James and the band, one of me holding up my drink; wasn't I making some face? She took one of me standing next to a statue of Johnny Cash. Were there more?

"You already have twenty-five friends and it's not even been three hours since I set you up."

I fall back down on the bed.

Well, it doesn't matter. I'll just close the account tomorrow. It's not such a big deal. I blow out a breath. I'd be mad if I weren't so sleepy. I make a note to myself to check Twitter, too. There's no telling what this girl has done when I wasn't paying attention.

"Somebody named Dixie likes your photo," she says. "She posted, 'Have fun, Al! We miss you.' "

I roll my eyes. Now Dixie will show this to everybody.

"Actually, Phillip responded pretty quickly," she tells me, as if this information will mean something to me. "He must have been sitting at his computer. I'm guessing he doesn't have much of a social life."

"It doesn't matter," I say, turning away from her.

"Of course it matters," she responds. "He was the love of your life."

"When I was twelve," I answer. "That's a lifetime ago."

"A guy named Ben wants to know if your father is aware of your drinking problem. Why would he ask that?" She pauses. "Oh, that's right, I made a little album of the pictures."

I start to get up to erase it all now, but I hear her close up her tablet and slide down in the bed. In a few minutes the light from the lamp on the table between us goes out.

"You want to talk about it?"

"About my drinking problem?" I ask, sarcastically.

"No, about Phillip."

"No," I reply.

There's a pause and I think, Finally, she's going to shut up.

"What happened?" she asks softly. "Why did you break up?"

"Blossom, it's late. I just want to go to sleep."

"Fine."

I hear her sheets rustle.

I've hurt her feelings.

I wait a few minutes and then I roll over to face

her direction. I can hear the traffic from the highway and Casserole snoring between us. Somebody is checking into the room next door to ours.

I close my eyes and still feel a slight spinning from the alcohol. It feels nice, actually, this little bit of buzz. I lie still and think about what it was like when Phillip came to the door the night of our senior prom.

He was so handsome in his rented tuxedo, his shiny patent leather shoes; so sweet standing there, holding the box with the wrist corsage he had bought. Small pink roses with just a stem of baby's breath. His hair was all slicked down and his face was cleanly shaven. He was wearing contact lenses and I thought he looked a little like Jimmy Fallon.

I remember just for a second taking my eyes off of him and glancing down the driveway to the limousine parked on the street in front of the house. I could see the driver, with his black jacket, skinny black tie, even the hat, waiting by the car. I could hear the others in the back, laughing and talking, yelling for Phillip to hurry up, that they were going to be late for dinner. And it was easy to see that it was going to be a special night for everybody.

"There was no breakup," I reply, breaking the silence. "Blossom, you still awake? You hear me?"

"Yes," she answers quietly.

Since I wasn't going to the prom and Daddy was

at the office composing the cold type for the next day's edition, Sandra made me answer the door and she waited until she knew he would be right at the bottom of the stairs before she made her grand entrance. She timed everything perfectly, choreographed it all down to the last second.

And I have to admit, it was grand; she was beautiful. Even as upset as I was, she captivated me, too. She wore a short pink taffeta dress with ivory silk piping that she had seen in a magazine and made Daddy order from New York. She'd bought silver sandals at the mall and she had a French manicure and matching pedicure. She'd had her hair and makeup done in Raleigh by real professionals. And, of course, she even had music playing while she walked down the steps, something she had downloaded onto a CD, a country ballad: "I Just Want to Dance with You" by George Strait, a singer and a song I will remember forever.

She had been playing country albums all day, searching for just the right song. Tim McGraw, Faith Hill, Randy Travis, Shania Twain. And she found exactly what she was looking for. And it was spectacular. *She* was spectacular. Standing there at the top of those stairs, she looked like a young Audrey Hepburn. She looked like our mother.

And of course, at the time, Sandra was only a freshman, not even supposed to go to the prom; but she'd figured out how to make sure she got there. And that was with Phillip Blake, the boy she claimed she didn't know that I'd loved from the time I sat beside him in homeroom in sixth grade, the boy she'd put under her spell so that she could go to prom and find a way to get close to Tommy Laughlin, the one she really liked, the captain of the football team, the most popular boy in school, the one she ended up coming home with.

Phillip Blake turned out to be just a means to another one of my sister's ends and I can't remember now whether I was angrier over the fact that she stole him away before I actually had a chance to have him, or that she broke his heart without even a thought. She walked down the stairs, took the corsage and wrapped it around her small wrist, grinned at me, and headed out the door. That damn CD playing over and over and over. Sandra wins again.

Of course, none of that matters now anyway. She dated Tommy Laughlin for a semester, became Homecoming Queen, went to the college in Chapel Hill, and married her wealthy tycoon in Asheville. And Phillip Blake left for Wake Forest University, married a pharmacist from Greensboro, and moved to High Point.

"There was no breakup because we never even went out."

And just like that, a wasted tear rolls down and across my cheek and I remember now why I hate country music.

Chapter Fifteen

"Rise and shine, new friend of mine!" Blossom pulls open the curtains and I am immediately blinded by the sun that is now streaming across the room. I bolt straight up in the bed.

"Would you look at this day!"

"Where am I?" I whisper, falling back down.

"You are in Music City."

"What?" I have lost my vision.

"It's a beautiful day in Nashville!"

How can she be chatty all night and then this perky in the morning? If I could see her I'm sure I would kill her.

"The sun is shining and the roosters are crowing!"

I will go to prison, but I don't care. I am going to kill her.

"Okay, okay," I say, making an attempt to rise. I fight with the sheets, knock over the lamp on the nightstand beside me.

"Oh, my," she says. And I hear her walk over and return the lamp to its original spot.

"Could you just close those until I can see something other than colored spots?" I cover my eyes until I hear the curtains drawn.

The glorious darkness descends once more and I blink a few times, trying to make out where she is standing so I can get my hands on her.

"You're not really a morning person, are you?"

I don't answer.

"Well, that's okay, most people aren't, I've learned. My dad put the television and a small refrigerator in the garage for me so I wouldn't bother him on Saturday mornings. And the hippies made me pitch my tent on the other side of the river from them because I am such an early bird. They got used to me, though. You will, too, I think."

This is our first morning together, and she's got a lot to learn about what I will and will not get used to. The first thing being that I will never get used to any early bird. It has been a long time—a very long time—since I woke easily in the morning.

"Blossom," I say through clenched teeth, "I do not like the light when I first wake up. I do not like noise. I like easing into the day. I like quiet. I like lying in bed for ten or fifteen minutes and thinking about getting up before I actually do anything about it. I do not like being called from my sleep with a high-pitched greeting and the assault of sunlight."

She is quiet for a second.

"It's okay," she assures me. "My grandmother is kind of slow in the morning, too."

"I am not slow," I say, throwing off my bed-covers. "And I am not like your grandmother."

I'm making my stand. I may like to sleep late, but I refuse to be compared to anybody's grand-mother.

"Uh-oh," she replies, acting as if she has finally detected the meaning behind the tone of my voice.

I still can't see because of the sun spots, but I hear scrambling noises.

"Casserole and I will just take our little walk, do our morning stuff, and give you time to wake up."

I don't respond. When I turn to face the door, near where she was standing when she yanked open the curtains, she has already departed with my dog, leaving me alone in our dark hotel room.

I yawn and fall back into bed. I blink a few times and can see the clock on the nightstand. It reads seven-thirty. I think about what time it was when we finally quit talking. Three a.m. I do the math: four and a half hours of sleep. I am tempted to pull the sheets over my head again, but she's going to return in ten or fifteen minutes and I will be forced to go through this bright-light assault again.

I clear my throat and sit up, rub my eyes, and glance around the room. There is just enough light coming from the crack in the curtains and from under the door so that I can see. I get up, stretch my arms above my head, exhale, and shuffle over to the bathroom. I do not turn on the light.

When I come out I glance over at the table where I plugged in my phone. I walk over to it to unplug the charger. And that's when I see I have seventy e-mails.

I sit down and scroll through the list on the tiny backlit screen. Dixie; James William; Tim Justice from the bank; Mary Dalton, the girl who cuts my hair; Ben; reporters from Garner and Smithfield; Patty Lewis, the librarian—they've all friended me, now that I have my own Facebook page. And they've all left me messages.

Look who's finally made it into this century!

Welcome, Al! We've been waiting!

What are you doing in Nashville and why are you drinking sissy drinks?

Your dad says hi!

Did you do the folo for the graduation story?

Say hey to Reba!

Stay out of the karaoke bars!

What are you doing in Tennessee?

Do people just stay on Facebook all day? I shake my head in disgust and stand up. I'm about to put my phone down and get dressed when I read the last posting.

Hi, Al, how's it going?

I sit back down.

It's from Phillip Blake.

Blossom wasn't lying; he friended me and he wrote a message. I sit down at the table, turn on the lamp, and go to Facebook, the password already remembered on my device. I forgo the news feed and click right on my page. What information about me could Blossom have posted? We've known each other all of two days.

Alissa Wells, Clayton, North Carolina. No age, no birthdate, no extra profile material. She did remember that I worked at *Clayton Times and News*, but she listed me as a reporter instead of assistant publisher. That's actually okay. And truth be told, the picture she chose isn't too bad.

It's the one of me standing under the Tootsie's sign, before we went in, before I got all sweaty and before the piña colada. I'm smiling and I have to admit I look happy. It's not so awful. She's even created the background using the night scene on Broadway, the flashing lights, the crowded street.

Blossom set my page up so that I appear kind of cool. It's better than anything I could have done. I decide not to close my account. Not just yet.

I stare at Phillip's posting. It's on my timeline, out there for everyone to see. He didn't send me a personal message. Phillip Blake has written me, and everyone knows he has written me.

I click on his name. And it seems that Blossom was right about him after all. It does appear that he and Hillary are not together. Phillip Blake is single again and he posted on my timeline.

Maybe I've been wrong about Facebook. I may actually enjoy it.

I rise from my seat and walk over to the window. I hold the curtains and take in a deep breath. If I was wrong about Facebook, maybe I am also wrong about mornings.

I yank open the curtains once more, letting the early sun stream into the room, and then, eyes closed, quickly draw them together. I take two steps back and fall into bed.

I am not wrong about mornings.

Chapter Sixteen

"Look in the HFR file," I tell Dixie when we're on the road. Blossom is driving, and I point out the sign to the interstate while I'm holding the phone to my ear. We've checked out of our room, had our breakfast, and are making our way to Memphis.

Dixie called just as we got into the car.

"Hold for release," I add, rolling my eyes. Dixie has been with the paper long enough to know what HFR means. "It's where we put the material that can't be used until it is released by the source." Daddy hired her when I was covering a beat out on the cotton farms last summer. I didn't have a say in this personnel addition. She's sweet, but as Ben says, she's about as sharp as a marble.

"Or at some other designated time," she calls back to me.

Well, what do you know? I guess she does remember the orientation.

"I see that written on the folder. Did you tell me about this?"

Or maybe she does not.

Ben's trying to find the information about the sale of a string of warehouses just west of Clayton. Everybody knows Reynolds Tobacco Company bought them months ago, but it's not supposed to go public until the purchase has been finalized. Toby Hillard, the real estate agent handling the transaction, asked Daddy not to publicize it until he had the contract in hand. From Dixie's questions, I assume the contract is in his hand.

"Oh, there it is!" Dixie exclaims. There is a pause. "Wait, you told me about that HFR file, didn't you?"

"I did," I answer.

Blossom is driving because she reminded me that she was the most awake this morning. She let me sleep another hour before she started packing and making a lot of noise.

It's fine with me that she's driving, though; I'm hoping I can actually take a nap as soon as I get off the phone with my colleagues. I've already learned that Dixie is only the first one with questions.

"Hey, Al." It's Ben. "You still in Nashville? I saw you on Facebook. Good picture of you with Johnny. Did you see my post?"

"I did. And no, to answer your question on my timeline, I didn't write a follow-up about the increase in our graduation statistics. James William was supposed to do that after he verified the numbers from the superintendent."

"James William?" There is a pause. "He said you were going to do that."

I lean my elbow on the door and rest my head in my hand. If I had a dime for every time I've had this exact same conversation.

"No, wait; he's nodding his head. He says he's working on it." He moves his mouth away from the phone. "Okay, 'bye, then."

Meaning James William forgot and he's now left the office to do what he was supposed to have already done.

"Oscar wrote a bright."

"About what?" My dad usually prefers writing the hard news, not fluff pieces, and especially not the short, amusing kind.

"Growing tomatoes," Ben answers. "He interviewed a lot of farmers, got tips from the gardeners. You know he hasn't grown a good tomato in a couple of years?"

I did know that, but regarding his writing a piece

about it, well, I have to admit, I'm a little surprised. When the news is light, Dad usually gets the funny stuff off the wire service or asks Ben to do something quick. And this update about his writing reminds me of how distracted he seemed at work before I left on this trip, how during the last week I was there he was not the first one at the office in the mornings, how he didn't stay late on the last few Fridays, the weekly meetings in Raleigh he attended but wouldn't discuss. I'm beginning to think something is going on with my father.

"It was real funny. Got a lot of phone calls and e-mails about it. Folks seem to like it. I think he might do a story on corn—guess he can't grow that, either."

"Ben, is Dad there?" I ask.

"Nah, he went for his coffee."

I glance at the clock on the dashboard. It is ten thirty in North Carolina. So he hasn't altered his daily morning coffee klatch with his friends at the Donut Shop.

"Does he seem okay to you?" I ask Ben, although he's not really the one to whom I should be posing that question. He isn't all that alert to subtle changes in people. Millie told me that his wife lost thirty pounds, colored her hair red, and got a tattoo, and he didn't notice for a month. It's not so hard to figure out why he's divorced.

"What do you mean?"

101

Why do I bother? "Is everything all right? Does he look okay?"

"Well, no."

I sit up and Blossom glances over in my direction with raised eyebrows.

"Why? What's going on?" I ask.

"About what?"

"Why would you say everything's not all right, that he doesn't look okay?"

"Well, Al, he's never looked okay, you know. His face is always puffy and he has all those allergies. His blood pressure has to be out of control all the time. Your father has never been a picture of health, if you know what I mean."

I sigh. He's right. Daddy sneezes more than any human I've ever known. He almost got on the David Letterman show for sneezing over twenty days straight, but after they booked him and just before he got on the plane, he stopped. Still, he is allergic to everything.

"Dixie, you got any more questions for Al?"

I hear her in the background talking, but I can't make out what she's saying. It sounds like she's still having difficulty locating some things.

"I know where that is," he tells her, his mouth away from the receiver. "No, that's all we need," he says to me and I can tell that he's about to hang up the phone.

"Have him call me, okay?" I say.

"Oscar?"

"Yeah."

"Sure thing, Al. Go to this bar downtown called Legends tonight. You'll love it." And he hangs up before I can tell him that I've already left Nashville.

Chapter Seventeen

"Well, maybe he just thought it was a good idea for a story. It sounds like an interesting subject, and you said that the reporter told you that he got a lot of positive feedback. Maybe he just got a tip and ran with it. What's that you called it again?"

"A bright." I've filled Blossom in on the phone conversation and my concerns regarding my dad's recent behavior. "Yeah, but he's never written that kind of feature. He's always said that if people want to read fluff they should buy a magazine, that the paper is no place for gossip or opinions. As he puts it"—and here I lower the tone of my voice a bit—*"Al, the newspaper is for the news."*

She laughs a little. And I hear my father's voice in my head and I can see him hunched at his desk, peering at me over his reading glasses, a pencil behind his ear, the latest edition of the paper in one hand, a cup of stale coffee in the other. "Al, if you want to be a real paper man, then you need to learn how to report the facts, not just entertain the masses."

I never pointed out to him that it wasn't really my aspiration to be a "paper man" or even a paper woman, for that matter. Running the *Clayton Times and News* was his passion, his love; I did it because it was set before me like our empty dinner table and math homework. Working for the paper, writing articles, doing layouts—this was not something I aspired to do; it was just the life that got handed to me.

"Maybe he's branching out, trying something new."

"Maybe," I say, but without conviction. Daddy is not one for branching out. He's been known to write enterprise copy, a story that digs a little deeper than the usual news—he even won a state journalism award for his coverage of migrant workers in the area—but mostly he prefers to stick to facts. He'll cut anything that he thinks might require a rowback or a correction. Daddy hates risk.

"What will you do when Oscar dies?"

Blossom's question startles me. I start to refute it, to say that's not happening for a long time, to reply that it's none of her business. Who does she think she is, to call my father by his first name? But after I open my mouth, I close it again. She comes with no agenda. Like everything she's asked or said in our time together, it's just a question. She's just a kid making conversation.

I take in a breath and consider my options.

"I guess I'll keep doing what I'm already doing, stay exactly where I am: selling subscriptions and ads, following the high school baseball team, taking photographs of Miss Clayton at the opening of the new Dairy Queen. I'll hound my reporters to get their stories in on time and sweat it out every week. Pretty much the same life I have now."

Blossom nods; but it's more than just a nod. There's a world of meaning in that gesture.

"What?"

"That's cool, owning a newspaper."

I wait.

"The *Newport News* folded a couple of months ago. I went to put in the announcement about Grandma marrying Tony and they told me they were calling it quits. Sure enough, a few weeks later they were selling off everything there. Sold the building to a T-shirt screening company."

"And your point being?"

She shrugs. "I guess you could move it online, right?"

"You're saying that I'll be taking ownership of a dinosaur."

She turns to me with another shrug.

I slouch down in my seat. I am listening to the economic forecast of my family's business from a seventeen-year-old—a seventeen-year-old waitress who practically dropped out of high school—and the sad thing is that she is right. When Daddy dies, the *Clayton Times and News* dies, too. And I'm fooling myself if I somehow think I am going to avoid either one of these impending deaths.

"I thought I wanted to be a carpenter one time," Blossom tells me. "I went with my dad to work sites, picked up nails, helped him measure wood, painted corners, that kind of thing. I was eleven, just about to finish fifth grade." She smiles. "He even bought me a little tool belt for my birthday; it had a pink hammer and a pink screwdriver, a set of paintbrushes. I carried on like that for months and he liked it. I knew he liked it." She takes a hand off the steering wheel and leans her elbow on the door; and I can see how she's enjoying the memories of being with her father, doing his work. I think of my dad and me standing in front of the open hood of his truck. "Here's the dipstick," he told me and I leaned as far as I could across the engine and put my hand on top of his.

"I learned a lot," she adds.

She moves into the fast lane and we both stare at the horse trailer we are passing. Two men are in the truck, one old, one young, and they sound the horn and wave once we get by them. Blossom signals and merges ahead.

"What happened? You smash your finger or finally just get bored?"

"What?" She doesn't seem to be listening to me;

she's grinning and waving at the cowboys behind us.

"Did something happen that made you lose interest in building things, or did you just finally realize that you were only trying to spend time with your dad, that you didn't really enjoy carpentry work?"

She shakes her head. "Oh, no, nothing like that. I was working mostly in the summer and then school started and then he lost his job and eventually moved out west. I always liked the carpentry work. Still do."

I watch her and wonder if a job working with her father is what she thinks is waiting for her in Texas. I turn back to the road ahead of us and remember how it was to be her age, how I went to the university just a half hour away and got a degree in journalism. I think about how I stayed at home, kept my job at the paper, sitting next to my father, never really considering whether or not it was what I wanted to do. And I suppose that is exactly what Blossom is doing, too. She is going to Texas to be with her father and fall back into what she remembers as being interesting and natural. I wonder if this will make her happy, and then I realize that I don't know what that means anyway, being happy.

I watch as we drive past tall green trees, pines, I suppose, maybe cedar, all lining the Tennessee highway. The rows are full and deep, making it appear as if the interstate was cut right through a forest. I think about travel before automobiles and four-lane highways. I think about the horse and buggy, the miles southerners walked just to get beyond the woods that hemmed them in. The men, the women, the babies born on the journey, all of them seeing nothing but a dirt path stretched before them, wide dark patches of firs and oaks, poison ivy and snakes, fighting the unbearable heat in summer, the elements, snow and ice in winter, just trying to leave.

How many people have taken this path? How many of them left the familiar East and South for parts unknown, for lives they couldn't even imagine? Sons and daughters refusing to do what their fathers had done, throwing aside the scripts written and handed down, letting go of the burdens; men and women, young adults, teenagers leaving their grieving mothers and heading west? Traveling light?

I close my eyes, no longer watching where we are going.

Chapter Eighteen

"She said they close at five."

We have arrived at Graceland.

I glance at my watch. It is just after four.

We are late to Memphis because we took our

time driving from Nashville, stopping at a few sights along the way. Just after we left Music City, Blossom wanted to see Loretta Lynn's Ranch and Coal Miner's Daughter Museum slightly east of Buffalo, in a little town called Hurricane Mills. We took a few photographs of the ranch, and we walked inside the estate but didn't take the tour. We set Roger on a fence to share the view, spent a little time in the doll museum, and bought a Loretta Lynn CD so that Blossom could sing along to her favorite tunes.

We drove a little farther and pulled off because I promised Casserole we'd stop at Sugar Tree and let him roam around Kentucky Lake. We bought snacks at a convenience store and had a picnic at Natchez Trace State Park, where there's a wrangler camp and miles of hiking trails and more than a couple of lakes. After lunch, we headed west and then south from Brownsville to see the Hatchie National Wildlife Refuge because I read in a newspaper I picked up at Natchez about the first nesting pair of bald eagles recorded in that county in Tennessee. It was late in the fledging season, but I was hopeful we might still get a view of the newly formed feathered family.

When we arrived, the ranger told us where we might find the pair with the fledglings, but a thunderstorm gathered over us, and if the birds were out, they quickly returned to their nest, refusing to make an appearance no matter how many times Blossom tried to call them to us. We had already walked at least a mile searching for the large nest before the storm came. We stood under the cover of tall trees near the river, but unfortunately there was no evidence of the eagles. Finally, when the lightning struck very near to where we had landed, we gave up and headed back to the car.

At first, I thought Blossom might complain that the trip had been futile and pointless, taking us so far out of the way from our pilgrimage west with nothing to show for our trouble; but over these last couple of days I've learned that Blossom rarely complains, at least not with me, and at least not on this journey. Plus, since she heard the story of the ashes I am taking to New Mexico, she has chosen to take on the role of Roger Hart's keeper, making sure to bring him along into every ranch or store we visit, to every restaurant where we dine, and along every path we walk. In Nashville she brought him to every bar where we listened to music.

She even takes pictures, holding up the box with his ashes at all of our stops. She reminds me of the school project in which a student brings a paper doll on all her trips and takes photographs of the doll, or sends it to extended family members living elsewhere and they take photos, to prove that it's traveled all across the country.

We did a similar story last summer, asking readers to bring along a copy of the newspaper on their vacations and to take a picture holding up the edition wherever they went. We called it "The *Clayton Times and News* Covers the World."

It turned out to be a good story until Ray Barber sent us a digital file of his edition showing up in all the strip clubs in Myrtle Beach. He labeled the attachment "The *Clayton Times and News* Covers My World," and there were photographs in which the paper was used to hide various female body parts, and, well, that put an end to our traveling news story right then.

Daddy immediately killed the running feature and disposed of the attachment; but I think Ben managed to keep a copy of Ray's file. I've found him and James William on more than one occasion sitting at his desk, giggling and whispering. When I've asked what they're doing, Ben always replies, "Just checking some local coverage," and then he and James laugh hysterically like it's the funniest thing they've ever heard. I quit paying them any attention about three months ago when I finally figured out they had forwarded the e-mail before it was deleted. Obviously they never grew tired of Ray's retort.

"We can come back tomorrow," I say to Blossom now, thinking we can spend the night in Memphis and drive to Graceland on our way out of town.

"It's kind of important that I visit today," Blossom replies, her voice trailing.

I glance over at her and she's facing the mansion behind us and I follow her eyes.

We talked about our trip to Memphis, both agreeing that Graceland was a significant stop-over; but we never discussed the expected day of our visit. I check the date on my watch. As far as I know, this day in June isn't important to Elvis. I don't understand why Blossom needs us to stop at Graceland today, but I suppose it's okay with me to pay for the ticket, visit the last hour of the day, and see what we can see.

I shrug. "Well, let's go, then," I tell her. "We don't have to stay long."

We find a shady place to park so that Casserole can enjoy an afternoon nap. Blossom, now clearly accustomed to bringing Roger along, sticks his boxed remains in her oversized purse. We pay at the shop, and as the last ticket holders of the day we move through the gates and enter the estate of Elvis Presley by ourselves.

We casually make our way through the foyer and living room, beyond the kitchen, to the TV room and pool room. As we move from location to location I watch as Blossom takes Roger out and sticks him under her arm. She stops occasionally, placing the box where she finds an empty spot, and takes a few photos with her phone. Finally, we wend our way upstairs to the Jungle

Room and in a few minutes Blossom leaves my side and I am standing alone in what has been reported to be Elvis's favorite part of the house.

Originally added to the back of the residence as a screened-in porch in the 1960s, the Jungle Room was closed in only a few years later. Elvis chose to decorate the space with green shag carpeting and furniture that was said to be reminiscent of his film scenes shot in Hawaii. I look around and smile. This must have been where Elvis gathered with friends and family members for some of his more happy times.

I take in the dark walls, the thick green plants, the exotically carved wood, and think of him sitting in one of the large chairs, drinking a beer, telling stories, feeling so proud of what he has accomplished. I figure Elvis's pride didn't have so much to do with the fame and the money. I don't even think it had to do with the music he made, the songs he shared, the films in which he starred. I think he must have been the most proud of what he had been able to give to his parents, what he had ultimately been able to do for them.

The stories that I've read all report that Elvis intended to make a lot of money and buy them the finest place in Memphis. With his earnings and newfound celebrity, he planned to rescue them from the impoverished life they led. Graceland was the fulfillment of that promise. And even though his mother, Gladys Love Presley, died only one year after the house and grounds had been purchased, there must have been some great sense of satisfaction for her famous son that at least she'd known luxury for a time. At least he had made good on his promise.

Vernon, his father, stayed on at Graceland even after Elvis died in 1977, eventually joining his wife and son in death a couple of years later. Once sentenced to three years in the Mississippi State Penitentiary for forging a fourteen-dollar check, a man estranged from his own father for most of his adult life, a man who'd been kicked out of the house when he was only sixteen years old, Vernon Presley had eventually been on the receiving end of a son's immense generosity.

And for some reason, standing here in this place, I get the feeling that this late addition—which resembles no other part of the house—must have captured and mirrored the huge shift of fortune they both knew but could not fully comprehend. The Jungle Room represented the new lush and luxurious life, their strange new normal, which would always feel like a wilderness adventure they could never have imagined.

I look around for Blossom. I want to ask her what she thinks of the space and whether or not a jungle room will be added to her dream house; but she is nowhere to be found. I wonder if she's gone down to the trophy room or out to Vernon's office, somewhere else on the estate. I hear some people coming my way and I move through the corridor, searching for her.

Finally, I walk around a corner and head down the stairs. I meet a few other tourists, wait for them to pass; and just as I'm heading back in the direction of the kitchen and pool room I glance out a window and see Blossom.

She has made her way to the Meditation Garden. She is at the grave.

Chapter Nineteen

"Did you know he had an identical twin born dead?"

I walked around the fountain and over to the grave, where I found Blossom kneeling with her head down. I stood beside her very quietly and since she's never looked up I'm surprised she even knows I am here; but now that my presence has been discovered I move closer, sit down beside her.

"Yes, I think I heard that before," I answer.

Blossom has stopped at the first gravestone. It's small and square, not like the others, not like the stones for Gladys and Vernon and Elvis, not even like the one on the opposite end, which I know to be Minnie's, the paternal grandmother.

She has Roger on the other side of her and she's holding something in her hands. At first I think it's her phone; but, having gotten closer, I can see it's much smaller than that. She has her fingers clasped around it.

"Jessie Garon," she tells me. "That was what they called him."

I nod, even though she cannot see me. I didn't recall from my limited command of Elvis trivia that Gladys and Vernon had given their dead baby a name; but now I see it before me printed on the bronze stone, the first loss for the young couple.

"I wonder what life would have been like for him," she says.

"Maybe they would have been a duet," I reply, but actually I find it hard to imagine two identical gyrating and singing Elvises. "Or maybe Jessie would have been his manager or the drummer or lead guitarist."

It seems unlikely, though, that the twins would have chosen the same path, sung the same tune. I glance up and see a Graceland employee, a guy dressed in a security guard's uniform, walking into the house. It's close to five so I guess he must be running everyone out and locking things up.

"Or maybe he would have been jealous and angry all his life," I say, "and caused trouble for the family like Roger Clinton did for Bill." I know what it is to be a sibling to the crowd pleaser, the extrovert. Jessie would have probably had it rough, always feeling like he was never quite as talented, never quite as important as his brother.

Blossom turns to me and her forehead is furrowed. It's suddenly obvious that she doesn't know about the president's brother. I start to explain but then I let it drop. It's not important enough to fill her in.

"I wonder if he felt guilty," she says. "I wonder if he somehow felt responsible for the baby's death, that he thought he took all the air or space that they both needed, that he thought he somehow kept him from ever being born."

I'm still thinking about Bill and Roger and how they aren't twins and are actually only half brothers and I'm getting ready to explain their relationship; but then I look at Blossom and I can tell she's not talking about the Clintons. She is talking about Elvis. About survivor's guilt, I guess. And then, peering at her like I am, being right beside her this way, I realize she's not talking about Elvis and his dead brother, either; she's talking about someone else. She's talking about herself.

I'm not at all sure what I should say.

"I've always thought I did something wrong, you know."

I drop my head.

She's thinking about her own baby, the one she lost after running off with the hippies, the one she said she miscarried the night she got back to Tennessee.

I remember our conversation at the restaurant

when we first met, and how she spoke of the loss so easily, so void of emotion, and I suppose I should have known it wasn't that inconsequential, that Blossom felt grief as surely as any mother would feel after such an unexpected death.

"I know I wasn't ready to be a parent; I wasn't even seventeen yet. And it would have been hard with me and Dillon. We hadn't really thought things through and there's no way he could have provided for me and a baby." She shakes her head. "It would have been a rough life for him."

I'm not watching but I hear her sniff. There are a couple of other visitors heading in our direction and I wonder if we should move from where we're sitting to give them room to pass.

"It was a boy," she announces. "Died in week fourteen."

I forget about the other tourists and let her continue.

"After the first trimester, the research says that he would have just begun to show reflexes—you know, fingers opening and closing, toes curling, his little eye muscles clenching." She pauses. "Knowing he should never be born."

I lean into Blossom, touching her slightly on the shoulder. "You don't really believe that, do you?"

She clears her throat, wipes her nose with the back of her hand. She shrugs.

"Your baby did not decide to forgo birth," I say

to her. "And you did not take his air or not give him enough space to grow."

Her head is still down.

"Miscarriage is not a reflex from the fetus, choosing not to be born. It's a bad thing that just happens and it's not anybody's fault."

She doesn't respond and I lean into her again.

"You didn't cause your baby's death."

One more time I lean into her, my elbow poking her in the side. "This was not your fault."

She's giving me nothing.

"Okay?"

She nods slightly and I'm glad to have that, at least.

"And for the record," I add, "I think you will make a terrific mother."

"Maybe later, but probably not at seventeen."

"I don't think that," I say. "I think you would have been just like your idol, Miss Loretta Lynn. You could have three children by the time you're nineteen and you'll do great."

She laughs a little at this.

"She seems like she's a good mom."

"Yes, she does. And just like Ms. Lynn, after you've had three or four you can sing, 'There's gonna be some changes made right here on nursery hill.' " I try to sing it in tune.

She laughs.

"You know the words to a country music song," she says, her voice sounding a touch lighter.

"Only because you have sung that song about a hundred times today."

I see the tourists walk away from the garden and head out the gate. The security guard is locking the front door of the house and glances over at us.

"I think we've been given the notice of last call," I tell her.

Blossom follows my gaze and sees the guard. We hear a clock chime five times and know our afternoon visit to Graceland is coming to an end.

"Lawrence Dillon Winters," she whispers.

She repeats the name as she places a tiny heart stone, a pendant she has been wearing, at the grave of Jessie Garon Presley. "Today is the anniversary of my baby's death. Lawrence Dillon Winters."

And I stand up and step back, giving a mother a little more time to say good-bye to her son.

Chapter Twenty

"He wants you to call him."

Blossom is lying on the bed in our hotel room.

We found a place in West Memphis after having dinner on Beale Street. We stopped in a bar and listened to some live music, a blues-singing piano man, but it had been a very full day and both of us were ready to find our place for the night. We didn't think we would come back to Memphis the following day and went ahead and crossed the Mississippi River to get to Arkansas.

I have just gotten out of the shower and I walk over to the bed we decided was mine, the one farthest from the window. "Who?" I ask. I sit down and drop my head and shake my wet shoulder-length hair, then I flip it all back and face her.

Casserole is asleep in the corner by the bed. He has eaten his supper and taken his walk, and now he is out for the count.

"You know who," she answers, adding a snap of her fingers, as if that would signal me to remember something that I clearly do not.

"Honestly, Blossom, I don't know who you're talking about." I drape the towel around my shoulders.

She holds the phone in front of me, but I cannot see the screen. I raise my hands and shake my head. Sometimes I feel like the age difference between us is too vast an expanse to cross. She's seventeen and I'm . . . well, clearly I'm not.

"Phillip Blake," she replies and I suddenly feel the air leave my lungs. "He texted you about half an hour ago. I didn't mean to be nosy, but your device was going off and I just happened to pick it up and read it."

I reach for my phone, which is still in her hand. "Why is he texting me? And how does he know my number, anyway?" I'm pretty sure I know the answer to this question, but I ask it nonetheless.

I read the message. It's really him. Give me a call, the text reads, and then it lists his phone number.

"How did he get this?" I ask Blossom. I'm going to need to examine a lot more closely what she has posted on my Facebook account. "How did he get my number?"

"I added it to your contact information." She stops for a second. "But just for friends." She grins. "Mostly just for one friend."

I place the phone on the nightstand and start to towel dry my hair, trying to resist the urge to look at the message again, which is making me want to jump around dancing and singing, *Phillip has my number. Phillip has my number.* I shake the thoughts from my head.

"As soon as I have time to figure it all out, I'm going to delete that account," I tell her, although I don't think I sound very convincing.

"Oh, don't do that. You've already got, like, fifty people following us on this trip. We've added about ten just since we got to Memphis."

"Why?" I grab the phone again. "What are you posting?"

I click on the Facebook app and find my profile page. Blossom seems to be posting to her own page, but because she lists my name, her updates are all showing up on my timeline, too.

Roger has fun at Kentucky Lake.

Roger enjoys the sights at Hurricane Mills.

Roger makes his way to Graceland.

Blossom has been taking the photographs and then tagging them for everyone to see.

"You can't post pictures of somebody without their permission." I scroll down at all the information she has provided under my personal profile data. My number is there, all right, along with my e-mail address.

"You gave me permission to use yours."

"I'm really not sure that is true. And I know that Roger Hart didn't give *his* permission."

"Roger Hart is not available to give his permission," she deadpans.

"I know, but this is wrong. It seems shady. It seems like we're exploiting the man and making a self-serving occasion of this trip."

"But that's not what we're doing," she responds. "This is his last hurrah. I bet he loves it, knowing so many people are watching him have this adventure."

I scroll over to her page to read exactly what she's written. Roger's last name is never mentioned, only that Blossom is with me and we're taking a friend back to his resting place. She took the business card off the top of the box before taking the pictures so there really isn't any clear way to identify whose remains we're carting around.

I click off the site and can't help myself. I go back to my messages and reread the text from Phillip Blake. My hands feel sweaty just knowing I have his phone number and that he has made an initial contact.

"Dad is excited that we're coming to see him," Blossom says, pulling me away from my thoughts of Phillip Blake.

"Yeah? Does he think you've taken up with a weirdo?" I can only imagine what this teenager's father thinks about her most recent photographs and posts.

"He didn't say," she answers. "Just that he hopes we are safe and that we will get to Amarillo soon."

"That's parental code for he thinks you've taken up with a weirdo," I inform her.

"Hmm-mm," she says. "I haven't heard of that code." She stretches out her arms and legs. She is the picture of a girl at ease and I'm glad to see she's no longer upset about her baby son and about today being the first anniversary of his death.

I put the phone down, connect it to the charger and then plug it in, and head back into the bathroom. I hang up the towel, comb my wet hair, and brush my teeth. I turn off the light, and when I'm back in the room, I check the locks on the door, give Casserole a pat on the head, click off the lamp on the nightstand between Blossom and me, and jump into bed. In exactly the same way it felt so good to fall on a mattress last night in Nashville, I am glad to be going to sleep in West Memphis.

"What are you doing?"

I slowly open one eye to look at Blossom. "What?"

"Why are you getting in bed?"

"I think you can figure that one out," I say to her as I punch my pillow and roll over.

She turns the lamp on the nightstand back on. I can tell she has something to say.

"You need to call him. Or at the very least text him back," she instructs me.

"For the last time, Blossom, I am not calling Phillip Blake. We are too old, and there is too much water under the bridge."

And just as I say this, my phone rings. Blossom is pulling out the charger and reading the screen.

"Phillip Blake," she reports, handing me my phone with a big grin and another snap of her fingers, leaving me to wonder how his name and number have been added to my phone contact list.

Chapter Twenty-one

I can't help myself. I place the phone in my lap, slide my wet hair behind my ears, smoothing it down, and pat my cheeks for a little color; and then I clear my throat, sit up, and straighten out my nightgown. Blossom gets up from her bed and heads into the bathroom. She turns in the doorway, makes the sign of a heart with her fingers, and then shuts the door behind her.

I pick up the phone, but then I realize I'm not quite sure how to answer.

Does "hello" make me sound too provincial, too stuck in my ways? Is it best to say something a little less formal, like "Well, look who it is"? Maybe I should try "Al here," making it sound like I do this all the time, get calls late at night. Or maybe it's best not to answer as Al, but try to sound more grown-up. What about "This is Al," I wonder.

The bathroom door flies opens and Blossom glares at me with her hands up. Maybe she has a good idea for a greeting. I wait, but she just mouths, "Answer it!"

Oh.

I put the phone to my ear. Blossom rolls her eyes and shuts the door. "Hello," I say.

"Al?" It is Phillip Blake. I recognize that voice; it is really him.

"Yes." I do not want to give too much away so I pretend I don't have his name and phone number staring at me from my screen; I don't say anything more.

"It's Phillip." And there is a pause. "Phillip Blake from Clayton."

"Phillip," I say, but I don't turn his name into a

question, the way I might have done in my imagination, if this weren't a real conversation, if he weren't really on the other end of the phone call.

"Hey," he adds.

"Hey," I say back.

"I saw you on Facebook," he tells me.

"Right."

"You're traveling to New Mexico."

"Right." I shake my head, disgusted with myself.

"So, how are you?"

I take in a breath. I can answer this one, I know. "I'm great, Phillip." I pause. "How are you?" I think maybe I'm on a roll.

"Well, I'm okay."

There is another pause. I realize that it's my turn again. "You still live in Winston-Salem?" I ask.

"High Point, actually. I moved a few months ago."

I hear him breathe.

"Hillary and I split up."

I have to admit I'm a little shocked that he just put that out there so soon in our conversation; but I guess his move to High Point must be related to the breakup, so that to name the town in which he lives is also to say he's not married any longer. It's weird, though. I'm surprised that he assumes I know his wife's name. ex-wife, I mean. And of course, I do know her name, but it isn't like he ever told me.

"Oh, I'm sorry to hear that," I say.

"Yeah." And there is that breath again.

"Did you ever get married?"

"No," I reply.

A pause. His pause, this time. I've got nothing to say for this part of the exchange. There is no expounding on my relationship status, that's for sure.

"So, you're going to New Mexico with somebody named Roger? That's great. Is this a vacation or a business trip?"

Good, back to something I can talk about easily. "Well, it's kind of strange." Okay, maybe this isn't something easy. "Roger is dead."

There is no response.

"I'm just returning his ashes, his remains, back to his home state."

"Oh, that must be hard. Was he a relative?"

"Uh, no, not a relative."

"A friend, then, somebody you cared about?"

I clear my throat again and I see the bathroom door open. Blossom has been eavesdropping. Normally, I'd be angry about it, except it's clear I need some help. Or at the very least a little moral support.

"Actually, Roger isn't anybody I know. I never really met him. I just found his ashes and a funeral home card with his name on the box, and, well, I just decided to take him back to where he belongs. Where I think he belongs, anyway."

"Wow."

I shake my head at Blossom to let her know this is not going well.

"That's pretty nice of you."

I shrug at my young roommate and she holds up both thumbs as if to say something like, *Good job, hang in there,* or so I think. Regardless of whether I'm interpreting her gesture correctly, I feel encouraged.

"Are you taking him back to his family?"

"Well, that's kind of the tricky part. I don't actually know where to take him. I have the name of the funeral home; but they won't tell me anything about him. So I hope that when I get there I can convince the funeral director to point me in the right direction."

"It's a mission of faith, then."

I have to say I haven't thought of this trip in that light, but I guess Phillip is right. "Yeah, I think that's a good way to describe it."

"You still working for your dad?"

"Yeah, still at the *Times and News*. And you?"

"I have an insurance company."

Another pause.

"Well," I say. "That sounds interesting." Although it doesn't so much, if I'm being honest.

"No, not really, but it pays the bills."

Is it me, or does Phillip Blake sound depressed?

"I'm sorry, Al, I didn't even realize how late it is."

I glance over at the clock on the nightstand. Blossom has left the bathroom and gotten into her bed; her head is on her pillow and she is facing me.

"Well, I'm in Arkansas, so it's not as late for me as it is for you."

"Oh, right. How has the trip been so far? Are you by yourself? Well, I mean, I know you have the box, the ashes—Roger, right?"

"Yeah, but I have my dog with me, too. And a friend is traveling with me to Texas." I look over at Blossom and wink. She winks back.

"Well, that must make it more fun."

Another pause.

"I've never driven across the country before," he tells me. "I've flown to California and Phoenix . . . Seattle . . . but I've never driven anywhere except to Florida."

"It's a great way to see the country, town by town and mile by mile," I reply. I sound just like a Greyhound Bus commercial.

"Yeah, I've heard that."

Probably on a Greyhound Bus commercial, I think.

"Well, maybe one day I'll do it," he says. "Maybe I'll just head out and drive all the way to the west coast."

"That'd be nice," I respond and roll my eyes at Blossom. I sound so stupid.

"I'm glad to talk to you, Al. You were always

such a good listener when we were in school together. That's what I remember, how easy you were to talk to."

"Thanks." This reflection surprises me and I make a funny face at Blossom.

"So, maybe we can talk some more, you know, once in a while."

I feel the flush rising from my neck to my face. Blossom is watching me intently. I slide down some in the bed, pulling the phone closer to me.

"That'd be nice," I repeat.

"Okay, then. I'll call you again, maybe when it's not so late. Or you can call me."

"Okay," I say.

"Okay," he responds. "Well, sleep well in Arkansas and be careful driving."

"Thank you."

"Good night."

"Good night."

I click the phone off, hold it to my pounding heart.

There are no words to express the way I am feeling right now. Without saying a word, Blossom turns out the light. I watch as darkness settles over the room. I close my eyes and breathe. In and out, in and out, trying to understand how nothing and yet everything in my world has just changed.

Chapter Twenty-two

I am dreaming of white flowers. A ground cover of Queen Anne's lace, clusters of fine, delicate blooms, tall bearded irises and datura, perfumed trumpet-shaped flowers that I know open only at dusk, callas and Annabelle hydrangea, iceberg rose and lilac, all white, all blooming and fragrant and alive. I am young in this dream, ten maybe, twelve, not yet saddled with disappointment, somehow not undone by death. And I am happy. I hardly even know this is me as I watch, as I stand in the midst of this garden of green stems, leaves, and stalks and stark white blooms. I am the girl in the garden but I am also watching her. And the air is sweet and the sky is perfect in its blueness, and I can breathe. And I am so full and so light and for the first time I can ever remember, I am completely unbroken.

I hold out both arms to my sides, lift my face to the sky, close my eyes, and twirl. I am laughing and twirling and loose in this wondrous moment, loose in this splendor, this unspoiled delight, and someone is coming to me, someone I am happy to see, and I'm just about to greet them, just about to welcome them . . .

"Rise and shine, sweet friend of mine!"

And the garden and the girl, the guest and the dream, wither in the light.

"What the . . . !?" I pull the pillow across my face. "Blossom, shut the curtains!"

"It's ten o'clock," she tells me, like I asked, like I care.

I don't move and I can hear the curtains close, as well as a long, dramatic sigh. "Casserole and I have already been out twice. You missed the free breakfast."

I grunt.

"I brought you coffee."

I try to bring back the whiteness, the flowery dream.

"And a banana and yogurt."

I try to make it all return.

"Do you really want to keep sleeping?"

She is not going to go away. The dream is gone, the feeling, the delight; but she is not. Blossom is not going away.

I pull the pillow away from my head and throw it in the direction of her voice. Casserole is now right beside me, breathing in my face. He's obviously eaten. His breath smells like chicken.

I reach my hand out and give him a pat.

"It's only about one hundred and thirty miles to Little Rock," Blossom says. "I thought we could stop for lunch there, take a tour of the capital city, let Roger see the governor's mansion. I think he needs a little more history on this trip."

"Of Arkansas?" I finally speak.

"Well, we've done mostly cultural stops."

I assume she means the bars and the live music venues in Nashville and Memphis. That's about the only culture I remember experiencing.

"Nature walks, a lake." I didn't realize Blossom was checking boxes for Roger's tour, that she had some kind of bucket list of things we needed to share with his ashes. "Church."

"Church?" I rise up from the pillow. "We haven't been to church."

"Well, there was Graceland."

I drop back down. So there was.

"I just think he needs to hear something about the past, visit a museum, maybe."

"You do know he's dead, right?" I throw the covers off of me and sit up. I yawn and stretch and feel my face. Casserole moves out of the way so I can stand, which I'm not quite ready to do. "We have his ashes, his remains. Roger is dead."

"He still ought to see a museum."

It's hard to argue with a girl like Blossom. I finally stand up, and I glance over at the nightstand, and with the little bit of light coming from the crack in the curtains, I can see my phone. I think of last night, of Phillip Blake, of his voice, of hearing him talk. To me. I remember how it felt to be in the conversation, to be connected to him. I remember how it was to say good night.

"There's the Museum of Discovery."

I'm surprised she's not asking me about the call. I'm surprised she's not wanting to know when Phillip Blake and I plan to talk again, when I'm going to call him.

"It used to be called the Museum of Natural History and Antiquities. It opened in 1927 on Main Street and its most popular exhibit was the head of a Chicago criminal."

I switch on the light and glance over at her. She's sitting at the table near the window, reading a brochure.

"It moved to city hall and then to MacArthur Park and now it's in a place called the River Market, which is next to the Arkansas River."

"The head or the museum?"

Blossom glances up from the reading material. She shrugs. "Both, I guess. There's also the Historic Arkansas Museum and the MacArthur Museum, and farther north from downtown is the Old State House Museum, which is the original state capitol building of Arkansas. It hosted the admission of Arkansas to the Union, a fatal Bowie knife fight between two sitting legislators, the vote to secede from the United States and join the Confederacy, and two acceptance speeches from the president."

"Well, you have certainly done your research," I say, scratching and yawning.

"I picked up some pamphlets from the office

when I went for breakfast and got you coffee. I've had a little reading time." She picks up a cup from the table and walks around the bed and hands it to me.

I take a sip. She's added milk, the way I like it. Blossom is certainly the attentive waitress. "Thank you."

She walks back over to the table, opens up the curtains a little, and glances over at me, her face a question mark. I squint at the morning sun, but I do not yell at her to close them. I start to move in the direction of the bathroom, but finally my curiosity gets the better of me.

"How come you haven't asked me about Phillip?" I stop and sit on the edge of the bed with my coffee in my hand.

She keeps reading the brochure, shrugs.

"You aren't going to ask me what he said or when I'm going to call him back?"

She shakes her head.

"You don't want to know what it was like to talk to him?"

"I think I know the answer to that one. You were smiling even in your sleep."

That's interesting.

"But you don't want to know anything?" I ask her.

She shakes her head.

I lean toward her, studying her. I do not understand this change, how she could be so excited for me one day and then completely uninterested the next. "Blossom," I say, "what's going on?"

I can see she has something she wants to say. She chews on her lip and shakes her head again. "I think the Old State House Museum is the best one."

And this time it is I who shrug, and who, without response, head into the bathroom to get ready for the day.

Chapter Twenty-three

It's raining hard by the time we get to the site of the Little Rock museum. We're sitting in the car on Third Street, drinking milk shakes we got at a drive-through. Blossom keeps taking her straw out of her plastic cup and sharing some of hers, vanilla, with Casserole. He's sticking his head between the two seats and waits patiently for the treat.

I'm not sharing mine. It's chocolate. I've tried explaining to Casserole that chocolate is no good for dogs; but he still seems disgusted with me and keeps glancing over in my direction with a kind of repulsed look and then turns back faithfully to Blossom.

We've been talking about my most recent phone conversation, the one I just had with my dad, who called me while we were ordering our milk shakes.

Not the one from last night, not the one with Phillip Blake. That one she has simply dismissed.

"He sounded okay?" She has the lid off her cup and is stirring her drink.

I nod and take a giant slurp of chocolate. I feel Casserole's disdain.

"So you were worried for no reason?" She pulls out her straw, heaping a spoonful of milk shake on the end, and holds it out for my dog to lick; then she sticks the straw back in her cup.

I watch this without a word. Most people would probably be a little grossed out about this exchange, but I happen to think my dog has only as many germs as the next person so I'm not at all bothered. It's just a tiny bit off-putting because I feel like Casserole is assigning a new loyalty to this teenager.

"I guess I was," I answer.

Daddy is fine, or so he says. He didn't call right away because he's been in Raleigh, attending a state legislature meeting. He claims he stayed in town because he was checking out a '57 Thunderbird he heard was for sale, but I clearly remember the one he had years ago and sold, saying it was just too expensive to keep running.

"Why didn't you tell him that we met the governor of Arkansas?"

I shake my head and don't answer. Following the motorcade as it drove up to the governor's mansion didn't really seem all that noteworthy, and even though what happened later certainly might be, I still chose not to say anything about that.

I had driven farther onto the governor's property than I should have as an unauthorized motorist, and after I realized as much, I stopped the car to turn around. But Blossom wanted a picture. Before I could stop her, she jumped out of the car with her phone trying to get a shot of who she thought was the governor. She landed badly, fell on the sidewalk near the front lawn, then lay there laughing hysterically while I yelled at her to get back in the car.

All of this quickly captured the attention of the security detail.

Their rapid response to surround Faramond, and the hour-long investigation that followed, would probably be interesting to a newspaper owner; but I chose not to give that report to my father. I start to remind Blossom that I don't really think having the car impounded and then the three of us—Casserole included—being taken to a locked room on the mansion premises actually counts as meeting the governor, but I decide just to let that drop.

"I'm pretty sure that one state police guy liked you." She takes a sip of her shake.

Casserole leans in.

"Which one?" I ask, surprised that she would think any of the security personnel exhibited anything other than sharp investigative skills. If I'm honest, I'm still a bit shaky from the entire incident. It was my idea to stop at the drive-through because I thought ice cream might calm me down.

"The skinny one who stayed behind with the car and then kept walking in and out of the room where they took us, jangling his set of keys like he was more important than the others."

I think about the men in suits, the uniformed officers, the room where they escorted us. We handed over driver's licenses, phones, the car registration, proof of insurance, even Roger's ashes, which they quickly returned. The agent Blossom is talking about was thin and balding, a bit fidgety, and I don't at all agree that he was interested in me. I think he was just trying to hurry along the entire investigation. He kept coming in and saying that the governor needed to leave, which apparently was a departure we halted with the illegal encroachment, the photo op, and Blossom's fall on the sidewalk.

He was clearly concerned about keeping the governor on schedule. He did look at me once, long and intently; but I think he was just making up his mind about whether or not he believed the whole "returning the ashes" story, which actually made a couple of the agents smile. Once it was clear that we were who we said we were and we had no weapons or ill intent and that the car wasn't stolen and that Blossom had permission from her grandmother to travel with me, I don't recall him giving me another look.

"Yeah, I don't really remember it that way." I watch the sheets of rain fall on the road ahead of us. I'm not sure Roger is going to make it to a museum in Little Rock. It's already quite late in the day. He may just have to be satisfied with an hour in the governor's mansion and the thrill of a near arrest.

"And what about your dad?" I ask, thinking about the second call she made after they found out she wasn't yet eighteen and asked her to go with them to another room, leaving me alone with Casserole and a silent police officer standing at attention in front of the door. She called her grandmother first, who said her travel with me was fine; but then they asked her to call her father as well.

"He was fine—told them I was coming to Texas and that Grandma was right to give me permission to leave." Another sip of milk shake for herself and then another for Casserole. He spills a little and quickly licks it up.

I nod.

"It's cool that they got hold of that funeral guy in New Mexico," she adds.

I have to agree. Mr. Harold Candelaria, owner and director of the Serenity Mortuary of Grants, New Mexico, confirmed that Roger Hart had been cremated at his facility in 2010; but he also told the Arkansas State Police that he did not know Alissa Wells or Blossom Winters and he could not establish that we were, in fact, in possession of his client's remains.

Still, I'm glad Mr. Candelaria knows we're heading his way. Maybe he'll find a Hart family member and have the contact information when I arrive. That would save me a lot of unnecessary research.

"That almost makes it worth that whole bit of drama, don't you think?"

I peer over at Blossom, who appears well at ease, make a face, and shake my head. I wouldn't really go that far. Almost being arrested for stalking the governor of Arkansas and trespassing on private property requires just a tiny bit more benefit than a name and number. Besides, I already had the contact information for the funeral home in New Mexico and I can't say when I'll quit checking my rearview mirror for police with their guns drawn or freezing up every time I hear a siren. So no, I don't really believe that side trip was worthwhile. That whole bit of drama makes me want to get out of this state capital as quickly as I can.

"But your dad sounded okay?"

I think again about the call. He sounded like himself, only, I don't know, cheerful, I think. And Oscar Wells may be described in many ways, but never cheerful. I should probably be happy about this, but it doesn't feel pleasant to me. I'm a little concerned, actually.

"Well, maybe we should just bag the museum idea," Blossom says, surprising me.

We both listen to the rain on the roof of the car and watch the wind kicking up in front of us.

"Besides, I got a couple of great pictures of Roger with the security guys. I think he's probably fine with that being our Little Rock adventure."

And I turn and watch as she takes a big slurp of milk shake and then holds the cup out for Casserole to finish it off. I don't even want to know about how or when she got those photographs. I gladly crank Faramond and point us in the direction of the interstate, getting us safely, and without incident, out of town.

Chapter Twenty-four

Fort Smith is about one hundred and sixty miles from Little Rock. It took us about three hours to get here. With the weather and interstate construction, our afternoon and evening travel was slow; but we made it, and it's another night in a busy highway motel.

Blossom wanted to stop in Clarksville, just south of the Ozark National Forest; but I was heading west and moving as fast as I could away from the capital of Arkansas. If it had been up to me, I would have crossed the state border and spent the night in Oklahoma; but Blossom wanted to spend some time in the city that boasted to be "where the New South meets the Old West." Plus she was charmed by the notion that the city's visitor center was a former bordello and thought we would somehow miss out if we didn't stop at Miss Laura's Social Club and pick up a few brochures and take another picture of Roger. The center was closed by the time we arrived, so I promised her we could check it out tomorrow and we picked our place for dinner and found another pet-friendly resting spot and we have checked in for the night.

There was a mall on our way to the motel and Blossom wanted to shop; so once we ate our dinner and arrived at the motel, I handed over the keys to the car, allowing her to drive back to the shopping center. Me, I'm going to make up with Casserole and hopefully return to his good graces. I told Blossom that a quiet evening would give me time to do a more thorough search for Mr. Roger Hart from Grants, New Mexico, even though I'm sure she saw right through me and knows that's not really who I plan to thoroughly search for.

I did finally ask her why she suddenly lost interest in my making contact with my old heartthrob and she just said that she didn't know for certain that Phillip was exactly who I might think he was. When pushed for more, she clammed up again, promptly denying that there was any clear reason for her sudden lack of enthusiasm, saying rather it was simply a feeling she had after seeing some of the pictures he had posted online. She didn't so much warn me to stay away from Phillip as she just thought it might be a good idea to check out some of the other guys who had friended me on Facebook. She even questioned me about my friendship with Ben from work.

He has sent me more than a few messages, and she thinks this activity has some deeper meaning, but I know it's just Ben needing help with his inserts and copy. All of his timeline posts and instant messaging are more reasons why I don't have a presence on social media. The man has worked for the paper for a decade and still doesn't know how to file a story or manage the cold type. He's a good guy; but like the others at the *Times and News*, he needs a lot of handholding.

"There's a good shot of you on here," I tell Casserole after I open up my laptop and get online. Blossom has posted a picture of my dog sitting next to a state trooper, taken once we were finally released from the mansion. I think I remember her asking the officer for a quick shot, but I was certainly not posing for any photographs; I was trying to get in the car and get out of there as quickly as I could. "You look all innocent, but I think they were on to you."

Casserole stands to check out what I am doing, yawns, and drops back down. He curls up on his stack of blankets, turning his back on me.

"Yeah, you pretend you like Blossom more than me, but just remember who took you in nine years ago when you showed up at my door so pitiful and needy. She might give you vanilla ice cream, but I've cleaned your poop."

I hear him make a kind of snorting noise and I know he understands exactly what I'm saying. I scroll through the photographs Blossom has posted. And what do you know? She did meet the governor of Arkansas! I click on and enlarge the picture and there she is right next to the man.

I guess at some point while I was sitting under guard in the locked room after they took her out to call her father, she was escorted to a part of the mansion where the governor was waiting for his security detail. How she got someone to take the photograph is beyond me, since I know they confiscated both of our phones when they stormed the car; but there she is, standing next to the state leader with Roger and two police officers nearby and now it's a post on her timeline.

"Did you know about this?" I ask my dog, turning the screen around to him, showing him the picture; but he doesn't look and he refuses to say anything incriminating about his new best friend.

I choose not to bear witness any longer to Blossom's photographic journal of the day and click instead on Phillip's page to check out his profile. There's not a lot of detail; but he does have a few photo albums and over a thousand friends. I take a breath, and then, I don't know, maybe it's the secret thrill of almost being arrested, but I seem to have a bit more confidence than I did yesterday. I exhale and start typing.

Made it to Fort Smith, I message him.

I click send and wait, watching the cursor blink. It blinks and blinks. I get up and go to the bathroom for a glass of water and I come back. It's still blinking.

I'm just about to give up, thinking this is a truly bad idea and that I don't really have jailhouse swagger because I would have cried like a little girl if I had been arrested and it doesn't matter anyway because Phillip Blake is not sitting at his computer reading Facebook messages.

Then: How far is that from West Memphis?

He's there.

About three hundred miles, I type. I'm not exactly sure of the mileage, but that sounds about right.

Did you stop anywhere?

Little Rock, I answer, without further detail.

I wait.

Did you really see the governor?

Blossom's posts must have landed on my

timeline. I have no idea what else she may have documented.

No, just his house.

A smiley face emerges.

I read something you wrote, he adds.

I'm not quite sure how to respond so I wait.

From the paper, he explains. I found some of your stuff online.

This makes me smile. Phillip is cyberstalking me.

You're a good reporter.

I post a smiley face in return.

I'm getting ready to go out. Want to talk tomorrow?

I glance over at the clock. It's not that late for him to be going out, and suddenly I wonder why I am thinking about what time he's going out and whether or not it's too late.

Sure.

You'll be in Oklahoma City by then, I guess, he writes.

At the rate we've been going, that's correct. Probably.

Okay, I'll give you a call. You can tell me about Little Rock. Or maybe you'll meet another governor.

I definitely need to read my timeline.

Okay.

And just like that, Phillip is gone.

I click over to my page and scroll down my

timeline; but I don't really see anything on my news feed about the governor's mansion. I guess Blossom hasn't posted it after all. There's the picture of Casserole and there's the selfie she took of us just before we saw the motorcade; but there's no shot of her and the governor. I'm about to keep searching when suddenly there is a knock at the door.

Chapter Twenty-five

"Just a second," I call out.

I check the clock on the nightstand—it's just after eight o'clock—and then my appearance in the mirror on the dresser in front of the beds; it's not great, but at least I still have on my clothes and haven't started to get ready for bed.

I run my fingers through my hair a bit, untangling some of the knots, and tuck my shirt in my shorts. I close the laptop and place it on the nightstand, smooth down the sheets on the bed, pick up the pillow I've tossed on the floor and put it back in its right location, and head to the door.

Blossom must have misplaced her key or else she has her arms full with stuff from the car and needs help getting in. But why she hasn't announced herself or started beating the door incessantly like she has done in the past, yelling lines from old television shows that she's been watching while waiting for me to wake up, I don't know. I wait, thinking the line is coming. She seems to like *The Andy Griffith Show* best, banging on the door talking about being Ernest T. Seconds pass and there's nothing.

I glance over at Casserole to see if he has a better idea of who is visiting us; but he's not offering any assistance. He seems quite comfortable all curled up in the corner on his bed and clearly doesn't smell danger.

I stand at the door and peek through the tiny hole, just to make sure it's my roommate. The image is distorted, the head looking a little like a giant balloon, but I can see that it isn't my roommate after all. It's a man, as best I can tell, a young one. He has long hair and I believe that's an earring in his left lobe.

"Can I help you?" I ask, my face smashed against the door.

"Oh, hey," he says, and he seems to know I'm peering at him through the peek hole.

"Hey," I reply, waiting for his answer.

"I'm looking for Blossom," the visitor announces. "Is this the right room?"

I can see he's pulling away and reading the room number posted on the door.

I lean in even closer, squinting.

"You work for the motel?" Maybe he's maintenance or housekeeping bringing us more towels; but that doesn't explain why he's asking for Blossom, and, from what I can see, he isn't wearing a uniform.

"No," he answers, without offering any more information.

"Are you a police officer?" I ask. Maybe the finest of Little Rock has finally caught up with us. *What if Blossom has an outstanding warrant? Or maybe after thinking about the two of us traveling together, the officers came to a decision that I'm a pervert who kidnapped a teenager and they drove all the way here to rescue her.* I try to look around the balloon-headed man-boy to see if there's a SWAT team waiting somewhere behind him.

What might the police have dug up on me? There were some parking tickets I sort of let go unpaid when I was visiting South Carolina during a guild meeting last year. And there was some mix-up a couple of years ago over the stolen identity of a Mr. Albert Wells from Jacksonville, Florida, who kept calling me at the paper and accusing me of using his credit card and making all kinds of charges on the Internet. I thought we had cleared up that whole situation; but now if the police are digging into my records and are standing at my door, I'm not so sure.

I try to remember where I put my phone and to decide who will get my one designated phone call once I am arrested. It'll be either my father or Joe Creech, the DUI lawyer in Clayton, who is the only attorney I know.

"What?" the stranger replies. He's young, I can tell now, a teenager, not much older than Blossom; and he's now trying to look at me through the peek hole, which obviously can't be done. "Why would you think I'm a policeman—is she in trouble?"

I see a giant eye staring back and it startles me, causing me to back away a bit.

"No, not that I know of." I wait and then lean back in a little more. "So, you're not with the police?"

He shakes his balloon head and I breathe somewhat easier. Although I probably should pay those parking tickets.

"Well, is she there? Can she come out?"

"Who are you?" I ask. "How do you know Blossom?"

And then the balloon head turns away and I hear him talking to someone coming up the stairs. Casserole perks up now. It must be Blossom returning from shopping.

"Is that her?" I ask my dog and he slowly stands, balances on his three legs, and stretches. I take that as a yes.

When I open the door, I see that the young guy has moved away from our room and is standing near the stairs. I can see Blossom stopped on the top step and the two are speaking to each other.

He's thin, wearing a black T-shirt and an old pair of khaki shorts. He has on flip-flops and his stringy brown hair hangs down his back. It's longer than mine but not quite as long as Blossom's.

I finally step all the way out of the room. Blossom is clearly focused on the guy and doesn't appear to see me. She seems a little surprised but not afraid of the boy who is now talking to her.

I clear my throat, but neither of them turns my way.

"Everything okay?" I ask.

She peeks around her visitor's shoulders. "Yeah, it's fine," she answers, offering me a smile. She has two bags in her hands and appears at ease standing a few yards away from me with a strange young man waiting between us. "There was a sale," she tells me.

I nod. The boy hasn't turned back around to face me, so I still don't have a good visual on him.

"I bought you a dress."

I glance at the bags in her hands. *A dress? For me?* I can't think of the last time I wore a dress and I don't ever remember having someone buy one for me. I must admit I'm pleasantly surprised.

"I'll be there in a minute and show it to you; I think you'll like it and I hope I got the size right."

"Okay," I say, still surprised by the declaration of her gift.

"It's yellow," she adds.

A yellow dress? I think. Well, that's something.

"I'll be there in just a minute," she informs me and smiles as if to say, *You can go now;* but I'm still not ready to step away. I'm still a little concerned about leaving her on the outside staircase with a boy I don't know. Plus, curiosity has definitely got the best of me. *When did Blossom meet a boy and give him our room number at a motel in Fort Smith that we just checked into?*

"You need me to wait out here for you?" I ask, hoping that she will at least make an introduction. "Or you want to come in the room and talk?" I'm holding the door open with my foot as I stand just outside. I can feel Casserole pushing against my leg, trying to get his own visual and, I don't know, maybe another milk shake.

"No, I think we'll go to the lobby."

The boy now turns in my direction and he smiles. He sticks his hands in the back pockets of his shorts.

I don't respond.

"Al, this is Dillon," Blossom says, finally.

Dillon. The old boyfriend from Newport, Tennessee. The father of her dead baby, the one she said was no longer in her life.

I have no idea what to say.

He holds up a hand, his greeting, and Blossom spins around on the stairs; and the two of them walk down the steps, as her bags bounce against her legs.

Chapter Twenty-six

The yellow dress, sleeveless with tiny narrow straps, a tight bodice, and a knee-length, flowing skirt, is made with a floral print, covered with white flowers, small embroidered ones, and it's flouncy and feminine. It reminds me of my recent dream of the garden of white flowers, so even though I own very few dresses, rarely wear them, and probably wouldn't have even selected this one for myself, I have to admit I like it.

Blossom made me try it on, pulled me to the mirror and made me look. It was slightly embarrassing to gaze at myself wearing a sundress, having a teenage critic behind me telling me to work on my posture, pull back my shoulders, lift my chin, don't wear a bra; but I did it, I stood there and examined myself in this lovely yellow dress.

Blossom apparently has an eye for fashion, and she's also apparently decided that I'm to be her project. When she asked me on our second day together about my wardrobe, thinking this road trip was not really a fair assessment of what might be in my closet at home, she became quite distressed to discover that I was actually traveling in my best work clothes, that the painter pants, oversized tees, and worn sneakers all are part of my daily attire.

Immediately, she began to gather information about my size as well as my measurements and declared she would fix me by the time we got to Texas. The yellow dress is the first installment of her makeover. And, well, so far, so good. I do like her taste, even if I don't really plan to wear this dress out in public, and I don't think I can ever go without a bra. I'm not chesty, but I feel more comfortable with a little restraint.

Dillon, it turns out, hitched a ride to Arkansas from Newport with various folks, the last being a guy joining the army in Fort Smith. Now that he's here, he's asked to ride with us to Shamrock, Texas, where he plans to get a job with a family member, a cousin or an uncle who runs a construction crew. Blossom admitted that she texted him when she left Tennessee, letting him know that she was going to visit her father, but she denies knowing that he would show up in Fort Smith, claiming he found out where we were because of the Facebook posts. He also finally confessed that he came because he thought Blossom was traveling with two men, Al and Roger; and even though they really aren't together any longer, he claims he couldn't stand it. So, he hitched a ride and found us. I think he's more than a little relieved that I'm Al and Roger is in a box.

When the idea was raised about him joining us, I was not at all comfortable with the thought of an additional passenger; but after hearing his request I admit I felt sorry for the guy. Besides, I feel somewhat indebted to Blossom because of the yellow dress. And it's only for a day, since we expect to get through Oklahoma City and across the state line into Texas by dark later today. And to Dillon's credit, he did apparently get up and leave early with Blossom to see the visitor center, allowing Casserole and me to sleep late, which seems to me to be an unexpected benefit of having him join us.

We gave him pillows and our blankets, but Dillon slept with—maybe I should say *in*—Faramond, which was the only way I was going to let him stay. Neither Blossom nor her young suitor seemed upset about the arrangements, although he did turn up about an hour after he left, asking for Roger, claiming he needed someone else with him so he would feel safe. And after he got the remains, he didn't bother us again. Funny what makes us feel secure. Some people need a gun or a dog. Apparently, Dillon just needs a box of ashes.

Blossom's ex-boyfriend says things like "it's cool, dude" and "jacked up" a lot, which is a little annoying; but I think I can manage for a few hours. I'm used to working with James William, after all, and "jacked up" and "cool" are not nearly as bothersome to me as some of his sports clichés. He writes and says things like, "That pop fly was a can of corn," or "They didn't take care of the rock," which I spend hours trying to translate in my edits. Besides, I sort of like Dillon, in a weird kind of way. He's extremely childlike, guileless, innocent. He takes everything I say literally, which is, I don't know, kind of refreshing.

When Blossom and Dillon returned from their tourist excursion to Miss Laura's Social Club, getting a number of quality photographs with Roger, Casserole and I had already checked out of our room and were waiting for them in the motel lobby. We gassed up at a station just off the interstate and are once again heading west.

I'm driving this leg of the trip and Blossom has decided to take the backseat with Roger and Cass. The rain has ceased and it's turning into a beautiful summer day. We've rolled down the windows and are listening to Dillon's playlist on his iPhone. Unlike Blossom and her country music, he prefers rock and roll.

"So, is it mainly road construction or building construction that you'll be doing?"

The first album has ended and Dillon is searching for a different one for our listening pleasure.

"Roadwork," he answers. "My stepdad's brother owns a paving company."

"In Shamrock?" I clarify. I studied the map before we started the trip earlier and it looks like Shamrock is just across the state line.

"Yeah, I think so." He nods and keeps scrolling through his list of songs.

"You're planning to do that kind of work all summer and go back to Tennessee in the fall?"

He shrugs. "Maybe," he says. "Do you like the Black Veil Brides?"

"Sure," I reply, making the assumption this is a rock band.

He makes his selection and places his phone back in the console between us. The music starts.

"Blossom says you run a newspaper."

"Well, I don't actually run it; my father does."

"Cool."

"Uh-huh."

He sings along to the song and then he stops. "Blossom thinks you're real smart."

"Is that right?"

"Yep, she said you use a lot of big words, but you don't make her feel stupid."

Well, that's nice to know. I glance in my rearview mirror and get a look at my passenger. She's got on headphones and is listening to her own playlist. From the way she's mouthing the words, I'm guessing it's the Carrie Underwood album. I figure I've learned the words to all the songs on Blossom's CDs. We've listened to the four she brought along with her for more than three hundred miles.

"Blossom's smart, too, but she don't like people to know."

I figured as much.

"Did she tell you I asked her to marry me?"

I nod. "After she found out she was pregnant."

"No, this morning."

Okay, well, this is news to me.

I turn to face Dillon. "And what did she say?"

He slides his hair behind his ears and shakes his head. Clearly, it was a no.

"I'm sorry, Dillon," I say softly, waiting to hear his predictable assessment of coming all the way to Arkansas to have his heart broken. Surely, for the teenager, this is as jacked up as things can get.

He shrugs. "Yeah, well, at least I get to ride all the way to Shamrock with her. And I really like you and Roger and Casserole; so it's cool." He closes his eyes as the music swells to a percussion solo and then he raises both hands and pretends to play the drums.

His ease with disappointment surprises me and I turn to face the road. I glance back in my rearview mirror at Blossom, who smiles at me, and then I look ahead, watching the green Arkansas landscape fade to the brown of the Great Plains.

Chapter Twenty-seven

We've stopped at the Oklahoma City National Memorial, but now that I have parked and turned off the engine near the entrance of the museum, no one is getting out of the car. The sun is shining; there is only a light breeze; it is a lovely afternoon. Yet we just sit here. Cars are pulling in and pulling out around us, people are coming and going, and we are staying right where we are without saying a word or making a move.

Blossom, who made the suggestion that we visit the memorial site, sits in the passenger's seat, just staring straight ahead without reaching for her door. Casserole and Dillon, both tired from the long walk we took only an hour ago near Norman at the Lake Thunderbird State Park, are curled up together in the backseat sound asleep. Roger has been taken from the console and placed in the front and is resting on the dashboard. And for some reason I can't explain, I am not moving, either.

I know that neither of my live human passengers was born yet when Timothy McVeigh parked a rental truck packed with four thousand, eight hundred pounds of explosives just across the street from the Alfred P. Murrah Federal Building and walked away. Of course they both know the story, are familiar with what happened here; but they learned it later, heard it discussed on anniversary dates or in their American history classes. It was never something they watched on the news or heard about as it unfolded.

They didn't see the images of police officers carrying out the bodies of the injured and dead children hours after it happened, and they didn't watch a national response of shock and disbelief when it wasn't a Middle Eastern terrorist who was later arrested for the bombing but rather a young Persian Gulf War veteran from Lockport, New York, who was responsible for the killing of one hundred and sixty-eight people and the injuries of over six hundred more. They know the event, sympathize with those affected, have a desire to understand and learn the details; but they didn't live with the story.

I, on the other hand, was fifteen, and I watched the evening news on April 19, 1995, with my dad, who covered the story for the paper. It was on a Wednesday, later in the day after the morning bombing; and we sat together on the sofa in the den watching the images of destruction, hearing the names of the victims, learning that a day care center had been destroyed and that a number of those killed were children. We didn't say a word to each other as we sat there side by side, Sandra somewhere else in the house, trying to learn some new dance steps. We watched the news without speaking and then he got up to pack and I stayed there, just like I am now, without moving.

He was leaving for Oklahoma City that evening just after Tom Brokaw's telecast broke for a few minutes so that the station could show some of the state's local news. He had one suitcase with him and his old leather bag that he took with him everywhere, the one that he still keeps hanging on his shoulder or the back of his office chair, the one that still holds his reporter's notebook, pens, and whatever relevant research he has collected. Our neighbor Millie called while he was packing to say she would be over in an hour, bringing us chicken pot pie and chocolate cookies, letting me know that the arrangements for our care had been decided before Sandra and I had gotten home from school.

I heard him say good-bye to Sandra and as he started to leave I finally got up from the sofa and followed him to the door.

"How long will this take?" I asked. I knew how important this news event was to my father, but I was not nearly as interested in a bombing in a place three states over as I was in knowing how long we would be without him.

He stopped and turned to me as I waited on the landing, the screen door propped open with my elbow.

"I'll be back by the weekend," he promised. "Millie will check on you every morning and she'll have you something to eat when you get home from school."

I nodded.

"You'll make sure your sister gets her homework done and gets to her dance class tomorrow afternoon."

Again, I nodded.

"I'm just going to be gone for a couple of days," he said again, this time with a bit more emotion than before.

"I know," I answered him.

"And so, you're okay?" he asked.

Of course I was okay. I was fifteen. By that time I had been staying alone with my sister for two years while my dad traveled to cover the news. I knew the routine. Millie came over, brought us something to eat. She checked on us in the morning and she called me just before she went to bed. I helped my sister with her homework, fixed our supper, cleaned up, washed the clothes, ironed what my sister picked out to wear, turned out the lights, and checked all the doors. In the mornings, I made sure Sandra got to school, and in the afternoon or evening, I made sure that she went to whatever party she was invited to or class she was registered for.

Because I was the oldest, I took care of things. I was responsible and dependable. I never missed a beat. I knew how to make breakfast and call 911. I was good with grammar and household emergencies. And this was Clayton, North Carolina; my sister and I were safe. I had never been afraid, never caused a fuss, never been anything other than the daughter Oscar Wells needed to keep things organized and working, to hold the family together.

And yet, I don't know, I can't even remember for sure why, but this time, this news story, this national event he had to cover and write about, this taking leave of us bothered me. I even started to cry. And I remember how Daddy stopped at the car and turned once more to look at me.

"Alissa," he said, one of the few times I remember him calling me by my first name. "Do you want me to stay?"

Every fiber of my being wanted to tell him yes. Yes, I wanted him to stay. Yes, I wanted him home. No, I did not want to be left in that house with this news, this terrible, horrible news still so fresh in my mind.

But ever the good soldier, I shook my head, waved good-bye, walked inside, and shut and locked the door behind me.

"You want to go?" Blossom pulls me from the memories of my fifteenth year and I feel her watching me.

There is just one tear that has rolled down my cheek and I wipe it away. I pull Roger down from the dashboard and place him back in the console between us. I shake my head. "Not really," I tell her.

"Then let's go west, sister. Roger Miller's museum is right at the state border and if we hurry we can get there before they close."

"You going to have a meltdown at his grave?" I ask, clearing my throat, pulling myself together, and turning on the engine.

Blossom rolls down her window and puts on her sunglasses. "Nah. He was a great singer-songwriter; but he won't no Elvis."

I nod and pull out of the parking space.

"Besides, this stop is for Roger. It turns out he and Mr. Miller have more than just a first name in common."

I wait.

"Mr. Roger Miller was cremated. The location of his ashes remains unknown."

I put the car in gear, switch on my signal, and make my left turn. We are heading out of Oklahoma City.

Chapter Twenty-eight

" 'Trailer for sale or rent, rooms to let . . .' " My dad is singing the words of his favorite Roger Miller song.

"That's the one," I say. I called him after our stop at the museum, and now I'm listening to him belt out the lyrics, although they sound a little tinny coming through my cell phone like this. I never knew he was a fan.

" 'No phone, no pool . . .' "

"Yep, that's still the one."

It took us two hours to get here and even though we're clearly the only tourists in Erick, Oklahoma, the museum hostess, Irene, seems anxious for us to take our leave. Since we arrived a few minutes ago, she must have looked at her watch and mentioned a dozen times that the place closes in thirty minutes.

I'm standing by the car and I can see Blossom inside trying to get Irene to hold Roger so that she can get a photograph. In spite of the fact that she must be late for some appointment, or nervous around the three of us, Irene is a good sport, even forcing a smile as Blossom takes the shot. I see her hand Roger back and then look at her watch once again. I check mine. Blossom still has fifteen minutes. She'll probably want to buy a CD or a nightshirt.

"I didn't think you liked country music," I hear my dad say.

"No, not so much," I answer, leaning against the front of the car. I look around the streets of Erick. It's a pretty slow day in Roger Miller's hometown.

"But Dixie says you've been to Loretta Lynn's Ranch, stopped at bars in Nashville, had your picture taken with Johnny Cash, and even took a tour at Graceland. Are you returning ashes to New Mexico or taking a guitar-picking hall of fame tour?"

He has a point.

"It's my passenger," I reply. "She's only a teenager and she doesn't sing or play an instrument as far as I know, but for some reason she likes the classics."

"Blossom?" he responds. I'm surprised that he

knows her name. I don't think I mentioned it to him in our past phone conversations.

"I saw her on your social media site. Was that part of the plan? Pick up hitchhikers?"

"You're using the Internet?" I ask, teasing him.

I hear him blow out a breath. "That's real funny."

"Yeah, well, I don't mean to be funny; I just can't believe you're looking at Facebook."

"I'm giving it a shot. It turns out I can learn a lot about people by just reading their profiles. Some of this stuff is just a waste of time, but I can see why it's important to keep up with the latest technology."

"I'm sorry. Am I talking to the publisher of the *Clayton Times and News*? Is this Oscar Wells, Oscar 'That Computer Will Make You Stupid' Wells? The one who still handwrites his stories in a composition book?"

"I know, I know," he replies. "Dixie's got me set up with these media sites."

"Dixie?" Well, that's a surprise. I thought it was Ben who was pushing for technological advancement.

"Yes, she's been real helpful that way."

Well, hooray for Dixie, I think. Maybe his hire of the single mom with one semester of community college wasn't a complete waste.

"Everything okay with this week's paper?" I ask.

"We lost a couple of ads to the *N and O*," he replies, letting me know that the Raleigh paper is still king in eastern North Carolina. "But we got a good feature on Senator Hill's widow and Ben did a nice job on the tobacco warehouse sale. I swear we should just change the name of the town to Reynoldsville, since all we seem to know how to do is grow tobacco. Hey, did you know Roger Miller died from lung cancer?"

I did not know that. I guess they didn't choose to mention cause of death in that little ten-minute video presentation I watched when we first arrived at the museum.

My daddy never was a big supporter of the tobacco farms that continue to prosper in North Carolina even though nationally cigarette usage continues to decline. We found out that most of the crop is sent overseas where there isn't as much legislation on smoking and where, as he likes to say, "we're popping cigarettes in babies' mouths just to keep big tobacco companies in business."

He's printed a lot of stories over the years about the hazards of smoking and the costs of lung and throat cancer to the state and has found himself more than a few times on the receiving end of angry op-eds and harassing phone calls from disgruntled farmers and unhappy businessmen. I think he's always thought growing up on a tobacco farm had something to do with Mama's tumors even though there has never been any scientific link between that particular crop and brain cancer. As long as he has run the paper, he has never liked what tobacco means to our hometown and he refuses to bow to the industry.

"So, you broke rank and wrote a bright?" I ask, changing the subject when I suddenly recalled Ben's report about last week's paper and my father's puff piece.

"You heard about that, huh?"

"From Ben."

"Yeah, it was just a silly thing I messed around with, about how squirrels got my last good tomato, just something to fill up space. Since you weren't here to cover the summer weddings or finish up that feature on the twin valedictorians over at the high school, I needed something for the split page. Ben and Jasper thought it was okay to add it."

"I heard you got a lot of good responses."

"Nah, nothing like that, just a few calls."

I glance over at Dillon, who is walking back with Casserole after their stroll down to the corner convenience store. He's got his hair in a ponytail and his earphones around his neck, he's eating something that is dangling from his lips, and I'm pretty sure he's talking to my dog.

I watch as a man comes out of the auto parts store that Dillon is passing, stops, and takes a very interested look. I can't say I blame him: there aren't too many long-haired, ear-pierced stoners with three-legged dogs walking the streets of Erick. My guess is that the Roger Miller

Museum doesn't really draw that sort of clientele.

"Well, Al, thanks for calling. I'm trying to get out of here before six tonight. A few of us are heading over to the baseball game."

I'm still watching Dillon and Casserole because the man who came out of the store has said something.

"Al?"

"Oh, sorry, Dad. You're going over to Zebulon to see the Mudcats with James William."

"Yeah, James and a couple others from the office."

Ben and Jasper, I suppose, since they're the only others who work there and follow the farm league. "And you're okay? Your blood pressure is all right?"

"Well, it's still too high according to Ned," he says, mentioning the family doctor in Clayton. "But we're trying a new drug; so I'm sure it'll be just fine."

I have quit listening and am now very distracted by what I can only guess is a confrontation between Dillon and some fine citizen of Erick, Oklahoma. Dillon is shaking his head and glancing around. Casserole is anxiously peering in my direction.

"Al, you there?"

"Yeah, yeah," I say, now feeling more than a little concern about what is transpiring a few hundred yards from me.

"Call me when you get to Texas," he says.

"Okay, then, have a good time. I'll talk to you later." And I click off the phone without hearing my father's good-bye.

Chapter Twenty-nine

"Everything okay?" I ask as Dillon heads in my direction. He's back to chewing on what turns out to be a string of red licorice. Casserole walks beside him and then heads to the other side of the car, waiting to be let in so that he can take his familiar place in the backseat. Dillon follows him.

"Yeah, it's all good. Casserole peed at the corner. He may want some water, though. It's pretty hot, huh?" Dillon peeks through the window.

I open the door on my side and find the water bowl. I fill it with water from the jug behind the seat, walk around, and place it in front of Casserole, who is indeed thirsty. He drinks almost the entire bowl.

"They had red ropes," the boy tells me, holding up the candy. "You want a string?"

I shake my head and help my dog get into the car. I walk back around and put the bowl back behind my seat. Then I close the door and glance over at the auto parts store. The man he was talking to just a few minutes earlier has gotten in a truck and appears to be leaving. He's staring in our direction and even from this distance I can see the scowl on his face.

"I just saw that guy stop you. I thought he might have said something to you."

"Yeah, he did." Dillon walks around and joins me. "Blossom still inside?" He nods toward the museum.

"Yes," I answer.

"Guess she's buying a CD." He laughs a bit.

"I guess."

He holds out the licorice and starts to chew another piece. "Wasn't he, like, a country singer or something?"

I nod. "Yep."

"Blossom and her country music."

"So what did the guy say?" I want to know.

"What guy?" He sucks a piece of licorice in between his teeth.

"The one at the store."

"He didn't say nothing, just sold me the red ropes. Two sacks for a dollar." He opens the plastic bag and shows me the purchase.

I'm a little confused. "No, not the guy at the convenience store, the guy at the auto parts store."

"I didn't go to the auto parts store." He steps away from the car. "Al, did you need me to get you something from the auto parts store?"

Why am I even trying?

"Not inside the store, the one you ran into. It

appeared as if he confronted you, like he said something to start a fight."

Dillon faces the direction where I have been eyeing the man with the scowl and watches as the truck pulls away. "Nah, I don't think so." Then he takes the red rope and swings it in a circle over his head. "What do you know? I could be a cowboy."

"Well, what did he say, Dillon?"

"Who?"

"The guy at the store." I need to just let this go, I know. But I can't.

"Oh, he said I looked like a girl."

"And what did you say?"

"I said, yeah, I know. And then I asked him how far it is to Shamrock."

"You agreed with him?"

He nods. "Sure."

"But why?"

"Well, Al, 'cause I kind of do." He stretches out his ponytail to show me. "Long hair throws people sometimes."

I shake my head. "But didn't that offend you?"

"Nah." He eats the end of the licorice. "That'd be kind of useless, don't you think?"

"Well, I don't know if it's useless or not, but I still think it is offensive. He had no right to say that to you."

Dillon shrugs. "It's not a problem," he says. "He was probably just having a bad day or something. And he was actually kind of cool. He told me Shamrock was less than thirty miles away."

I shake my head in disbelief. "It doesn't bother you when people say stuff like that to you?"

He shrugs. "Been looking like this for a long time. Kind of used to it by now." I watch him as he chews the end of his licorice.

"I didn't think people ever got used to that kind of thing."

"What?"

"Crass remarks, stupid observations, unwarranted comments."

"Unwarranted?"

"Yeah, unnecessary, unprovoked."

"You do use big words."

I shake my head and sigh.

"Well, what do you do if somebody says something . . . unwarranted to you?"

His question certainly is a fair one. He takes his place beside me and we both lean against the car.

"I tell them to mind their own business."

"That's cool."

"And I may say something else."

"Yeah?"

"Yeah."

"Well, good for you, Al."

I step away from the car and face Dillon. "You're telling me that if someone says something to you that's mean or hurtful, you don't say something back? You don't protect yourself?"

He shrugs. "Why would I need to protect myself

from what somebody says?" He slides his hand through his hair and tightens up his ponytail.

"I don't know. I guess I just always thought you had to stop that kind of behavior, let folks know what you will and will not put up with."

He scratches his chin, apparently considering what I am suggesting.

I glance over. Blossom is finally leaving the museum. Irene peeks through the window and flips the sign on the door from Open to Closed. I hear her turn the lock.

"There was this boy at school when I was in first grade and he used to beat the crap out of me every day. Billy Jackson was his name. He'd wait until all the teachers were gone and then he'd just pounce on me. I used to pretend I was sick, just so I wouldn't have to face him." Dillon shakes his head. "And then one day my stepdad made me tell *him* why I was afraid to go to first grade."

"Did you tell him?"

"I did, yeah."

"And what did he do?"

"He beat the crap out of me, too."

"What?" The lives people lead, it still amazes me.

Dillon laughs. "Yeah, it's jacked up; but it's like I figured out that my stepdad hit a whole lot harder than Billy Jackson so I quit being so scared of him. And then, when I quit being scared of him, he quit picking on me." He puts his hands behind his head and stretches his neck. There is just a little stubble growing over his lip. He really is so young.

"So, what you're saying is that when you appear not to be affected by the behavior of others, when you don't shrink at their offensive remarks or bullying actions, they don't bother you anymore?"

He stares at me, looking confused. Then he takes out another string of licorice. "Nah, I'm just saying that stuff people say doesn't hurt nearly as much as getting the crap beat out of you." He stuffs the candy in his mouth and grins in Blossom's direction. "Hey, baby."

I watch her smile. "Hey, Dillon."

He waits for her to approach, then the two of them open the car doors and take their seats, leaving me outside, looking in.

Chapter Thirty

Blossom and Dillon are saying good-bye to each other and I've snuck away. I have the two of them in my line of sight, but I'm far enough away that I'm not eavesdropping on them and they can't hear me call Phillip.

We've stopped at a hotel, a Best Western, just off the interstate, where Dillon's uncle is supposed to meet us in about an hour. We got here early, and I am about to make my first telephone call to the boy I have loved since I was twelve. I stick the phone in my back pocket and wipe my sweaty hands on the sides of my legs and then give them a good shake. I roll my head around, loosening up my neck, trying to get up my nerve.

I watch as Casserole glances over in my direction and then drops his head into a clump of clover. He thinks I won't do it.

The last time this happened I was fourteen. It took me all afternoon to get up my nerve. I must have walked past the phone in our kitchen a hundred times, then upstairs to my room and then back down again. I paced and practiced what I would say. I drank full glasses of water and fixed my hair and brushed my teeth, did a few sit-ups, and made the trek again from my room to the kitchen and then back to my room again. I still remember watching every minute tick past on the clock in the den as I paced by it.

It was early November and Phillip and I were study partners in biology. I still don't know how that partnership came to be, but at the time I was certain it was divine intervention, and only an hour after the assignments were given I was already planning our wedding. The science project was to dissect a frog in class, and even though I had helped organize a school PETA committee and could have been excused from the biology assignment due to my noted ethical conflict, I would have gone gigging with Dad at the Neuse

River and brought in my own toad if it meant I could stay Phillip's partner.

The classes and the dissection went fine; we made the incisions and we talked and laughed and I acted all grossed out like the other girls, but the truth of the matter is that I have never loved science like I did the week we studied amphibians. I was practically ready to become Mr. Daniel's assistant. I lived for that class and I rocked the project.

For the final assignment we were supposed to answer questions and fill in a blank illustration of the frog and label its parts. I had done most of the paperwork before the class was even finished, toiling away happily while my partner cleaned up our experiment and stopped to talk to some of the other guys on the football team who had gathered in the back of the room.

However, before class ended and we left for lunch, we had not completed the two essay questions that we were to work on separately, one question for each of us. When the final test was passed out, I had chosen to write the essay on the frog's morphology and physiology and Phillip was answering the question about the frog's life history. We could not turn in the project until all the illustration blanks had been completed and all the questions were answered. It was supposed to mean that the study partners would meet sometime after class to finish the project, an idea

I was greatly in favor of; but Phillip left class with his teammates without taking his copy of our final assignment and without making a start on his essay question.

By that evening I was both desperate to talk to Phillip again and nervous that we wouldn't have the project completed. We needed to communicate; and since he clearly wasn't making the call, I knew that initiating a conversation and completing our biology project were entirely up to me.

From four in the afternoon until eight I walked to the phone and tried to dial the numbers, making all kinds of excuses about why I couldn't call Phillip and why Phillip hadn't called me. There was football practice and other homework. There was an early dinner and time with his friends. Maybe he was taking a nap. Maybe he was helping his dad.

There were lots of reasons I made up as to why we hadn't spoken to each other. And for four hours, home alone while Sandra was at some pageant rehearsal and Daddy was finishing up an article on the elections, I tried to make the call. By eight, with both of my family members home, sitting at the table and waiting for dinner, I had written his essay and completed the entire project for us both. He didn't call and I could not. I turned in our papers the next day and he never even asked what else had been needed. The last exchange we had regarding our assignment was a high-five when we got our final grade, a solid A for us both, two weeks later.

I take in a breath and touch the screen where his contact information is listed from the call he made a couple of nights ago—one touch and the call is made, and yet I found it only slightly easier than having to hit every number. I hear it ring and watch as Dillon and Blossom stand facing each other. There is a slight breeze and Dillon reaches up and slides a piece of hair out of her eyes. She tilts her head and smiles.

"Is this Al?"

I clear my throat, somehow not expecting him to know it was my number. "Yeah, hey."

"Hey, I've been waiting for you."

My head feels a little swimmy. "We're in Texas."

Casserole hears what I have said and looks at me. He shakes his head and walks a little farther away, so he can't hear any more, I suppose.

"Oh, okay."

"Yeah, we decided not to stop in Oklahoma City."

"Huh, Texas, that's far from Fort Smith, right? You must have driven a lot today."

"Yeah, maybe five or six hours?"

"Oh, that's not as bad as I thought."

"No, not so bad." A line of trucks passes on the interstate and it suddenly gets noisy. I hold the phone closer to my ear.

"What's it like there?" I think I hear him say.

I look around, wanting to answer his question as truthfully as possible. "Flat, mostly brown. We're just over the state line, about an hour and a half from Amarillo, in a little town called Shamrock."

"That sounds pretty."

"It does, doesn't it?" This makes me smile because I realize that I have liked the name of this place since Dillon told us where he needed to go.

I peer over at my young traveling companions and they're still facing each other, still talking. Dillon has his hands in his pockets and Blossom has dropped hers at her sides. She is a beautiful girl, long brown hair, all that jewelry; she is forthright, confident.

"That's where you're going next?"

"What? Oh, yeah. That's as far as my passenger, Blossom, is going. I'm dropping her off at her dad's and then I'm going on to Albuquerque."

"You staying in Amarillo?"

"I don't know, I haven't really thought that far ahead."

"Hillary went to a conference in Wichita Falls once. Is that close by?"

I have no idea. "Yeah, maybe." Okay, I lied.

"I've never spent much time in Texas. I've been to Dallas and Houston, but that's really it. I hear Austin is nice."

"Uh-huh, great barbecue."

"Well, not as good as the White Swan."

This makes me laugh and I'm about to say something about the diner in Clayton that has been around longer than I've been alive, but there is a noise on my phone and I have another call. I look down at the screen. Blossom. I walk back around the corner so that she can see me; but she and Dillon are gone.

"Uh, Phillip, I have another call coming in. Can we talk later?"

"Sure, Al. You got my number."

And I hang up. "Yes, I most certainly do," I say to Casserole, who has made his way back to my side.

Chapter Thirty-one

"Hey." I have clicked to the other call and I'm still walking in the direction where I last saw Blossom and Dillon. They had been waiting just outside the motel office, standing in the parking lot. Now the whole area appears empty.

"You talking to somebody?" Blossom says over the phone.

I still don't see them anywhere.

"I was walking Cass." I glance over at my dog and shrug innocently. He knows I'm using him as a cover, but what is he going to do, tell somebody?

"Uh-huh."

And suddenly I have the strangest feeling that I am being busted by a seventeen-year-old.

"Where are you?" I ask, trying to find the two of them.

"Dillon's uncle is here."

And that's when I see them. An old truck is parked on the other side of the office and Blossom is waving in my direction.

"Hey."

"Hey," I reply. I click off the call and head over.

The man we are meeting is leaning against the truck and the first thing I notice is how much space he seems to take. It's not that he's big—he really only carries a medium build and isn't much taller than Dillon—but his stance is wide and he has his hands at his sides, his elbows out, and his fingers looped in his belt. I feel his eyes moving across me and he doesn't change a thing about how he is standing as I approach.

"Dude, this is Al," Dillon says. It's an introduction, but without giving me his uncle's name, it's not a complete one.

"Ronny," the man says, raising his chin at me in what I can only guess is a sort of cowboy greeting. He appears to be about my age and he's wearing old jeans and dusty boots, a John Deere hat, and a Shiner Bock T-shirt. He has a mustache and a tattoo of a green mermaid on his arm that seems to move up and down as he flexes his muscles, which he's doing a lot.

"Nice to meet you," I say, stopping next to Blossom. I pinch her on the arm lightly and she glances over and I notice she seems a little nervous.

"What happened to your dog?" Ronny asks and I look down at Casserole, wondering if I've missed something since he was sniffing around the hotel.

"How did he lose his leg?"

Oh, that. I forget that having three legs is a disability, since Cass still has one more than most folks I've seen.

"Don't know. He showed up that way."

Ronny nods, giving a look of mild interest. "Good thing you don't do dogs like horses."

And while I'm trying not to edit that sentence or ask the question about what is done to horses, Casserole nudges me, asking me to leave it alone; and then it dawns on me that Ronny is suggesting my dog would be shot if he were a horse.

"Dude," Dillon says, and the way he says it makes me think that his rules about not being offended by what people say to him must not apply to three-legged animals. His simple one-word defense of Cass makes me smile.

"What?" Ronny replies and elbows his nephew in the ribs. He grins and I see something small sticking between his teeth.

"So you girls are traveling all the way from Tennessee?" It's a toothpick and he pulls it out and gives Blossom a long look, apparently making the choice to leave my dog alone.

"Newport. My dad lives in Amarillo," Blossom answers, the tone of her voice surprisingly timid.

Ronny nods his head, sticks the toothpick back in his mouth. He keeps leering at her and she takes a small step closer to me. "What you driving?" He finally takes his eyes off of her and glances around the parking lot like he'll know the car when he sees it.

I feel a little protective of Faramond and don't want to point him out.

"He's on the other side," I say.

"He?" Ronny slides the toothpick from side to side in his mouth.

"Faramond. It's German for 'protector of the journey,'" Dillon announces. "Al named him when she was eighteen." He eyes me and grins.

Ronny slides his hand down the front of his jeans. "What, is it some Nazi car?"

"It's a Volkswagen," I tell him, feeling more than slightly defensive. "Nineteen ninety-eight, two-door, automatic transmission with a 115 horsepower." I take a breath. "Cherry-red hatch-back."

He makes a face. "Nineteen ninety-eight?" But he doesn't say anything else, like how old Faramond is or how old I am or whether or not because of our age, one or both of us might be shot if we stayed in Texas.

I don't respond, but something starts to nag at me. I glance back over at Dillon. He doesn't seem like the same boy I met yesterday. He doesn't seem at all like the young man I have come to like. His shoulders are slumped and his eyes keep darting in the direction of the interstate, like he's expecting someone else to arrive in Shamrock.

"Well, boy, your daddy said you need hard work to keep you out of trouble—already knocked up one girl." Ronny spits his toothpick on the ground and turns around to open his truck door. "But that wouldn't be you, would it?" He grins and winks at Blossom, who does not respond. He turns to Dillon. "You got any bags?"

He shakes his head.

Ronny stops and stares down at his nephew's flip-flops and shakes his head. "Well, you ain't paving no roads in them." He blows out a breath. "I guess we'll have to stop at the store and get you some decent shoes. You'll already owe me before you even start to work."

There is a pause. Dillon doesn't move, and for some reason I cannot name, I lift my chin and step forward.

"Stepdad," I say.

Ronny gets in the truck and shuts the door. "What?" He peers down at me from his high perch.

"It's his stepdad who told you that, who sent him here, not his dad."

He studies me for a second. "What do you know about Dillon's daddy?"

"I don't know a thing; I just know you stated incorrectly that your brother is the young man's father and that is not true."

Ronny shakes his head and starts the engine. "Get in, boy," he says to Dillon.

I cannot name this feeling that has come over me, but I have clenched my fists and tightened my jaw and I'm pretty sure that I could take Ronny if he got out of the cab of his truck and wanted to give it a go.

I turn to Dillon. "You can go on with us if you like," I say. "I mean, I don't know what's in Amarillo, but you can stay there or you can go with me to New Mexico or I'll take you back to Tennessee." Casserole rises from his seat and steps in front of me, standing guard as Dillon and I hammer out these negotiations.

The boy smooths down his hair and shakes his head. "You'd do that, Al? You'd let me ride a little further?"

I nod.

"Cool," he says and then steps around me next to my dog, placing his hand on Casserole's head. "Sorry, dude. Looks like I've got a better offer."

Ronny revs up his engine. He waits a minute like he's trying to think if he just got duped and then he starts to roll up the window. "This is the only time I'm coming out to get you. Don't call me again, boy." And he hits the gas, throwing gravel and kicking up dust in our faces.

Not a one of us moves as the truck speeds out of the parking lot, until I feel Blossom's arm around my waist, her fingers sliding up my spine. "I need to get a feel of this," she says. " 'Cause I haven't seen a backbone like that since Grandma cocked her shotgun and met a thief at the front door. My women are tough." And she smacks me on the behind, almost knocking me over.

Chapter Thirty-two

The horizon on the Great Plains is so vast that it has been said that during an Amarillo sunrise and sunset a person can actually see the curvature of the earth. We arrived in the largest city in the Texas Panhandle just as the western sky blushed in the setting sun. We stopped in a parking lot at a diner at the first exit off the interstate because I had never seen that shade of red and because Faramond was smoking. I waited until the crimson streaks faded before I opened the hood and then all of us simply stood at the side of the car in a white cloud watching the earth as it turned.

We had originally planned to spend the night in Shamrock, even booked a room; but after meeting Dillon's uncle and after our contentious encounter, none of us wanted to stay. Blossom and I agreed that Ronny seemed angry and just unstable enough that he might return to the Best

Western hoping for a fight or to kidnap his brother's stepson. And either Ronny Blevens has a reputation for unseemly behavior in Shamrock, Texas, and the manager knew our fears were not unfounded, or he was simply glad that the five of us weren't staying, because we were refunded our full amount. We left not long after Ronny sped away.

Amarillo, it turns out, is only an hour and a half away from the town where Dillon was supposed to start his new life, and Blossom was sure her father wouldn't mind us showing up tonight instead of tomorrow. He's waiting for us now; but I'm not sure my car can make it any farther. The smoke coming from the exhaust pipe is white and has only a slight smell, but not one that I can clearly diagnose until I get a closer look.

"Faramond could have water in the combustion chamber and may have blown a head gasket," I tell my two passengers when I can finally stick my head under the hood. "Or there is a leak in the intake manifold runner," I add. "But I can't really tell." When I pull my head out, wiping my hands on my pants, Blossom and Dillon are standing back staring at me.

I continue. "Or it could be a cracked cylinder head. If it's a leak, the water is simply mixing with the air and that's easily repaired. If it's a blown head gasket, that means I'll have to get a

190

mechanic because the oil is no longer protecting the bearings and that will ruin the engine completely if it's not replaced." I glance back at Faramond's insides. "Or I may have misdiagnosed it completely and it could just be the radiator overheating from driving so far and maybe he just needs coolant."

They look at me like I'm teaching calculus and they signed up for art appreciation. It's pretty evident that I've lost them.

"We can wait to see if it's just overheating from losing water or we may need a tow," I sum up. "I'll call Triple A." And I walk over to the driver's side, take out my purse, and find my card. I pull it out and start to dial the number.

"Let me call Dad first," Blossom says, stopping me. "Let me see if he can meet us and then maybe he knows a mechanic in town you can call." She raises her chin, pointing to the diner behind me. "I'm kind of hungry, anyway."

I glance behind us and I have to admit the thought of dinner sounds pretty good to me, too. I leave the hood open, letting the engine block cool, and open the windows for Casserole, explaining to him that he needs to wait with Faramond and provide a little moral support to the protector of our journey. Roger is safely stashed on the floor of the driver's side. Blossom calls her dad and the three of us head to the diner, Dillon leading the way.

There is a buffet at the Petro Travel Center; and in less than ten minutes we are seated with full plates of steaming, mostly fried food.

"What do you know about Amarillo?" Blossom asks me.

I ponder the question. I realize I don't know very much about Amarillo at all. "I know Oprah showed up here when she got sued for saying something bad about hamburgers and that she hired Phil McGraw to help her analyze members of the jury." I take a bite of pork-fried chicken or chicken-fried pork. My mystery meal actually tastes pretty good.

"Dr. Phil knows Oprah?" Dillon pipes up. He hasn't said much since we left Shamrock and I'm glad to hear he's not rethinking his decision to leave Ronny.

"Dr. Phil doesn't just know Oprah, he owes Oprah," I say, remembering the Dallas-based jury consultant's newfound fame. "She introduced him to the world."

"Cool," Dillon says, nodding and eating a piece of biscuit.

"Amarillo was incorporated in the late 1890s." Blossom begins reading from her paper placemat that gives the history of the town in which we have landed. "It is the fourteenth most populous city in the state and also the seat of Potter County. The city was once the self-proclaimed Helium Capital of the World for having one of the country's most productive helium fields." She holds up her plate so that she can continue reading. "Natural gas was discovered here in 1918 and oil in 1921."

Dillon nods and chews. "Helium grows in a field?"

Ah, I think, *the boy is definitely back.*

"What does the name Amarillo mean?" I ask, dismissing Dillon's question and enjoying the little history lesson with our dinner.

"Spanish for yellow," she answers, still reading, her fork in her hand. "Probably comes from the yellow wildflowers that were blooming everywhere in the spring and summer when the town got its name."

"Or maybe because the first color associated with helium was yellow," I add, recalling the story of the first sighting of the element that I learned in my high school chemistry class.

Dillon is staring again and I can see the wheels turning in his brain.

"Helium doesn't actually grow in a field," I answer before he can say anything else. "It's a by-product of natural gas."

He nods, pondering my science news.

"The airport has the third largest runway in the world and is designated as an alternate landing site for the Space Shuttle," Blossom continues.

"Cool." Dillon has apparently chosen to let his helium questions go unanswered.

"Why did your dad come here?" I ask Blossom, deciding I would rather hear more personal than city history.

"He wanted to be a cowboy," she said, putting her plate back down on the history mat and diving into her dinner.

"I thought he was a carpenter," I note.

"He is," she explains. "But he first came to Texas to work with cattle. He met some guy in Newport who told him about some ranching jobs out here."

"He was a cowboy when I met him," Dillon adds, stuffing the rest of his biscuit in his mouth. "He drove to Tennessee that first Christmas we were together, remember?" he asks Blossom.

She nods.

"He was wearing this great big belt buckle because he had won some roping event at the rodeo. He had a bunch of horses. He was cool." He sits back against the booth, still eating.

"He's still cool," Blossom responds.

Dillon nods.

"But he's not a cowboy anymore?" I ask, wondering what happened.

"Hurt his knee," Blossom answers. "But he still rides."

I look up at the door to see a man entering the diner. He's tall, with a medium build, wearing jeans and a long-sleeved Western shirt. He's taken off his cowboy hat, holding it to his chest, a stance of respect, and I can see he has short wavy blond hair, like a young Robert Redford. He's leaned down to speak to the older woman running the cash register at the front and she smiles and reaches out to touch his arm while he says something that must be funny. She throws back her head and laughs and just at that moment he glances up and catches my eye. I feel my stomach make a little flip.

"Why are you blushing?" Blossom notices I have quit eating and follows my line of vision. She puts down her fork, turns back to me with her eyebrows raised. "How do I keep missing this?" And she stands up from the table and walks to the door. Where is she going? I wonder. And what is she getting ready to do?

"It's him," Dillon announces, when he sees the two of them greeting each other at the entrance. "The cool cowboy."

I have just spotted Blossom's dad.

Chapter Thirty-three

He looks like her or she looks like him; I can see that now that she has brought him over to our table and the two of them are standing side by side. There is the same quiet ease to him, a certain measure of confidence without coming off as cocky or arrogant. They smile the same way, with a similar tilt of the head; and I can see that they

195

are tender with each other. He is, of course, taller; but it would be hard to miss that they are father and daughter.

"Al, this is my dad, Lou Winters."

I wipe my mouth, hoping I don't have fried dinner stuck in my teeth, wishing I had brushed my hair or taken a shower or, heck, lost a little weight. "Hi," I say and extend my hand.

He takes it and gives a kind of small bow without looking away. His hat is still under his arm. "Al, I have to say that you are not at all who I expected."

"It's short for Alissa," I reply, since I am used to the surprise my name will sometimes cause.

"And now I know." He smiles with the slight tilt and squeezes my hand while elbowing his daughter as if the gender confusion was her fault.

"And you remember Dillon." Blossom moves aside and announces the other person at the table.

Dillon is grinning. "Hey, Mr. Winters, 'sup?"

He drops my hand and this time the smile appears a wee bit forced. "Dillon."

It's awkward for a second because we're sitting at a booth and for him to join us means he has to sit with me, on my side, and I don't know the protocol for making room. Do I ask first and slide or do I make the presumption he is joining us and slide without asking? I am completely out of my comfort zone here.

"Dad, why don't you sit next to Dillon?" Blossom says, saving me from myself.

She takes her place beside me, and Mr. Winters—Lou—moves in next to Dillon. It's worked out just fine and we all have a seat; but I have to admit it still feels a bit awkward.

"So, you're having some car trouble?"

I exhale rather more loudly than is customary, because I suddenly realize I haven't breathed since our introduction. I answer with just a nod.

"Tell him about the smoke," Dillon says, prompting me.

"Well, it was white," I say.

Lou nods with understanding.

"I figure that means—"

Dillon interrupts me. "She can tell what's wrong with a car by the color of the smoke. And because it's white it's either a blown gasket or a cracked cylinder." He's grinning and nodding at me like he's now the calculus teacher. "Dude, that is so cool." And he pushes a strand of hair behind his ear.

I shrug. There's not much else for me to add.

Mr. Winters watches Dillon briefly and then turns to me. "We'll take a look after we eat. I brought my chains if we need to tow it. I don't live far."

The waitress arrives before I can give a better description of what's wrong with the car. It's pretty obvious she knows Blossom's father. She flirts a little, calls him "hon," and brings him a large iced tea before he even makes the request.

"I guess I'll go ahead and get me a plate," he says to the three of us and to the waitress, who has placed her hand on his shoulder.

"The pork is better than the chicken," she leans in to tell him and I glance back down at my plate and wonder again which one I chose.

"Good to know. Thanks, Lacey."

And she winks and walks away without asking anything else of Lou or any of the rest of us.

Blossom watches her father. "You eat here a lot?" She gives him the look of someone who knows the flirting language of waitresses better than most.

He blushes slightly. "Once in a while," he answers and stands. "Can I get anybody anything?"

"The French fries are way cool," Dillon says. Then Lou casts a slightly disgusted look at his daughter.

"No, thanks," I say, and Lou smiles at me and gives a nod. I watch him walk to the buffet.

I no longer have interest in my fried food and start to eat my salad instead. I feel Blossom watching.

"What?" I ask, not completely sure why she's staring at me.

She bites her lip and shakes her head.

"Do you know a Lacey who isn't a porn star?"

I ask, confident that this will make a fine deflection.

And it does. She laughs.

"How old is your father?" I tend to forget how young these two are and how old I actually still am.

Blossom shrugs. "Forty, forty-two? Something like that."

"And he's never married again?"

I watch him at the buffet line, leaning down, spooning green beans and creamed corn onto his plate. He stands back up when Lacey comes over to him.

Blossom shakes her head. "There was one woman one time, Pam. Pammy." She takes a bite of her food. "I never liked her."

I keep watching him as he moves around the buffet, taking a piece of the meat that Lacey is pointing out.

"But I don't know about now. He does look like he's lost some weight and that's what happened when he dated Pammy, so maybe he's found somebody."

He's gone over to the bread station now, stands there for a second or two, but walks away without a biscuit or piece of corn bread. He is certainly showing restraint. I look at the two fried hush puppies on my plate and place my napkin over them.

"What about your dad?" Blossom asks and I'm

not sure if she's talking to me or Dillon. But then I see her looking at me.

The question comes as a surprise. I haven't thought about my father dating anyone for a long time.

"I think he's always been too busy—you know, married to his job—since my mom died." But the truth is I don't really know why he never dated anyone else, why he never got married again. I only know it would have been terribly difficult with Sandra and me. With my sister there was hardly enough room in the house for me; I can't imagine her making space for another woman. I'm pretty certain that would have never worked out and I'm also pretty certain my father knew it.

"You all aren't through yet, are you?" Lou is back and he slides in easily next to Dillon.

"Dude, I ate, like, a whole cow," Dillon answers.

I am about to say that I'm through as well, but my phone starts to ring and when I reach down to answer it I recognize the number right away.

Phillip Blake is calling me again.

Chapter Thirty-four

"You still in Shamrock?"

I feel my face redden and notice that everyone at the table is watching me. I give Blossom a look asking her to slide out of the booth so I can take my call privately. She won't move at first and I hear Phillip ask, "Is everything okay?"

I wait, rolling my eyes at Blossom, who finally slips out.

"Excuse me," I whisper to everyone, pulling the phone away from my mouth, and best as I am able, I slide out and head toward the door.

"Al, you there?"

"Yes, hey, and no, we made it to Amarillo."

I can't seem to find a quiet place to take my call so I end up walking out, pushing the front door open with my elbow.

I glance around the parking lot and over to the tree where Faramond is parked. I see Casserole standing up in the backseat, eyeing me through the opened window. He heard my voice or smelled the fried chicken on me. Either way, I know now which direction I have to go.

"I thought you were staying in Shamrock."

For some reason, his comment surprises me.

"Well, we were, but we decided that since we were already so close, we'd just drive the extra ninety or so miles and get all the way to Amarillo." I decide to forgo the story about Ronny. "We're having dinner." And as soon as the words leave my lips I realize that I sound like someone who doesn't want to talk. Now he will probably say he's sorry for interrupting and allow me to get back to my meal and I may not ever hear from him again.

"You eating at that big steak house?"

Guess I figured that wrong.

"What's that?"

"The big steak house where they serve a seventy-two-ounce steak and you don't have to pay if you can eat it all. It's near the interstate, something with Texas in the name. Wait, I'll Google it."

"Oh, okay." I have made my way to Faramond and I reach in the rear window and give Casserole a pat.

"Yep, here it is. The Big Texan," he tells me. "Seventy-two ounces, can you imagine?"

I'm about to say that no, I cannot, but he keeps talking.

"Some girl won the big steak challenge—ate three of them in twenty minutes."

"That's quite a feat," I reply, wondering why this is interesting to Phillip.

"Yeah, you can watch the video on their web-site."

There is a pause and I think that he must be

doing that very thing. *Maybe I should try the "eating dinner" sentence again.*

The pause continues and I clear my throat, trying to move the conversation along, or at least remind him that I'm still here on the other end.

"Anyway, it's funny. You should watch it."

"That is exactly what I'll do, then, a little later this evening."

"So, I'm calling because I found out where you can get an address for the remains."

"What?"

I can see Blossom staring at me through the window of the restaurant. Casserole sniffs my hand and then looks up at me, confused that there are no leftovers.

"Your dead guy, the one you're returning to New Mexico."

I glance down in between the front seats and see the box. "Roger Hart." I say his name because he's more to me than a dead guy or just remains.

"I know you're the great researcher, being a journalist and all, and I figured you had already tried the usual methods for finding the address."

I don't say anything.

"You did, right? You Googled and ran searches on those websites."

"Yes, I did a fair amount of checking before I left North Carolina." This line of questioning, this phone call, it is all quite unexpected.

"Yeah, well, did you do a property search?"

"A what?"

"Property search. Did you go through the records in the county where he lived?"

I have to say I did not think of that. I tried calling the funeral home, tried to look up his obituary to find family members' names, tried a few websites that promised they could find anybody; but I never found a real clue before leaving on this trip.

And yet, reflecting upon it now, I kind of think I didn't want to get in touch with anybody before I left. This was part of the adventure, not knowing what or who I might find in New Mexico.

"With running audits for insurance, that's one of the ways we find out about people."

"You look up their properties?"

"Yeah, it's just a way to validate whether or not they own or rent. It's a criterion we sometimes use when we make risk assessments."

I had no idea that insurance salespeople researched their clients this way. It sounds a little creepy to me; but I don't say this to Phillip.

"So, I didn't check anything out about your guy because I didn't remember his name; but I just thought about it and wanted to shoot that idea over to you. You can do a property search."

"Well, that's a great idea, thanks, Phillip."

"If you want, I can get my girl to look it up and e-mail you what she finds."

Phillip has a girl? Should I be offended that he has a girl?

"No, I thank you very much, but I'll look into this as soon as I can get to a computer and find the county files."

"Good, then," he says, like I'm a client or a new insurance salesman or maybe the girl.

"All right. Thanks for the tip," I say and shrug at Casserole, who is watching me, waiting for the conversation to end so that he can get his dinner.

"Let me know if you find out anything."

"I will do that," I say.

"So, I may come to Clayton for the Fourth of July," he notes.

I turn my back on Casserole. "Oh, well, that'll be nice."

"Yeah, Mom is always bugging me about coming home, so I thought I might drive down for the holiday."

"Well, I know she'll be glad to see you."

"You'll be home by then, right?"

I place my hand on the front of Faramond. The warmth of his hood is comforting to me as I feel a little faint.

"I will be home next week," I reply, wanting to say, *I'll come home right now if you're going to be there;* but I know to show a little restraint.

"Okay, well, the Fourth is still a couple of weeks away so maybe we'll talk again before then."

I truly do not know what to say, but somehow "yep" comes out of my mouth.

"Let me know if the property search comes up with anything; I'll be interested to see if it does."

"I will check on that and I'll text you."

"Or message me, either one."

"Okay, thanks, Phillip."

"You're welcome. You can pay me back by buying insurance from me." And I think I hear a slight laugh.

"I would be honored to buy insurance from you." I don't even know what that means.

"Okay, have fun in Amarillo."

"Yeah, thanks for the tip—and thanks for calling."

And I click off the phone and turn back to my dog. "How'd you like a seventy-two-ounce steak?" I ask him; but he does not respond.

Chapter Thirty-five

Lou built his house all by himself. It's small, about eleven hundred square feet; but it's open and airy, with lots of windows and high ceilings. It's framed with a pitched roof, has hardwood floors, and is decorated in a Western motif, with horseshoes and cowboy pictures, ropes and rodeo trophies lining the shelves on the walls. He's proud of it, you can tell, because he slides his fingers tenderly and knowingly across the surfaces and takes out his handkerchief to wipe along the top of the crown molding as he talks about how hard it was to find the right wood and how long it took to locate high-quality gypsum plaster to fill in the ceilings and walls.

His kitchen is simple but ample—a big gas oven and stove and plenty of counter space, two sinks, a stainless steel refrigerator, and a dishwasher—and he claims he uses everything because he enjoys making pots of stew and baking pies. Blossom agrees that her father knows his way around the kitchen and promises that if I stay long enough I will come to know that fact for myself; but I haven't quite decided if I will stay past tomorrow.

If I can get Faramond up and running, I would like to get to New Mexico as soon as possible, find out where to deliver Roger Hart, and then hurry back to North Carolina. I told Blossom that my dad needed me at work, but the truth is I want to get back in plenty of time before the Fourth of July and Phillip's return visit to Clayton. Suddenly, I feel a new purpose in being at home.

Lou has given me his bedroom for the night. Blossom has the spare bed in his office, and he and Dillon are sleeping in the barn out back, which Lou assures him has more to offer than just a stack of hay. I told him I was happy to sleep on the sofa in the den; but he insisted that I have his room, even placing an old blanket on the floor for Casserole and clearing a space on his dresser for Roger.

It's quiet here where Lou lives, out from the sprawling neighborhoods along the interstates and twelve miles beyond the city center. He was given the land by the rancher who had employed him for more than ten years after he first arrived in Amarillo. The man is old now, well past eighty, with no children and only a few cows and bulls, Lou says, and is giving away his ranch parcel by parcel to cowboys and cooks who have worked for him.

Lou got his property just after the rancher's wife died. He offered to pay the old man a decent price and, when refused, encouraged him to wait at least for a while to make sure this wasn't just an impulsive act fueled by his grief. But the rancher had made up his mind. He surveyed the land, portioned off the acreage near a small southern creek, and deeded it over to him. And Lou said he continues to do the same thing every year or so, pulling in the fences for the cattle, tightening the grazing land, and giving parcels of his land away to friends and employees. In my opinion, that's a fine way to leave this world, handing over land to others, being able to watch them build or farm, or just enjoying the satisfaction that comes in giving things away.

I like it here, though I cannot fully articulate

why. This part of the Lone Star State is flat and brown and dusty and has no natural barriers to the winds that sweep across the area coming from all four directions. It is the Great Plains, the panhandle for the second largest state in the union, and some people are, I'm sure, frightened by the long views and the threat of storms, while others, like myself, I suppose, discover a kind of contentment. It does feel lonely out here, but also strangely calming. I am at peace in this place, as if something bound in me has been loosened.

Blossom says it's the way you can see so far, the horizon bending in sight; she says she always feels safe here because she thinks she will be able to see trouble coming and have time to prepare. In Tennessee, she explained, just before we said good night, there are too many trees, too many places for danger to hide.

"I love the hardwoods," she said, "don't get me wrong; but sometimes I grow weary trying to anticipate what's going to fall from the branches or who's waiting to jump from behind the trunks. West Texas gives you the long broad view, and for me there's some comfort in just seeing things for what they are." Now I know why she came here after the baby died. This land left her nothing to work on but her grief.

Tonight the sky is black and I have found I am unable to sleep so I have come outside and I'm seeing stars I have never seen before. The Milky

Way and all the constellations are so prominent and visible, stretching from top to bottom, that I cannot see where the earth ends and the heavens begin. It is almost more than I can stand. I am heading back to bed when I see a small light glowing from a landing not too far away. It's a cigarette burning, and since I don't think Dillon smokes, I suppose that Lou is awake, sitting just beyond where I stand, apparently watching the same stars that have just overwhelmed me.

"Can't sleep?" I ask, as I approach him, walking carefully in the dark. He is sitting on an old swing attached to a frame, the kind we hang from rafters on porches in the South. There is a wicker chair beside it, but I stay standing for now.

"Oh, hey," he says, appearing a bit surprised that he is no longer alone. "Yeah, sometimes I have a little trouble." He takes another drag on his cigarette and then drops it and steps on it, grinding it in the dirt. "What about you? Is the bed okay?"

I glance behind me at the house. "Yes, it's fine," I answer.

"You want to sit?" he asks.

And I move over to the seat and sit down. I'm wearing my pajamas, but I grabbed a blanket from the bed before walking outside and I pull it around my shoulders.

"It's really quiet out here," I say.

"Yeah, it's a bit different from living in the city, that's for sure."

"You like it, I guess." I try to imagine every night this dark, every evening this silent.

"I do, yes," he replies. "But I know it's not for everyone."

"Yeah, I know some people who would go crazy not having the sounds of traffic or neighbors." I think about James William at the paper telling me once that he left the television on all the time at his apartment because he needed noise to feel like he was still alive.

"The wind drives a lot of folks out of West Texas," Lou informs me. "Lots of people lose their minds because they think they hear voices, children crying, women screaming; and some days and nights, it goes on for hours."

There is no wind tonight. I wonder if I would be affected in that same way by the harsh desert elements. "It doesn't bother you?"

"Nah, I like it, makes me feel like something new is blowing in, change is brewing."

"You like change?"

"Sometimes," he answers. "Not all the time, but sometimes, yes."

"I haven't changed anything in my life in a long time," I say. "I've lived in the same house all of my life, held the same job, kept the same car."

"Yeah, I thought the car had a few stories in him."

I shrug, even though I'm sure he cannot see my

expression. "Not so many stories," I say. "Just a lot of miles."

There is a pause. I close my eyes.

"You've lived in the same house all of your life?"

I know how that surprises some people.

"Bought it from my dad when he wanted to move into an apartment downtown. I just like living there and didn't see any point in leaving."

"Well," Lou responds, "that makes perfect sense to me."

I remember the discussions we all had, Daddy explaining he didn't want to live in the house any longer, that he wanted to be able to walk to work. And I remember the three of us hammering out a payment schedule, since I ended up having to pay both him and Sandra, who complained she was getting left out and wanted the same opportunity as I had to buy our house.

Of course Daddy and I both knew that Sandra never intended to move back to Clayton, that she'd never liked our house, claimed it was puny and old. But when she found out I was getting it and that I was paying my father a small sum to take it over, she packed a bag and left Asheville to come home and "make things right."

She had just taken her real estate license exam, and she showed up with ideas about when to sell it and what we needed to do to stage it for potential buyers. She walked around touching the furniture, turning up her nose, opening closet doors and looking inside. I followed her from room to room and quickly informed her that I was not selling our house, and even though it was going to strap me financially, I agreed to pay her what she thought was fair to keep her name off the deed and her husband, the financial adviser she talked to once an hour, off my back.

"It's a good house," I say now, wondering where I might have gone if I had allowed Sandra to sell it. For some unexpected reason, I am feeling a little defensive that I live where I live.

"That's nice," Lou responds. "A good house is real nice."

And I realize that with Blossom's father I have nothing to defend.

Chapter Thirty-six

"The Milky Way includes at least thirty constellations," Lou says, breaking the silence and jarring me out of my thoughts about the house where I live and my sister who tried to move me out.

"Thirty?" I repeat. I had no idea.

I think about what I know about the galaxy of stars and planets stretching across the sky. It isn't much. I remember that it's called the Milky Way because with the naked eye one cannot distinguish individual stars, only a hazy band of light. I know that until the 1920s astronomers believed that the Milky Way consisted of all the stars in the universe, but after a huge argument between scientists, Edwin Hubble, of Hubble Telescope fame, proved that it was only one galaxy and that, in fact, there were billions of others. His conclusion, of course, unnerved the science community. Everyone was shocked to discover that there is more in space than we will ever understand.

I have only seen the Milky Way once or twice in my life, once out on a farm deep in Johnston County when I was interviewing migrant workers and stayed late talking and listening. The stars filled the sky as I drove home, causing me to stop and pull over just to see them all. And the other time was when I slept on the beach as a young girl with my mom, watching as the moon dipped below the horizon, the ocean reflecting starlight. I can't see the Milky Way from my house or anywhere else in town because the night is lit up with streetlights and traffic traveling east and west along the busy corridor traversing through Clayton.

"It's quite something," I say, feeling insignificant under a wash of so many galaxies.

"The band divides the night sky into two almost equal hemispheres and the light from the Milky Way actually originates from unresolved stars."

"Unresolved stars," I repeat. "That sounds like they might need therapy."

"And some of the dark regions, like the Great Rift and the Coalsack, are areas where light from the distant stars are blocked by interstellar dust," he continues.

Lou Winters knows his Milky Way.

"I'm sorry. Sometimes I get a little carried away and ramble on about the sky."

"No, don't apologize. I like it." And I do. "I like the names of things that I don't know anything about, dark regions like the Great Rift and the Coalsack. Those are good names," I say.

"Blossom said you're a writer."

"A journalist, really."

"That's the same thing, isn't it?"

I think about it. "Well, writing is generally required for journalism; but it's more about reporting facts. I guess when I hear the word 'writer,' I think about the creative kind."

"Reporting facts is creative," he notes, but without really convincing me. "I would have a difficult time trying to write a story about something that happened even if somebody told me everything to write down."

"Tell me more about the Milky Way." I don't feel like talking about my work. I'd rather hear about the stars.

"Okay, but you asked for it."

And I pull the blanket even tighter around my shoulders and tuck my legs beneath me.

"That band of stars and planets is said to lie in

a region the astronomers call a green valley, which means it is populated by galaxies in transition from the blue cloud, where new stars are being formed, to the red sequence, which are galaxies that lack star formations."

"Green valley," I repeat, wishing I had taken the astronomy class that was offered at the university instead of focusing only on my major, trying to graduate early so that I could do more at the paper. "How do you think they decide on the names of these galaxies and regions and clusters of stars?"

"I don't know. Maybe they realize how complex everything is in space and so, just to simplify it for those of us not as smart as they are, they use the least complicated ways they know to describe things."

"Blue cloud, red sequence." I peer up at the sky, trying to see colors. "Green valley. Yeah, that's pretty much Space for Dummies."

We pause again in our conversation.

"The area of the sky obscured by the Milky Way is called the zone of avoidance."

This makes me laugh. "Well, I suspect that if scientists are really trying to find life on other planets, they ought to start there," I reply. "Because that's not a bad place to hang out."

"You avoiding something?" he asks.

"Only the hard stuff like truth and intimacy."

I hear a slight laugh.

"Blossom really likes you," he tells me, in a pretty abrupt change of subject. From stars to daughters.

"Yeah, well, I like her, too. She's a smart girl."

"About some things," he replies. "Others, well, I'm not so sure."

I know he's talking about Dillon. Lou has been nothing but polite to the young man, but it's clear he's not happy that we've brought him along.

"I don't really think they're a couple anymore," I tell him.

"Then why is he here?"

It's a fair question. I think about how to answer it. I try to remember how he suddenly appeared out of nowhere to join us.

"I get the feeling he doesn't have anywhere else to go."

I think about how Dillon looked when he showed up, how eager he was to see Blossom. Maybe it wasn't just because he wanted them to become a couple again. Maybe he seemed in need of just something as simple as a little kindness. I think about how quickly he bonded with Casserole, how protective he's become of Roger. I remember how sad he was in Shamrock, how nervous he got when Ronny showed up.

"I don't know what his expectations are for Amarillo, or anywhere else for that matter, but I think he's been pushed out of Tennessee and he's just trying to find a place to land."

I hear the chains on the swing squeak and watch Lou light up another cigarette. I can see him when he strikes the match. He's wearing his hat, and looking even more like a star from the Western movies that my mom and dad used to watch together.

"I thought after she lost the baby that she was through with Dillon Montgomery; I know I was."

"Well, I don't think it's the same relationship." He asked her to marry him again just today and she, sternly but carefully, said no. But I don't mention this to Lou.

Blossom and I haven't talked about it, but I get the feeling that she's moved on and that any kindness she's offering to her ex-boyfriend is just that, simple kindness, without any expectation of something more to grow between them.

"He's not playing with a full deck, that boy," Lou notes. He takes a drag and I see the light of his cigarette grow and fade.

"Well, maybe not, but he didn't abandon her when she was pregnant," I remind him.

"Yeah, that's true," he agrees.

"And he's basically harmless," I add. "Kind of like a puppy."

"I suspect I'd have less trouble keeping your three-legged dog," he responds. And there's the chuckle again. "Which reminds me, I checked your car."

He must have done that while I was taking a shower.

"I think it's just a leak. I can probably replace the gasket tomorrow. But if you want, you can take my truck to Grants and stop by on your way back east, pick up your car. That way I can make sure it's okay. You know, test drive it around here before you hit the highway back to North Carolina."

"That's a nice offer," I say. "But I don't want to put you out."

"Well, I suppose I need to confess there's an ulterior motive to having you come back."

And I'm glad we're sitting in the dark because I'm sure I'm turning red. "What's that?" I manage to ask.

"Well, if you stop on your way back through, I have a better shot of sending Dillon home with you."

The heat that flared in my face is surely starting to fade. "Oh, sure, I told him I would give him a ride back to Tennessee. That's fine." I feel as flat as an old balloon.

"It also means I might get a little more time with you."

"Oh," is all I can think to say.

"Well, I'm going in, try and get some sleep with the harmless puppy."

"Oh," I say again. "Okay," I add, glad to have another word. I hear him get up from the swing and suddenly feel him close.

"Sleep well, Al," he says, touching me on the shoulder as he passes by.

And just like that, he's gone, and I'm left sitting alone in the quiet night, the stars even brighter than when I first arrived.

Chapter Thirty-seven

It's a five-hour drive to Grants, New Mexico, from Amarillo, Texas, and I'm sure I can get there by the early afternoon. I took Lou up on his offer, left Faramond in his care, and I'm driving his truck, planning to stop back in Texas before I head home. Casserole and Dillon stayed behind with Blossom; and so, for now, it's just me and Roger heading west in a short-bed Ford.

It's a beautiful day to be on the interstate and I'm glad for the peace and quiet. I enjoyed having company when I was on the road before, but right now I am grateful for some time to think, a few hours to ponder the things Lou said last night and to consider what I will find in New Mexico. I need to think about what I will do with Roger and, of course, I plan to replay the phone call from Phillip in my head a few more times. I glance over at the box of ashes.

"Well, apparently you owned some property," I say out loud. "I Googled the county records before I left Amarillo," I explain aloud. "And what do you know? You're in there," I tell him. "You own two acres near a place called San Rafael; so I finally have a place to start."

When I first found the ashes, I called the funeral home director whose business card was attached to the box. He put me on hold for a few minutes and then came back on the line to explain that his establishment had in fact handled the cremation of Roger Hart, but that he could not release information to anyone other than family. Harold Candelaria, his name was. When he learned that I simply wanted to return the remains, he promised to call family members. After not hearing from him for days, I called him back, only to discover that he had no current phone numbers on file and as best as he could tell, there were no family members to reach. The remains, paid for in full, were mine to do with what I wanted.

I Googled Roger's obituary and found nothing, then used several people-search websites, but never came up with a name or address. I left Clayton less than a week ago with only the name of the funeral home in the town where he was cremated and just a glimmer of hope that Mr. Candelaria would give me something more when I showed up at his door.

Now, however, I have vital information. I have an address. I have a place to go. All because of my conversation with Phillip yesterday. And I reach down and pat the box, relieved that I have a destination for my passenger's remains.

As I drive, I take in the vast horizon and the endless blue sky. I think about Phillip's phone call and I consider once again his suggestion about the property records. I wonder how long he thought about it before he called me, if he did his own research and came up with nothing but still wanted to let me know of his idea. I wonder if he really wanted to give me the suggestion or if that was just his cover to let me know he was coming to Clayton; but of course it doesn't matter. He's coming home and he's asked to see me and I cannot believe my good luck. It's like having a dream finally come true. I let out one long breath.

And then, I think about last night and the conversation about stars and the Milky Way with the father of a girl I only just met but who is now clearly my friend. I think about how easy it was to sit and talk with him, covered in his blanket and sheltered by the darkness, how funny he is, how sweet he was to cook my breakfast this morning.

"So, there's Phillip," I say to my silent companion. "The guy I have loved since I was twelve, the guy who has never paid a bit of attention to me and is now helping me find your home and has basically asked to see me when he comes back to Clayton."

Just to say his name makes me feel all funny

inside. I think of how he looked on prom night almost twenty years ago—that classic tuxedo, the small arrangement of flowers in a box in his hand that I wanted so much to be mine. I think of our high school graduation night and how he hugged me and swung me around, saying what a good friend I had been, leaving me breathless. All four years of college, I pined away for him, the boy I loved. I think about his pictures now posted on Facebook, how he hasn't changed very much, how handsome he still is, how grown-up and smart he sounds, and how I seem to be getting one more shot at happiness.

I shake my head as we drive across the line to the last state I will have to traverse before I head home.

"And then there's Lou," I say to Roger, worried that I may have lost him since I wandered off in my thoughts. "He's the father of my friend who kind of made a pass at me last night, although I'm not completely sure that's what it was."

I think about how he watched me at dinner, how he laughed at my jokes, took to Casserole right away, how he changed the sheets on his bed and tidied up before letting me in, his arms full of linens and laundry as he moved away from the door, giving me room to enter. I think about our late-night conversation, how he talked about the stars and planets and the simple, easy way he spoke of his love for his daughter. I think about his sturdy hands and the stillness he did not push away.

I think about breakfast, the smell of eggs and bacon pulling me from the bed and how I finally got to be the one who woke up Blossom, knocking on her door and letting her know what a beautiful day she was missing, how hard and long I laughed when she came to the table, drowsy and uninterested, asking me what happened the night before that caused me to be so perky and cheerful so early in the morning.

I am definitely confused by recent events.

I glance down.

"What do you think?"

But of course Roger doesn't answer.

"I bet you were in love. I bet you died a young man in love with your childhood sweetheart and she took you with her to the ocean, where she wanted to live, where you had never been before. And I bet she was saving your ashes to mingle with hers but in some grand, tragic way, she died, unable to see to it that your remains were scattered together."

I think about this scenario, wondering if even with an address I will ever find out anything about how Roger Hart died and why he ended up in Wilmington, North Carolina, when he was cremated in New Mexico, about two thousand miles away.

"Or maybe there were two lovers, two women that you were unable to choose between; and one of them stole you after your funeral, slipped the box under her arm, and drove you home with her, while the other one still cries for you. And when I give you to her she will cling to this box, promising to keep you always with her."

Then I have this crazy fantasy of Phillip and Lou sitting in a funeral home chapel, both of them mourning my death as my lovers without either ever knowing about the other one sitting only a few pews away. This thought, I have to say, makes me laugh a little. I'm just envisioning Phillip throwing himself on my casket when my phone rings. My father.

"Hey, Daddy, what's up?"

"Just wondering where you are," he says.

"Tucumcari," I answer, reading the signs as I pass.

"Where's that?"

"New Mexico," I reply.

There is a pause.

"So, you're almost done."

I think this is a question, so I answer, like the dutiful daughter I am. "Almost done."

"Good."

And then there is another pause.

"When will you be home, then?"

I think about the trip so far and how long it will take me to return to the Southeast, knowing I plan to drive as quickly as I can.

"Three or four days, I suppose."

"That's good," he says again. "The VW okay?" He knows about the smoke.

"Yeah, it should be fine. Blossom's father is taking care of it."

"You mean you can't handle the repair?"

I smile. What daughter gets to hear that from her dad? "He just had more time," I explain.

"Oh."

I wait. Something about this conversation doesn't sound exactly right.

"Is everything okay, Dad?"

"Yep, it's fine. I just wanted to see when you'll be back, how to assign next week's stories."

This is just like him. He has a list and he needs to mark things off.

"What are you looking at?" I ask, wondering about the stories he intends to cover.

"Drought," he replies. "State's water table is still low. There's a scandal with the police chief, and the school is getting remodeled over the summer."

I'm sure I'll be assigned the story about the drought. James William will be all over the scandal. I don't know who will want to write about the remodeling.

"Well, be safe and hurry back," he says.

"Okay, I'll talk to you later."

"Yep." And he hangs up.

I shake my head at Roger. "There'll be no two

lovers crying for me," I tell him. "Just my father and the citizens of Clayton, North Carolina, wondering why no one told them the high school got new toilets."

And I lean back against the seat, hit the gas, and keep heading west.

Chapter Thirty-eight

Grants, New Mexico, is seventy-eight miles west of Albuquerque and just over sixty from Gallup at the state line with Arizona. It sits near the pueblos of Acoma and Laguna and shares a mountain with the people of Zuni. It is near the Continental Divide and an area known as El Malpais, Spanish for the Badlands. You pass this area on the interstate, a black basalt terrain created by volcanic forces over the past million years.

The landscape on both sides of Interstate 40 is black and stark and, according to the material I have read, displays the best continuous geologic record of volcanism on the planet. To see it, however, is to feel like you're looking at the remains of the Apocalypse, the trenches and cones covered in molten lava, miles of endless barren land.

The small community of Grants was first a ranching one, the region shared by Spaniards and Indians, farming and shepherding cows and sheep. Then in the 1880s a railroad camp was founded by three Canadian brothers named Grant who'd been awarded a contract to build a section of the Atlantic and Pacific Railroad through the region. Logging soon became the big employer for the people of Grants as lumber was taken from the nearby Zuni Mountains and sent by train to larger cities like Albuquerque and Santa Fe in need of the wood.

In the 1930s, as logging declined, the high desert area gained fame as the carrot capital of the United States, growing and then trucking the crop to outlets all across the country. And finally, in 1950, the greatest economic as well as social change came to the area. A Navajo shepherd named Paddy Martinez discovered uranium ore on a mesa near the community of Grants, announcing his finding to the leaders in town and forever altering the little village of loggers, farmers, and railroad workers.

At first there was a great mining boom, bringing in lots of companies and developers all seeking fortune from the uranium-rich hills. There were churches built as well as bars and a few nice restaurants. Subdivisions were developed, schools came; Grants was turning out to be one of the fastest-growing towns in the entire state, becoming the lead producer of uranium in the entire country.

Lots of people from all across the world came to work in the mines: engineers, scientists, human resources specialists, and, of course, miners. Lots and lots of young men came to Grants, some from elsewhere in the state, others from across the country, eager to make money, unconcerned about what they were digging out from the mountain, and completely ignorant of what mining might do to the environment or to their health.

Grants continued to prosper, growing in population from about twelve hundred to twelve thousand, until the 1980s, when the mines began to close, one after the other, the recession hitting and the government finally acknowledging the grave consequences of the work done to extract the mineral from the mountains. Mining companies closed up shop, and the owners and managers, the engineers and white-collar workers, left for brighter pastures, leaving the miners and their families with open mines, contaminated water-sheds, scarred hills, and the residual consequences of lung disease and cancer. The town almost died.

However, today, according to the brochures I have picked up at the Chamber of Commerce, there is new blood in Grants. The little community is now touted as a retirement haven, trying to bring in new residents and more money. Grants pushes the tourism angle, promising great hiking at its local mountain, Mount Taylor, the largest peak in the region, great sightseeing at several national monuments and pueblos, and a fine city golf course just on the outskirts of town. It's a stop along the famous Route 66, promising tourists a town with a great hidden spirit.

I stopped at the Chamber of Commerce to get a better feel for the place—it's the journalist in me, the natural-born researcher—and later, at a gas station near the interstate, a clerk told me where to find the funeral home. It's exactly where she said it would be, across the street from an empty parking lot and standing between a dilapidated motel on one side and a liquor store on the other. I pull in and park in the lot across from the Serenity Mortuary. And then I kill the engine in Lou's truck and roll down the windows, choosing to stay a few minutes just where I am.

I've decided to stop here because I want to meet Mr. Harold Candelaria, let him know I'm still searching for Hart's family, before heading out to find the property Hart apparently still owns. Since Mr. Candelaria has already learned from the police in Little Rock that I am on my way, maybe he will ease up with his information and share more with me about Roger. I thought it might be the better place to start. And since I am a reporter, after all, I should know how to get the story.

I put the box on the dashboard.

"You remember anything about this place?" I

ask Roger, but then I think better of showing him the funeral home. I return the box to the passenger's seat.

"I'm sorry, that was thoughtless of me. Of course you remember this place. It's the funeral home."

I pat the top of the box.

"Well, I think I'll just go in there and have a look around." I glance down at him.

I roll up the windows a little but leave them cracked just because I'm used to doing that for Roger. I've been doing it since I set out on this trip. I get out of the truck, lock the doors, and walk across the street to the front door of Serenity. A chime rings when I open the door, and in a few seconds I hear a man call from the back of the building. "Be right there," he says.

The place itself smells like bouquets of old flowers even though all I see are a couple of arrangements of plastic ones, while the walls are adorned with pictures of canyons and mesas, a few of Jesus. There is old living room furniture in the foyer: two large chairs in a floral print, a rug, and a small table. Everything looks to be in need of a little housekeeping, with dust on the tops of frames, dirt in the corners. There is an office on the left and an entrance to the chapel on the right. I can see a narrow lectern with an open book, and over the door a sign reads, *Peace to All Who Enter Here.*

I have been in only two funeral homes before this one, Harvey's Chapel in Clayton and the Rosewood Mortuary in nearby Benton. Both were approached by the big funeral corporations now taking over many of the small-town family funeral homes; but both declined the offers. I went to school with old Mr. Harvey's sons and now they run the place, the older of them, Charles, handling sales and working with grieving families, and the other one, Darrell, in charge of the embalming and body preparation. Even as a boy Darrell was slightly freakish. I sometimes think that neither he nor I had much of a chance to do anything but follow in the footsteps of our fathers. This thought makes me glad I was born in the house of a newspaperman and not a funeral director.

"Can I help you?"

Harold Candelaria has entered the foyer from the back of the building. He's wiping his hands on a handkerchief and when he extends one to shake mine I'm a little reluctant to take it. I guess I'm still thinking about Darrell Harvey and all that embalming fluid.

Chapter Thirty-nine

"Weren't you arrested in Little Rock?" he asks as he sits down in a big leather chair behind his desk.

I take the seat across from him. "No, not arrested," I reply. "It was just a misunderstanding," I add.

"Always is," he says, sounding like he doesn't believe me. His chair tilts back as he leans away from me.

Mr. Harold Candelaria appears to be in his sixties. His face is weathered and his hair is all salt-and-pepper, slicked back and cut just above his neck. He's a big man, tall and wide shouldered; and he's trying to be cordial, but it's easy to see he doesn't really want to talk to me. He reminds me of the Big Tobacco businessmen back home. They looked just the same whenever I tried to ask questions, as I did at a town hall meeting where they met to disclose information about the warehouses they intended to build, insisting that the entire city was going to benefit from their business.

I had announced myself to those businessman as a reporter with the *Clayton Times and News* and I was immediately met with a look of disdain and what felt to me to be a closing door. The man I'd introduced myself to looked right over me and took a question instead from Larry Goads, a farmer who had sold his property to the business-man for a large sum of money and had agreed to be in the crowd that night to lend his support. Apparently, Big Tobacco knew my father's stance on bringing their business to town and wanted nothing to do with the small local paper. I was not allowed an interview.

Now I address myself to the matter at hand. "I just need the name of somebody in the family," I say to Mr. Candelaria. "I don't want to know anything about how Roger Hart died, if he had debts or left any sums of money to anyone. I just found his remains and want to give them to someone in the family who might know what to do with them."

The funeral director clasps his fingers together and places his hands over his belly. He seems to be sizing me up. "Aren't you a newspaper reporter?"

The question surprises me. "How did you know that?"

"After you called, I checked you out. Alissa Wells from Clayton, North Carolina. You work for the local paper there." He grins, looking every bit like he thinks his moves are smarter than mine.

"Well, yes, that's me; but I'm not doing this for the paper."

He nods, still grinning, like he wants to see me try and get out of this.

"What I told you on the phone is true," I say,

leaning toward him from my chair. "I found this box of ashes with the name Roger Hart and your business card. I just want to return his ashes to his family."

"Uh-huh," he responds. He just sits and watches me.

"Why would you think I'd be doing a story about Roger Hart?" I ask.

He hesitates, and I decide to wait, letting him have all the time he needs.

"Well, see, I don't really know the answer to that. I just know that over the years we've had lots of reporters from all over the country come here and want to dig up information about the miners. Some of them want to get the families all agitated and eager to file lawsuits, and others just want to write a story about how we've ruined the environment, how bad mining is for a town, maybe win themselves a Pulitzer or something."

I have to admit there is evidence of a good story here, about the pitfalls of uranium mining, and more than a couple of lawsuits to be filed in this old mining town. Surely Mr. Candelaria is telling the truth about his reluctance to share any information with a stranger, especially a stranger with a press badge.

He goes on. "And see, about a month after I find out that we've got real interest coming from Canadian and Japanese companies to pick back up the work that was being done in the mines, I get a call from you out of nowhere, a small-time reporter claiming to find someone's ashes, wanting names and numbers. And I know from experience that every time companies hear we've made the news—some article somewhere about the dangers of uranium mining—those companies drop and run like they just got caught with their hands up a married woman's dress. They don't want nothing to do with a city in the news."

I can't help it, but this makes me laugh. "Their hands up a married woman's dress?" I have to admit that's funny.

He's just watching me. I know I've got nothing to lose.

"Mr. Candelaria . . ."

"Harold," he says, interrupting, and smiles. And I almost think it seems genuine this time.

"Harold, I think a piece about uranium mining and the dire consequences of its excavation both to the environment and to the workers would make a fine story. And you're right, it could win a Pulitzer."

I sit back in my chair and drop my hands in my lap.

"But that's not a story I am trying to write. I report on car crashes and the style of gowns that brides are wearing this year. I write about the best pumpkin recipes and when trash is scheduled to be picked up during the holidays. I report on the weather and the traffic and local politics." I take a long breath, depressing myself with this assessment of my work.

"I don't cover Grants, New Mexico, or the business of uranium mining; I cover Clayton, North Carolina, Johnston County, and maybe Zebulon and Smithfield, but not Durham or Raleigh or Chapel Hill. I write local stories, Harold, not national ones, and certainly not southwestern ones. Frankly, they don't interest people in my hometown—and even if I did decide to write about what is happening in Grants, New Mexico, the publisher of the *Clayton Times and News*, my father, Oscar Wells, would rip the story to pieces and tell me to write for the place I live and the people who don't care about anywhere else."

I take another breath.

"The truth is, Mr. Candelaria, I called you with an honest request. I discovered Mr. Hart's ashes when I bought the contents of an abandoned storage facility. I found your business card and his name on the box that contains his remains. I just want to return what I have to his family. I have no hidden agenda. This is not some hoax to gather names for a petition. I just want to return a man who's met his end to those who might wish to lay him to some final rest."

Either Harold is feeling sorry for me or he believes that what I've just told him is the truth. He softens.

"Look, after hearing from you, I tried to call the numbers I had on file. Every one of them is disconnected or has been changed. The truth is, Miss Wells, I'm not trying to be hard to get along with. I really don't have any information to give out."

"But surely somebody in town knows the family. This isn't New York City. You only have a population of about nine thousand."

"Well, even with such a paltry population of nine thousand, we don't all have Sunday dinners together. Our children don't all share the same classroom." He shrugs, and there's a little sorrow in the gesture. "I don't know Mr. Hart's family."

I just lost the connection. I've done all I can do.

Mr. Candelaria checks the clock on his desk. He's given me as much time as he intends; I can tell I'm about to be dismissed. Then I hear a phone ring from the back, but it seems as if another employee has come to work.

"Look, I don't mean to be a troublemaker." I'm trying one more time. "I'm actually just trying to do a nice thing here. I found the ashes and your card and that's all I've got to go on." I don't mention the property records I only recently discovered. "I'd just like to get the ashes to somebody who might know what to do with them."

The funeral director takes in a breath, gives me another long, hard look, stands up, and walks around the desk. "Give me a minute," he says and heads out the door.

I sit and wait, and I hear him talking to someone. It's only five minutes before he walks back in.

"Here's the record from the cremation. There's all the information I have about Mr. Hart's family; maybe you'll have better luck than I did."

I stand to face him and take the file he's holding out to me. I drop it on the chair and take his right hand in both of mine, giving it a firm, hearty shake. "Thank you, Harold; thank you very much."

And with that, I head back to Roger.

Chapter Forty

"Harold wasn't lying, after all," I tell Roger after I've finished calling each of the numbers listed in the file Mr. Candelaria has given me. There are only three and all three are disconnected or no longer in service. "So, it looks like you have a nephew from Gallup, an ex-wife in California, and a stepdaughter with no address given. All other family members are deceased." I glance over to the box beside me. "You were kind of a loner, I guess."

I turn the contract over and read the back, see who paid the final bill. There's a name listed that doesn't match any of the three on the front, Georgia Pointer, but there is no contact information for her, just a signature and her name printed in neat block letters.

I take my chances and open up my computer to Google her. "Well, what do you know?" I tell Roger. "There she is." I find a pen and a piece of paper in the glove compartment of Lou's truck and write down an address for Ms. Georgia Pointer, living in Milan, New Mexico, the next town over from Grants.

But first, I crank up the truck and put the address from the properties search into the GPS.

"Here we go."

From the funeral home it is only about fifteen minutes to the last known property owned by Mr. Roger Hart. I take a right on the main street through town, passing old buildings boarded up, relics of a better time. There's a Catholic church, a park with a nice lake in the center, a few offices, two fast-food restaurants, and another liquor store. I make a left, cross over the interstate, and head south. Eight miles out of town I am directed to turn right on a road listed as FR 37; but I don't see it. I drive up a few hundred yards, turn around, and look again.

"You want to give me a sign?" I ask Roger, who is really no help at all.

There's a narrow driveway on the right, but it can't possibly be the road I'm supposed to take. I go back toward town, turn around again, and drive as slowly as I can. I inch toward the driveway while the synthetic voice of the GPS assures me this is where I'm supposed to turn. So I do. I make a right and head west on a dusty, bumpy, unpaved dirt road, finally coming upon the sign—*FR 37*—that confirms I am indeed heading in the right direction.

One mile becomes two and then four and I feel the sweat beading across my top lip. Lou's truck has an air conditioner and I've cranked it up; but I am facing the afternoon sun and I am more than a little nervous that I might get lost in these desert hills or drive up on some motorcycle gang's property. I keep going.

Finally, I hear the words I have been waiting to hear, the announcement from the voice of the GPS telling me I have arrived at my destination. I see a narrow driveway to my right and make the turn.

I feel a little bad that I'm taking Lou's truck on such poorly maintained roads, but I'm also a bit relieved that this isn't Faramond being forced to drive the rocky terrain. I'm almost certain he would get stuck in one of the deep ruts that Lou's truck seems to be able to move across without sinking.

"Did you drive this every day?" I ask Roger, thinking he must have had to replace his automobiles yearly if he lived out here. I think about how it must have been in the winters. I wonder how he ever managed to drive on this path when the monsoons came. "You would need a tractor to pull you out if you got stuck in mud out here."

And as soon as the words leave my lips, I see a tractor standing in the middle of a field to my right. It's an old one, a rusty red Ford with a snowplow still attached, the weeds growing up and through it. I stop and glance over. I look down on the passenger's seat and reach for the box, hold it up. "That yours?" I ask my silent companion. And it makes me smile to think of him seeing his old farm equipment again after such a long time.

I place the box on the dashboard now and use one hand to steady it so that it won't slide off. We drive about five hundred more yards, and then the driveway ends and there is nothing there but the remains of a corral, a few boards still connected in places on fencing that circles a long wooden trough. There's a worn spot in the dirt. Maybe a trailer was parked there, or a small house was torn down, everything taken away. I stop and park. I turn off the engine and get out of the truck, taking Roger with me.

It is late in the afternoon, the sun is sinking behind the hills known as the Zuni Mountains, I've learned, and the western sky is turning shades of pink. It is quieter here than even what I found at Lou's place, and I hear only the sounds of ground squirrels and songbirds. I close my eyes, take in a deep breath, open them, and then place Roger on the hood of the truck.

"This is quite a spread," I tell him, glad to be

where we are, glad to have found his property, the place I am sure he lived before he died.

A hawk flies overhead, circling us, welcoming us; and I take Roger and walk past the corral and out beyond where I parked. There is a faint sound of water and I head in that direction. Ponderosa pines tower over this secluded piece of land; green-topped mesas lie ahead. I know a little bit about these mountains because I read everything I could find about this area of New Mexico before making this trip, hoping to find clues as to what Roger's life might have been like. And of course, researching facts is a reporter's idea of fun.

I know, for example, that the Zuni Mountains are surrounded by red sandstone and that the range sits on the Continental Divide and forms part of the southern end of the Colorado Plateau. I remember reading that the string of hills is about sixty miles long and forty miles wide and that the highest peak is Mount Sedgwick, though I'm sure the Native people call it by another name. I know the land has been logged and mined and that more than a few landowners grew rich as a result.

I glance around at the unbelievable beauty surrounding me. However Roger Hart lived his life, if he lived here—and now that I'm here, I'm quite certain that he did—he lived with some of the most breathtaking views in the land.

"How did you get this place?" I ask him,

wondering if the acreage has already been claimed by county or state, its driveway so close to the marked territory of a national forest.

"Are you Zuni?" I ask, but that seems impossible. Surely his people would have buried him in the traditional way, not sent him to a white man's funeral home, sending his body away to be cremated and then picking him up in a box. I also believe that the people of the pueblo would be much more careful with a loved one's remains and would not have allowed them to end up in a storage building at the other end of the country. But maybe I'm just a romantic that way. Maybe he is Zuni. Maybe he pulled away from his people and just got lost while living out here by himself.

I walk a bit farther in the direction where I hear running water, but I cannot find it. I see small paths running up the hills, deer crossings, I guess, and openings in the pines; but I cannot find a creek or river, although I can hear one. I stop in the field and look up to the sky until, finally, I decide to turn back. The sun is setting. I need to leave.

I stop for a second, the late afternoon breeze picking up around us, and lift Roger up, high above my head. I turn from the direction I was going—east toward Grants—back to the west toward the mountain, and I stop again. I close my eyes and stand quietly for a few seconds. And then I turn to the north and then to the south. I do not know what is leading me, but I want to pray for the soul of Roger Hart. So I do. I pray for a restless spirit and I ask the maker of these hills and trees and fading sun to bring peace to this son, this spirit of a man who I now know is from this place. I make one final turn and, with the box still in my hands, I head back to Lou's truck.

Chapter Forty-one

"He didn't really have anybody," Georgia Pointer is telling me after she has flipped through the file that the funeral director gave me. She's in her sixties, I think, boxy with short white hair and a streak of pink down the middle. She wears glasses and has three diamond studs in each ear.

We decided to meet at the Denny's near the highway. She was driving home from a meeting in Albuquerque and she likes the Grand Slam breakfast for dinner. We order our meals and Georgia fills me in on Roger, the man I have delivered back home.

"He moved out beyond San Rafael when he came back from Vietnam," she explains. "Bought the piece of land from an old rancher. Was married for a few years; but he couldn't even remember exactly why they broke up, just said the desert was too hard for some people and that his wife never quite got used to the dry, hot air."

"Was he originally from New Mexico?" I ask,

taking a sip of coffee and glancing around the restaurant. There are a few truckers at the counter, some tourists making a stop off the interstate. There don't seem to be many locals.

"Not born here, no," she says. "But I think he was part Navajo. Like I said, came back from Vietnam and made his home up on Zuni. That was, what?" She looks for me to fill in the blank, so I do.

"Nineteen seventy-five?"

She nods. "Forty years ago. That's long enough to call this place home, don't you think?"

I shrug. In North Carolina, your parents have to have been born in the town for you to be called a local; otherwise you're still thought of as somebody just passing through.

Our dinners arrive and we both dig in. I ordered pancakes, and I reach across the table to grab the syrup.

"He drove a cement truck for two or three decades, retired from that job when he was seventy, I guess. He was my patient for two years," Georgia tells me before taking a bite of egg and bacon. "He was a little standoffish at first, but after he figured out I wasn't going to report him to the IRS for not paying taxes or call any of his kin while I cared for him, we got along just fine."

Georgia was his hospice nurse when Roger was admitted with a diagnosis of bone cancer. He refused aggressive treatment and died before having to make the hard decisions about long-term care and moving out of his house.

"I think he willed his trailer to an old buddy from AA, left the land to the government. He didn't have much else to give away. After he died, I called his ex-wife and his nephew. I think there was a child he raised for some years, too. But none of them really wanted anything to do with him, so I had him cremated and paid the bill myself." She takes a drink from her glass of water. "I know Harold pretty well, and he gave me a discount because of all the business I bring him."

A hospice nurse and a funeral director, I can see the connection.

"Anyway, like I said, Roger was a loner. Worked in the mines, went to war, drove the truck, stayed up there underneath the mountain all the time, came into town for groceries and gas, but that was about it."

I eat a bite of pancake. It sounds true enough.

Then I ask the sixty-four-thousand-dollar question. "But how did he end up in North Carolina?"

She finishes her mouthful and swallows, peers out the window facing the interstate. She shakes her head. "I'm afraid I don't know the answer to that one, sheriff."

And that makes me laugh a little, since I've never been called that before.

"Did you ask Harold who picked up the ashes?" she asks me.

"Well, Mr. Candelaria wasn't all that forthcoming," I explain. "And in the files it just reports that the ashes were picked up a couple of weeks after the cremation, doesn't list a name."

"I'll call him tomorrow," Georgia tells me, taking another big bite of her nighttime breakfast.

I nod.

"Was there a service?" I ask.

She shakes her head. "Not that I recall." She seems to be thinking about it. "The chaplain visited a few times," she remembers. "But I don't think they ever agreed on what he wanted when he passed. Knowing Roger the way I did, I seriously doubt he would have agreed to a gathering on his behalf and having people stand around making up stories about him."

She takes another bite.

I drink some coffee.

"He loved the wolves," Georgia says.

I wait for her to finish.

"There's a sanctuary down the road from his place in a little town called Candy Kitchen. He used to volunteer there when he was first retired. He talked about them all the time, the wolves, how wrong people were about them out here." She wipes her mouth with her napkin. "Ranchers hate wolves. It's a big fight in the Southwest; but Roger loved them, talked about them like they were family. I don't know, maybe they were."

I've eaten all the pancakes I can handle, and I push aside my plate. It's nice to hear real memories about Roger, but I'm not really getting any more information than I started with. "I guess I was hoping for a reunion of some kind."

"What's that?"

I didn't realize I'd spoken out loud and I know I must seem a bit surprised by Georgia's question. I shake my head. "I don't know what I was thinking," I confess to the hospice nurse. "I guess I had this thought that there would be some family member desperate for the remains of their loved one. I think I was imagining that there would be something that would cause all this to make sense."

"A happy ending," she notes.

I shrug. "I guess."

Georgia takes a drink of water and puts down the glass. "I used to think I knew how to help make a right kind of death for everybody."

"What do you mean?"

"I used to think I could lead people to forgive or be magnanimous with their hearts, tell their loved ones that they loved them, stay engaged in life as long as they could, do life review, make good choices, let go of their burdens." She shakes her head. "But I eventually gave up on my ideals. I realize now that most people die exactly the same way they live. Angry people die angry.

Broken people die broken. Lonely people die lonely. Burdened people die burdened. I can't change any of it even if family members are desperate to be a part of something they have waited for all of their lives. I can't make a person's path twist the way I think it should go."

I can tell she isn't finished, so I don't respond.

She puts down her fork, wipes her hands on her napkin.

"What I'm saying is that we don't always get the happy endings we want; but that shouldn't change what we try to make right."

I shake my head, not sure what she means by that last comment.

"You brought back Roger's ashes because you felt inclined to do it, just like I feel inclined to be a nurse who works for hospice. There is no grateful, grieving wife for Roger. There is no child that has searched desperately for his father, to whom you now deliver great comfort by returning the remains. Roger died just like he chose to live, alone, in the desert near the wolves, and you are bringing him back. That's the happy ending. And you and Roger get to share it."

"I think my head hurts," I say. I need a little time to think about all of this.

"I got your number in my phone. I'll call you after I talk to Harold." She pats her belly. "That was a grand slam." And she smiles.

I pick up the check and start to exit the booth.

"My treat," I tell her and she seems pleased.

"You staying in town?" she asks.

And I nod in the direction of the Holiday Inn next door to the restaurant. "I'm here for the night."

"Well, I hope you sleep good and that you have a safe trip home to North Carolina." She gets out of her seat and stands next to me. "You taking Roger back to his place?"

I nod. "I guess I have to if I'm going to have the happy ending."

She smiles and slaps me on the back. "That's it," she says. "And don't forget, sheriff: live how you want to die." And she heads out the door.

Chapter Forty-two

My sleep is fretful. There are doors slamming around me all night; I can hear the traffic from the highway and I can't get Georgia's words out of my mind. *Angry people die angry. Lonely people die lonely. Died just like he chose to live. Alone.*

When I do nod off, I dream of howling wolves and old men walking down dirt roads, old men who will not speak to me even as I keep running from one to the other, asking them where they are going and who they expect to find. They just keep walking to nowhere and I keep chasing them. I finally fall into a deep sleep just as the sun is rising, my mind and body exhausted from all the running and tossing and turning.

I'm twisted in my sheets but dead to the world when the banging on my door bolts me upright. I shake my head, trying to clear the images and the cobwebs and remember where I am, since there have been so many beds in so many places this past week. *Was that another dream or is there somebody at my door?*

When the banging starts up again, I'm pretty certain that even in this state of disorientation, I am likely to do harm to a hotel maid.

"Al, wake up."

How does the maid know my name? I stay where I am.

"Al, get up, it's Blossom. Open the door."

"Blossom?" I wipe my eyes, untangle myself from the bed linens, and stand at the door. *Was she with me last night? Are we still traveling together?*

I peek through the small hole in the door and it's definitely Blossom. I glance around the room: one bed, one suitcase—I'm pretty sure she didn't come with me from Texas.

"What are you doing here?" I ask as I let her in.

She walks in with Casserole, who seems slightly put out to be up so early, but maybe a little happy to see me, too.

"Is something wrong with Cass?" I bend down and give my dog a hug. He sits down, allowing

252

me full access as I probe him from end to end. He seems fine: two ears, two eyes, one nose, three legs, no blood or bandages. I stand back up, slide my fingers through my sleep-matted hair, and try to straighten out my nightshirt while Blossom closes the door behind her.

"Do you have your phone on?" she asks.

I left it charging in the bathroom. Apparently, my ringing phone was one of the few sounds I *didn't* hear during the night. I turn back to Blossom and shake my head. "Why? What's up?"

She takes me by the hands. Everything feels a little off about her appearance and about how she's behaving. Her clothes and hair are disheveled, like she's been up all night; she seems tired and nervous, evidence to me that this is not the Morning Blossom I am accustomed to. In the days that we've been traveling together, I have never seen her look like this. It's all a little unnerving.

"It's your dad," she says.

Not good news, that's pretty clear. Nope, not good, not good at all.

"What about my dad?" And I feel a kind of thud hit my chest. My legs feel a little wobbly, and my pulse picks up.

Blossom leads me over to the bed and I sit down. Casserole comes over beside me as if he's fulfilling his role in delivering this bad news. I look from him to her, and back again.

"He's in the hospital," she tells me as she kneels in front of me next to my dog. "He's had a heart attack and he's having surgery this morning."

"What?" The words hang over us like they're stuck in balloons.

"He had a heart attack last night. Everybody tried contacting you, but no one could get through. I finally got a message on Facebook."

"How—?" I don't finish the question; I'm just shaking my head at the news.

Blossom is explaining how she found out about it. "When I opened your account in Nashville, a couple of your contacts friended me. James William and Dixie."

My head is just shaking, back and forth, back and forth. None of this is making sense.

"Dixie messaged me because she couldn't reach you and then I tried to call; and, well, I just decided to come here and tell you in person."

I'm still shaking my head, still trying to make sense of this. What a horrible way to wake up.

"He was okay when they took him in; I just talked to your sister a little while ago. She's there."

"You talked to Sandra?"

"Dixie gave her my number last night; she knew I was going to see you so she called with reports every couple of hours. I just talked to her about an hour ago when I was at the truck stop and she said he had been taken to the operating room for surgery, that they had finally stabilized his blood pressure and the doctors were pretty sure he was in good shape for the operation." She waits. "You okay?"

I look down to see her hands on mine. I nod.

"You want to call her?"

I nod again.

Blossom reaches in her back pocket, takes out her phone, touches the screen, and hands it to me. I hear it ring and then I hear my sister's voice.

"Sandra?"

There is a sigh. "She found you," she says.

"Yeah."

"Is your phone not working?"

"It's in—" And I stop; these are not the details that interest me. "How is Dad? What happened?"

"He was at some silly town meeting and got all upset about something, and just passed out. They rushed him to Raleigh, and, well, it's his heart."

"And he's in surgery?"

"Yes, they took him in about an hour ago. We're at Rex on the seventh floor in Raleigh. There's a blockage, but they think they're going to do bypass surgery—open it up or put in a new artery, whatever it is that they do. Are you coming home today?"

How do I get home today? "I'm in New Mexico," I explain.

"There's not an airport there?"

"I . . . I . . ."

"Look, never mind. Just get here when you can. I'll call you when he's out of surgery; but I have to head back to Asheville tomorrow. I've already missed getting Kaitlin to camp. I need to be home, so you need to get back here as soon as you can."

"I will," I reply, feeling guilty and punished at the same time.

"All right. I'll call you later. Or I'll have somebody call you."

She says good-bye. And the line goes dead.

I turn to Blossom.

"Well, at least we know who got the charm in your family." She smiles.

I start to cry. I slide off the bed and land between Blossom and Cass. And I cry because my father has had a heart attack and I am not there and I cry because I've driven all the way to New Mexico with the ashes of a stranger and I have just been told that there will be no happy ending and I cry because my sister is with my dad and not me and I cry just because that's all I can let myself do.

Instantly, there is an arm around my shoulders and a furry head in my lap.

"It's going to be okay," Blossom says, comforting me. "He's going to be okay."

Why I think a seventeen-year-old can read the future and give me something to hope for and believe in, I don't know, but for right now, it's her words and her prediction to which I cling.

Chapter Forty-three

There were thirteen messages on my phone, most of them regarding Dad; but there was also one from Georgia, the hospice nurse, who called me just before Blossom arrived with the news about my father.

Dusty Lennon picked up the remains of Roger Hart fifteen days after they were returned from the crematorium to the mortuary. Harold gave them to him because the three contacts he had listed as next of kin didn't want the ashes, and he was just glad that someone cared enough to pick them up. Dusty, it turns out, is the same friend who was deeded Roger's trailer and the same friend who decided to drive to North Carolina, get a boat, and—well, after that we don't really know what Dusty Lennon was going to do because he never told anyone his plans.

He died on a dock at a harbor near Wilmington, from a stroke or aneurysm, something quick and fatal, and in his belongings there was a card from the Serenity Mortuary, where Dusty had prepaid his funeral. Unclaimed by anyone in the southeastern state, he was, therefore, shipped back to Harold, who had forgotten by that time, a year after the first death, that he had ever given him Roger Hart's ashes. Dusty had started payments on a sailboat and had been working on it for months, Harold told Georgia; but no one, it seems, knew about a storage unit rented by the New Mexican when he arrived in North Carolina.

Dusty Lennon had a daughter in Albuquerque and there was a service in Grants for the Vietnam vet and recovered alcoholic, friend to Roger Hart. Harold said that it was held in the chapel at the mortuary a couple of years ago and he recalled that it was a well-attended and polite service that included the local honor guard playing taps and presenting Dusty's daughter with an American flag. Georgia was also given Lennon's daughter's phone number and address, which she included for me in her message.

I can call the daughter if I'd like to see if she knows anything about the ashes, and I suppose I can send her the other things I found in the storage unit and placed in my garage if she wants them. There isn't really anything of value in there; but I don't know, maybe she'd like her father's tools and books and the blankets, tent, and few pieces of camping equipment. I suppose, thinking about it now, that Dusty was living on the boat he'd bought while he was making repairs. Makes sense that he'd have left the bulk of his possessions somewhere else.

"I'll go down with Casserole while you check out," Blossom tells me from the hotel bedroom while I am listening again to Georgia's message.

"Let him walk around a little before we head out. It was a long drive this morning."

We are going to scatter Roger's ashes at the place he called home, the spot I visited yesterday, and then Blossom will drive her father's truck back to Amarillo. Casserole and I will hitch rides with truckers back to North Carolina, all arranged by Blossom and her grandmother's husband, Tony, hopefully making it home by tomorrow evening. The part where I am reunited with my dear old Volkswagen, Faramond, has not been worked out.

Jumping trucks from Texas was how Blossom got to Grants, and she knew she would find me at the Holiday Inn because she'd added the "locate friend" app to our smartphones after the near arrest in Little Rock. She told me about it at the time—we were almost to Fort Smith by then—but I'd forgotten all about it.

"Wow, you're right, it is beautiful out here." Blossom has her head stuck out the window, right next to Casserole's, who is sitting in her lap. Both of them have their noses in the air; the wind is blowing back her hair and his fur as I speed along the state highway. They're so cute together like this, my two passengers, that I am given a moment of mercy and I feel almost light and unburdened.

"I wonder why his friend thought he would want to be near the ocean." She's pulled her head in from the car window and slid over toward me, giving Cass his own place on the seat.

"Maybe he was just taking him for a trip—you know, sailing for a year or something—and then he was planning to come back to New Mexico."

"I guess," Blossom replies.

"Maybe it was something they had always talked about and never got around to doing."

"Do you think that happens a lot?"

I turn to her. She is so young it breaks my heart. "I do," I answer, suddenly thinking about my father. He has always planned to go fly-fishing in Idaho, talked about it every spring and forgot about it by the end of every summer.

I face the road again, determined to get him there next year. I will make all the arrangements and I will drive him there myself. That is exactly what I will do.

I see the turn to Roger's property now, and slow down, make a right, and head west on the forest road I traveled yesterday and ran all last night in my dreams.

"It's only a few miles," I say to Blossom. "But you might want to roll up your window; it's dirt all the way and it's pretty sandy."

"My dad always says a dirt road is a good teacher of patience," she informs me as the truck cab starts to fill with dust.

"And my dad says taking a dirt road is a sure way to lose your lead." I look over at my passenger. "He doesn't like to be slowed down."

"Then I guess a heart attack will really be hard for him."

I think of my father lying in a bed held down by tubes and surrounded by IV poles and monitors, and I speed up, the moment of mercy and relief I felt earlier now gone. Even though my first pickup toward home isn't for another couple of hours, I feel the need to hurry.

I make it to Roger's driveway and up to the corral and stop. I kill the engine and we all four get out—Cass, me, Blossom, and Roger, who she is carrying close to her chest. The dust from our arrival settles and we just stand for a few minutes near the truck. Once again, I am startled both by the stark beauty and its silence.

I watch as Blossom looks around, her first experience in the Zuni Mountains. She catches my eye. "Sweet," is all she says, and she holds the box of ashes in both of her hands like she is offering a gift.

"So, where do you think we should do this?" I ask her.

She takes in the view for a few more moments. "What do you think, Cass?"

And my dog turns to her and then starts walking in the same direction I went yesterday. Blossom looks over to me and shrugs and we follow. The sound of running water I heard earlier is still there.

We have walked just a couple of hundred yards when Casserole stops and sniffs the air. Blossom and I stop and wait behind him. The thought crosses my mind that he doesn't actually have any real inside spiritual knowledge about the right place to scatter Roger's ashes, he's just trying to find a good place to poop. But when he starts walking again, like a good soldier I remain in line.

When we arrive at the narrow creek whose presence explains the sound of running water I could hear from where we parked, I turn to my dog. "Good job," I say. Then I notice a butterfly, a monarch, flitting about near him and it makes me think of the carving on Roger's box, the one that started me off on this pilgrimage.

"Well, I guess this is it," Blossom says. She looks over to me. "Do you want me to leave the two of you alone?"

I walk over to her as she holds out the box and I touch her hands and shake my head. I open it and take out the bag of ashes. I remove the tab that keeps the bag locked and hold it open. I pause because I'm not quite sure what to say.

"Roger Hart," I begin, "thank you for bringing me to this place. Thank you for your service as a veteran and for being with Dusty when he died. Thank you for sending me Blossom and Dillon, and for keeping us safe in our travels. May you be free and at peace." I wait a second to see if Blossom has anything she wants to say, and it looks like she does.

She clears her throat. "I don't know anything

about you, Roger, except what I've learned from traveling with you. I think you were a good man, and that you were kind, and I hope that wherever you go from here, you find your friend. You shouldn't be alone." And she nods at me to let me know she is finished.

I hold the bottom of the bag and let the ashes drop. A breeze picks up just as they are falling and takes them toward the creek; and somewhere off in the distance I hear the howl of a wolf.

"Welcome home," I say and I feel Blossom's hand as she slips it into mine.

Chapter Forty-four

It is two o'clock in the morning and I am somewhere between Memphis and Nashville, Tennessee, in my third vehicle since I started off from Grants. It's the last leg of my journey back to North Carolina, and I'm riding with a man named Milton. He'll drive me all the way to Raleigh, where I will meet Ben, who will take me to the hospital and bring Casserole back to Clayton. I haven't quite worked out how I'm going to get home after I see my dad, but if I've managed to hitch rides with strangers all the way from New Mexico to North Carolina, I shouldn't have too much trouble getting a twenty-minute lift home.

Milton drives a semitrailer. His vehicle is

tandem axle with a sleeper behind the cab, where Cass and I are riding; and connected to the fifth wheel hitch behind us is an oversized load on a lowboy trailer. Milton is from Jacksonville, North Carolina, a retired Marine who likes the old R&B classics and driving at night. He has a shiny brown bald head, a broad frame, and a wide smile. We met in Russellville or Conway, I can't remember exactly, but somewhere in Arkansas in the diner at a big truck stop off the interstate.

The waitress at the diner let me bring Casserole inside, even though it's technically against the rules, because she claimed she had a three-legged dog once when she was a girl. She slipped him leftovers from the plates of her customers and bagged up pieces of hamburger and pork chops for us to take on the rest of our trip. She even refused my tip, handing me instead a roll of one-dollar bills. I'm pretty certain she thought I was homeless or lost, and she's a sucker for women traveling alone.

I had been dropped off by Clyde Tessler, the trucker who drove us from Oklahoma and who was heading north to Belvidere, Illinois, where he was returning from a trip to California. He had dropped off a load of new Jeep Patriots to a dealership in Los Angeles and was in a bit of a hurry to make it home for his granddaughter's sixth birthday. He apologized for not staying with me at the diner until Milton showed up; but I knew he didn't want to wait and I reassured him that Casserole and I would be fine.

As I sat in the Arkansas diner with my dog and the minutes ticked by, I did wonder what might happen if Milton didn't make it. Cass and I were stuck in a town where we didn't know a soul. But Luna, the waitress who gave me the doggie bag and her tips, also slipped me a number for a women's shelter nearby; and I was certain that as long as we stayed during her shift, she wouldn't steer us in a wrong direction or even leave us alone.

Before Clyde picked us up, I rode with Tony, the husband of Blossom's grandmother; and we talked about Newport, summer construction, the decline of Western civilization, and how Casserole and I would be in the safest hands and best-maintained rigs on the road. Tony made all the arrangements for us to get back to North Carolina. He was easy with his promise that both of the others offering us rides were kind and courteous and longtime big-rig drivers. The three of them had started trucking at the same company years earlier, and although they went in different directions over the years, they were all still driving rigs, and all still friends.

So far, I have learned about the Motor Transport Workers, the union for drivers; laws regarding the required weight and inspection of loads; and the names of different tractors and rigs; as well as what it's like to own your own fleet. I found out that truckers still use the CB radio occasionally, but rely more on smartphones and social media to stay informed about traffic and road construction.

I also learned about open-heart surgery since both Tony and Clyde had stints and bypasses, Tony a triple and Clyde a quadruple. Both of them claimed that the surgery is a piece of cake and that my dad should be fine. Better than fine, actually, since a person's blood flow is so much greater after the operation. It turns out that a lot of truckers have heart problems, which I'm sure has to do with their lack of physical activity and the really bad food.

Milton tells me that we should be in Raleigh by noon. He's encouraged me to sleep, but I've been having trouble stilling my mind since we left New Mexico. I've talked to Dixie and Ben. And Sandra gave me the report after the surgery, saying that everything was fine, that the doctors were pleased with how things went and that she was leaving to go back to Asheville just as soon as Dad was out of recovery. Dixie was planning to stay the night, even though I know that must be terribly inconvenient for a single mother with small children; but she insisted she'd worked it all out. I could hear more concern in her voice than in my sister's. I feel lucky that we have such dedicated employees at the *Clayton Times and News*.

I texted Phillip somewhere in Oklahoma to tell him what has happened and he finally replied as I crossed the border into Arkansas, interrupting a conversation I was having with Clyde about electric cars and whether or not there will ever be a truly viable option to gas-powered motors.

So sorry about your dad, Al, he wrote. Have you heard anything about how the surgery went?

He's in recovery, seems to be okay, I typed.

Good to hear.

I didn't reply.

Are you driving back?

Riding with truckers, I answered, glancing over at Clyde, who had quit talking about hydrocarbons and filtering the fats in biodiesel fuel. I guess he figured it made sense for me to have only one conversation at a time.

I can't wait to hear about that! Phillip wrote.

And I read the sentence over and over before knowing how to respond.

Interesting, for sure, I finally decided.

Call me when you get to NC.

K

And I stared at my phone like it was my life unfolding in my hands.

"Must be your fellow," Clyde said, taking his eyes off the road for just a second and looking over at me. He had a big grin plastered across his face.

"Just an old friend," I said, but I knew I didn't sound very convincing.

"I have a lot of old friends," he said, "but never one to make my face turn that shade of red."

Then he winked at me. And went back to talking about biodiesels and how he had invested some of his earnings into soybean and safflower farms, hoping that someday the popularity of alternative fuel sources would make him rich.

I close my eyes now, throw my arm over my head, and listen to the road passing beneath me. I think about my day. It started with Blossom and me saying good-bye to Roger, tossing his ashes high along a winding creek in northwestern New Mexico. And now I'm somewhere in Tennessee, sleeping in the cab of a rig owned by a trucker whose last name I don't even know.

Daddy is in the hospital, Phillip Blake and I are talking and texting like we're a couple, and I suddenly think of Luna, the waitress in Arkansas, and what she said when she insisted on handing over her tips. She pushed the wad of cash into my hand and said, "Honey, even if you don't need this money right now, just take it, because in a minute, or a day, everything you thought you knew about your life could unravel like an old pair of socks. You never know when you're going to need a little extra something to darn the holes."

I reach down and pat the pocket in the front of my jeans. Having the money isn't so important— I have enough of my own to make my way— but her priceless wisdom just makes me smile.

Chapter Forty-five

"You look different."

Ben is staring at me even though he should be paying attention to the road.

"I'm still me," I say.

He shakes his head like he's stumped, then turns and finally faces the direction a driver ought to face. Forward. "Yeah," he says. "I guess."

I pull down the visor anyway to see if something is off about my appearance. After all, it's Ben telling me this, the guy whose wife divorced him for not noticing her makeover.

But I look like I always do: plain, pale, determined, and wrestling with uncontrollable hair. I try to smooth it down on the sides a bit, slap my cheeks to give them a little color. There's not much I can do without a shower and makeup, so I just pop the visor back up.

"So, truckers, huh?" He taps his fingers on the steering wheel.

"Yep, all the way from New Mexico."

The previous day of my life is a blur. Saying good-bye to Blossom, hopping from vehicle to vehicle, meeting the three drivers. I probably didn't sleep but two or three hours because of all the things I was thinking about: how I will retrieve my car, all the conversations about Roger, wondering about his friend's daughter and whether she knew about the ashes, worrying about Daddy.

"Did you take any drugs?"

"What?"

"Drugs? I heard truckers are the best dealers in the country."

I have not heard this.

"Nope, not the ones I rode with. Straight as arrows, these guys." And I think I must remember to get Tony's address so that I can write him a thank-you note.

Ben nods. "Prostitutes?"

"What?"

"Did you see any prostitutes?"

I roll my eyes. "I'd have to say no to that question as well. No prostitutes, no drugs, just twenty-four hours of bad country music." I pause. "Make that fourteen hours of country music and ten of Ray Charles, T-Bone Walker, and the Drifters." Milton had a collection of CDs like I have never seen before.

Ben nods, appears a bit disappointed. He speeds down the interstate, changing lanes, as we head toward the hospital.

I feel like I have seen nothing but highway and scenery out windows for months; but it really hasn't been that long.

"So, tell me about Dad," I say, wondering what Ben can tell me about what occurred before the heart attack.

He turns to me again and shrugs. "Nobody really knows what happened."

"Sandra said he was at a town council meeting?"

"County commissioners," he says, correcting me. "They were voting on changing the name of the park. The county got a big gift from a corporation doing some business here, and the commissioners thought putting the company's name on the park sign would convince them to bring all the jobs to Clayton."

"Let me guess—Reynolds?"

"That's the one," he replies. "They're expanding, and they like what Johnston County has to offer." He smiles and it sounds like he's reading a press release.

Big Tobacco, I think, my father's nemesis.

"I don't know why O.W. is still convinced that cigarettes are bringing down our society."

I start to explain about my mother and her cancer and the tobacco; but it doesn't matter because there's no logic to my father's obsession with these companies. Even without a connection between brain tumors and smoking, he refuses to let go of blame.

"He'd just like his hometown to be known for something more than growing tobacco," I explain. "He thinks we sell ourselves short by catering only to those companies."

"Well, those companies are what's keeping our town's economy going," Ben responds. "And if he wants to keep the paper, he needs to start writing some supportive stories."

I look over at Ben. "Why? What's going on with the paper?"

He won't face me. "Everybody knows what's happening to small-town newspapers, Al." He shrugs. "I'm just saying if he'd do a little more to show gratitude for the businesses still operating in our county, he wouldn't be so nervous every month trying to pay the bills."

I don't reply.

"Tobacco is still lucrative and all those companies have diversified. It wouldn't hurt Oscar to write about the good things they do."

The thought of Oscar Wells involved in crony journalism or writing positive-slanted feature stories about Big Tobacco almost makes me laugh. He'd let go of the *Times and News* and go to work for the *News and Observer* out of Raleigh before he'd do that.

Ben is still talking. "They give a lot of money to the schools and the parks in the towns where they are. Shoot, they just built a four-million-dollar sports complex in Winston-Salem and gave tons of money to the college for a new library. Think about what they could do for Johnston County."

"You sound like you've been drinking some tobacco-flavored Kool-Aid since I've been gone." I pause a second and then lean toward him and whisper, "Are you taking bribes from Virginia Slims?"

He takes his hand off the steering wheel and waves me off. "I smoke cigars, Al. If I was writing puff pieces for bribes it would be for Gurkha. Now, I'd sell my soul for a year's supply of a box of their Beauties."

"I have no idea what you're talking about," I reply. "Just tell me what happened at the meeting where he had the heart attack."

Ben takes the exit and continues to head in the direction of Rex Hospital. "I don't really know. I got the call after he collapsed."

"Was he there alone? Didn't James William go?" I thought he had let the young sportswriter take some of the political stories.

He shakes his head. "Dixie was there," he answers and says nothing more.

"Oh." It's not particularly odd that the administrative assistant was with my father while he was covering a local story; but it seems a little odd the way Ben has just clammed up. "She called you?"

He nods. "They sent an ambulance and just took him straight to Rex." He says this as we are arriving at the parking lot of the hospital. "He stood up to say something and then just fell back. He stopped breathing for a few minutes but Doc White immediately did CPR and got his pulse going again in less than a couple of minutes."

For a second I am very grateful that Dr. White, a retired physician from the area, decided to run for a seat on the county commission.

Ben pulls into a parking spot and stops the engine. He turns to me. "He's going to be okay, Al," he says reassuringly, and I reach over and squeeze him on the arm.

"Thanks for meeting me and bringing me over here," I tell him. Then I let go of his arm and glance in the backseat at Cass. "And thanks for taking him home; poor guy, he's exhausted."

"Not a problem," Ben says. "Your key still in the same place?"

I nod, knowing he's been in a few times when I needed something and didn't have time to go. "Frog planter by the back door."

He's staring at me again. "You sure you didn't do something different to your hair?"

I open the car door, shaking my head. "No, Ben, it's the same." And I thank him again, though not before wondering exactly what it is that he's seeing.

Chapter Forty-six

Daddy is still in the intensive care unit of the hospital. He's hooked up to monitors and IVs, has a catheter, and is getting oxygen; but he is off the ventilator and breathing on his own. There have been no complications from the surgery and his vital signs are stable. I am told that he will likely be moved to a cardiac step-down unit later today or tomorrow, where he will stay for three to four more days and then be released.

He was sleeping when I arrived, but I spoke to the nurse, who gave me a complete rundown of what has happened and how he is doing; and I have been sitting by his bed for about a half hour just watching him, trying to decide whether I should punish myself more for not knowing this was going to happen or for not being here when it did.

He looks small and pale, resting against the stark white sheets and pillow on the hospital bed. There are bruises up and down his arms and his face is puffy, swollen, which the nurse has explained is not uncommon after heart surgery. He twitches a bit as he sleeps; and I wonder if he's dreaming, writing news and commentary, or if it's simply all the drugs that are pumping through his system.

As I stare at my father, I see him in a light I have never seen before. He is vulnerable and without expression; I realize how much he has aged over the years. Wrinkles across his forehead, lines around his mouth, thinning hair, prominent blue veins on the tops of his hands. Without my knowledge, and certainly without my consent, my father has gotten old.

In my mind's eye, he is still a young man, ordering folks around, laughing at ridiculous jokes, trying to teach me the news business. In my mind's eye, he is tall and carries himself like a soldier or an athlete, strong and unwavering. But now I see that he is not that man, hasn't been that man in years. I simply chose not to notice.

"Hey." He wakes up, startling me. He tries to sit up a little. He glances around like he's disoriented and starts moving around in his hospital bed.

"Wait, what are you doing?" I ask, nervous that he's going to pull out an IV line. "Just lie back. You're fine."

"I'm not fine," he says, his voice hoarse and ragged.

"You need some pain medicine? Are you hurting?"

"No, I was just looking for . . ." He pauses, turns back to me, shakes his head, confused. "Never mind."

I smile at him. "Hey," I say and place my hand on his arm.

We just look at each other for a few minutes, both of us glad to see the other, it seems.

"Welcome home, Al," he says, his voice still raspy.

I pull my hand away. "You know, if you wanted me to come home you could have just asked. All this wasn't really necessary," I say, teasing him.

He clears his throat, tries to cough, reaches up and holds his chest. It's obvious that he's in pain. I watch him and can't help but cringe, thinking of how it must feel to move when you have just had your ribs sawed in two. "Can I have some water?" he asks.

"Sure." I reach for a pitcher on the bedside table next to him and pour him a cupful. I hold it so that he can take a sip with the straw.

He raises himself up, drinks a few swallows, and then pulls away, lying back down against the pillow. "That's good," he tells me. He closes his eyes and I think he might be going back to sleep.

I hold the cup in case he wants a little more.

"When did you get back?" he asks with his eyes still closed.

I glance up at the clock behind his bed. "Little less than an hour ago."

"You drove all the way from New Mexico?"

I shake my head. "It's complicated," I answer. "I left Faramond in Amarillo; I rode home with truckers."

He opens his eyes and blinks a few times like he's not sure he recognizes me. "You can explain that later."

I smile as I put the cup back on the table. "Okay," I say.

There is a pause.

"How are you feeling? Is it bad?"

"It's no walk in the park, that's for sure." He manages a wink.

"So, Daddy, what happened? Have you been having problems and just didn't tell anybody or did you get so mad at the commissioners you blew a gasket?"

He closes his eyes again, blows out a breath. "I wasn't really sure what it was," he replies. "I'd been feeling, I don't know, funny for a couple of weeks, thought it was just nerves or my pressure; I didn't know."

Nerves? This doesn't sound like my father at all. "What's that about?" I ask him.

He looks at me like he wants to tell me something but then turns away. "Just the usual stuff," he tells me, not at all convincingly.

"What is it, Dad? Is there something wrong at the paper? Are we in trouble?" I do not understand what has him upset enough that he would have a heart attack.

He slowly shakes his head, closes his eyes. "The paper's fine," he answers.

"Then what?" I want to know.

And it seems like he's going to answer, when there is a knock at the door.

I hear the familiar voice. "You feeling better this afternoon?" And Dixie sticks her head in. When she sees me the expression on her face changes just a bit and I think that either she's picking up on the same thing Ben seemed to notice, that I'm different somehow, or she just wasn't expecting to see me.

"Al, hey, I'm surprised to see you." She walks in but remains standing at the door.

"Hello, Dixie." I get up to give her a hug. "I hear I owe you quite a lot of gratitude."

She pulls back a little and shakes her head. Her face flushes. "For what?"

"For staying with Dad when Sandra went home, for being with him at the meeting when this happened. You have really gone far and beyond your job responsibilities." I pat her on the arm. "Thanks so much. And look, I know he feels the same way I do—let us pay you for all of this time you've spent helping out."

She shakes her head, waving away the suggestion with her hand. "No, I wouldn't take any money for this." And I watch as she glances around me to get a look at Dad. She smiles.

I turn to my dad and he nods and then there's this sort of awkward pause in the conversation.

"Well, we can talk about that later; but since you're here, I think I'll run down and get a bite to eat." My stomach has been rumbling since I arrived; I haven't eaten since Arkansas. "Hopefully, the food here isn't as bad as it's rumored to be in hospitals." I turn to my dad. "You want anything? Magazine? Soda? Typewriter?" I grin.

He shakes his head. "I'm fine," he replies.

"Okay, how about you, Dixie? Want a cup of coffee or something?"

She's still watching Dad and then turns to me. "No, I'm fine, too."

I look at Dixie and then at my father and I have the weirdest feeling that I am missing something. I stand watching for a few minutes, shrug, and then head out the door.

I'm halfway down the hall when I figure out that I'm not that hungry after all. I need to talk to Dad.

After returning to his room and pushing open the door, I see Dixie leaning over, kissing my father, and I practically fall back into the hallway.

"Wow, I did not see that coming," I say, sounding exactly like Blossom when she discovered the romance between Tony and her grandmother. Except it's not true. Not really. I saw it coming from miles and miles away, but I wasn't paying attention.

Chapter Forty-seven

"Who else knows about this?" I ask.

I am alone with my father. Dixie left so that we could have this conversation. She looked every bit as embarrassed as I did to find out about the two of them in this way.

I stood at the door staring at them for a few

seconds, trying to wrap my head around what I was seeing, trying to make it into something else —a friendly hug, a shared whisper, anything but what it actually was—and then the nurse came and I just left. I found my way to the cafeteria, even though my appetite had deserted me, and bought a bag of chips and a candy bar as I was not exactly in the mood for the healthy kale options they were offering. I tried to text Blossom to tell her what I had seen, but she never texted back so I took my chips and chocolate back to a half-empty waiting room and ate them while watching an afternoon soap opera on the television there.

When I got back to Dad's room in the ICU, Dixie had gone. Frankly, I'm so confused I don't know what is best. I don't even know why it matters who knows.

Dad shakes his head. "We haven't told anybody," he answers. "But I think Ben and James William figured it out."

So that was why Ben acted so strangely when he drove me to the hospital, and why he wouldn't look me in the eye when I asked him why Dixie was at the commissioners' meeting. And if Ben knows, Dad is right, James William knows, too.

"When did this start?" I have taken the seat by the bed again.

He slowly reaches behind him for the pillow, rearranges it slightly. He grimaces and I stand

and move closer, adjusting it so that it gives him more support. "That good?"

He nods. He takes in a breath. "Not long after she came to work at the paper," he finally answers. "I didn't mean for anything to happen between us; we just immediately had this connection."

I think back. That was more than a year ago.

"You've been having an affair with Dixie for a year?" I return to my seat, plop back down.

"Technically, Al, it's not an affair since neither one of us is married."

He's got me there, but it just feels so inappropriate, my father and Dixie Weston, involved with each other.

"She's—" I try to recall how old Dixie is, try to remember what was written on her application when she came to the paper.

"Thirty-two," he answers before I can figure it out.

"Thirty-two? That's—"

"Younger than you, I know." Apparently, he's prepared for this conversation, whereas I am completely in the dark.

"Her children are, like—"

"Six and two. I know. I've spent a fair amount of time with them both. I know this is unsettling for you and I'm sorry. I haven't known how to tell you."

I can only shake my head. *My dad is dating a woman thirty years younger than he is, a woman with two small children. He's twice her age!* I hate to admit it, but this is more shocking than finding out he's had a heart attack.

"Did you tell Sandra?" I want to find out if my sister has been in on this little romance, if she found out the same way I did.

He seems surprised and shakes his head. "Why would I tell Sandra?"

I shrug, feeling a bit of pleasure at hearing this.

"Like I said, we haven't told anyone, and besides, I haven't seen Sandra in months."

"She was here for the surgery," I tell him, wondering why he wouldn't remember this.

"Oh, well, I didn't talk to her," he responds. "And I'm pretty sure Dixie didn't tell her."

I think about Sandra and Dixie meeting, how my younger sister probably thought of her as the help, asked her to fetch things for her, make arrangements for her, oblivious to anything that did not directly alter the axis of the earth that she thinks revolves around her.

She will not be happy about this at all. She will think of it as some blight on her reputation, and even though I am pleased that she'll come completely unglued, I do not want to be around for that little enlightening conversation between my dad and his youngest daughter. As hard as this is for me, I'm certain it's been easier for my father to break the news to me than it will be to break it to Sandra.

"I don't really care about Sandra and what she thinks. I haven't told her because I don't think it's any of her business."

I'm nodding, since I totally agree.

"But you, Al, I haven't told because I do care about you and what you think."

I stop nodding.

"Well, I don't really know what to think," I tell him. "It's kind of a surprise, you know."

He bites his lip and looks away.

"Wait," I say. "Is this part of the reason you've felt nervous and upset? Has worrying about my reaction to you and Dixie caused your blood pressure to spike? Is it the reason for your heart attack?"

He shakes his head. "I wanted to tell you before you left; but I just couldn't." He closes his eyes. "I've wanted to tell you for a while, but I just couldn't ever find the right time, the right way."

"Well, having a heart attack will certainly get my attention." I sigh. "It must not feel very good to Dixie that you're embarrassed about the relationship and won't tell anyone."

He seems surprised. "Al, I haven't kept this a secret because I'm embarrassed."

I don't really believe him, but I don't say this.

"Honestly, I could care less about what other people think about me. I have very deep feelings for Dixie. I love her. In fact, I asked her to marry me a month ago."

"Marry?" The room starts to spin.

"Yes, marry me."

"For heaven's sake, Dad. If you're not embarrassed about the age difference, then why haven't you told anyone? Why is it such a secret?"

I watch some of the lines in his face soften. "Because of you, Al."

"Me?"

"I guess I kept hoping that you'd find somebody and you'd have a meaningful relationship and then you wouldn't mind so much that I had one."

"Wait, what?" Suddenly, the conversation has taken another surprising turn. "You put your life on hold because you thought I couldn't take you being involved with someone? You sacrificed your relationship with Dixie because of me?"

"No, that doesn't sound right," he replies. And he appears to be gathering his words before beginning again. He takes in a breath and then exhales. "I just wanted you to be happy, and I didn't want to make things worse by me being happy."

I shake my head. "But why do you think I'm unhappy? Why do you think that I need a relationship to be happy? And even if I was unhappy, why would your happiness affect me anyway?"

He seems to be thinking. "It's not that I think you're unhappy, exactly. But I don't think you're happy, either."

All of this seems to be coming out of nowhere. I feel off center and out of balance. The lack of sleep, the trip out west, the hospital, the sugar spike from lunch, finding Dixie and my dad . . . as the nurse comes in to announce that Dad is doing well enough to be transferred, and that a room is ready in the step-down unit downstairs, all I can hear is Dillon's voice rumbling in my head: "Dude, this is jacked up."

Chapter Forty-eight

I am home and nothing has changed but everything feels different. Old Joe sits and stares at me from the hallway, only he's blind so it's not really staring. It's the feline cold shoulder; I'm used to it and I don't press for affection. I know he'll come around when he feels he has punished me enough. Casserole greets me and then heads back to the bedroom, choosing to retire for the day without supper.

There is a little dust on the shelves, mail and newspapers piled on the kitchen counter, a long note from Millie telling me how much my cat ate while I was gone and that she watered my plants inside and out. It's a bit stuffy so I turn up the air-conditioning.

A couple of sodas and a few containers of leftovers are in the fridge. Ben dropped off my suitcase by the front door and there is dry food in the dog bowl, water in the dish near the sink. It is quiet for an early evening hour and I pour myself a glass of wine, take a seat at the table, and pull out my phone.

I turned it off when I was with Dad at the hospital, and with everything that happened, everything I saw and then discussed with him, I never turned it back on. I wait until the screen lights up and check the messages. Blossom texted three times, wants to talk, of course, is glad I am home safely, and is eager to hear about my dad's condition. She was out with Dillon when I tried to contact her earlier, she wrote me.

Ben needs information right away to make sure the paper comes out in time. I glance up at the clock. He called a couple of hours ago; I'll get back to him in the morning. The futures calendar isn't done and he's not sure how to manage the makeup, the arrangement of headlines and illustrations. My gym membership, which I bought at the beginning of the year but never used, apparently runs out at the end of the month. And Dad managed to phone, just making sure I made it home (which I did thanks to Jasper, who was willing to come up to the hospital and drive me back to Clayton).

The last message came in about an hour ago. Phillip called; he wants to know if my dad is okay. And I don't hesitate to call him back.

"Hey," he says, when he answers. "How is he?"

It's like we've been in touch for years, not days. This is the first time I've smiled since lunchtime when Milton dropped me off at the All-State Truck Stop on the outskirts of Raleigh to meet Ben.

Before we parted, Milton handed me a CD by Bill Black's Combo, a white band that was popular with black listeners in the early days of rock and roll. "Smokie, Part 2," the band's first single, was released in 1959 and rose to the number one position on black music charts. He gave me the album because I'd told him that I had been to Graceland. It had been a religious experience, I'd said, though I didn't give the details.

"If you like Elvis," Milton said, "you need to hear his roots. Bill Black was a great influence on the King, helped him get started. White man who sounds so black they wouldn't put his photograph on the album covers. You'll like it, I promise."

And I took his offering, gave him a hug, and smiled.

I had traveled all the way across the country and made it safely back to Clayton. And it was all because of the kindness of strangers: Tony, organizing my trip home; Luna, with her bag of pork chops and rolled dollars; Clyde, hurrying home to be at his granddaughter's birthday party; Milton, and his extensive knowledge of rhythm and blues and Bill Black and Elvis. It all just made me smile.

But since then I've been pretty down. Sitting in a hospital room, seeing my dad after surgery, discovering his secret romance, which he's hidden from me because he thinks I'm unhappy—that was the rest of the day, and I haven't felt cheerful since the truck stop on the outskirts of Raleigh. Until now.

"He's okay," I tell Phillip, taking a sip from my glass of wine. "They moved him from ICU this afternoon. When I left, he was in a regular room watching CNN, eating a cherry Popsicle."

"Cherry Popsicles are good."

There it is again. I'm smiling. "Well, it's not a hot fudge sundae from the Dairy Barn; but it's close."

There is a pause and I watch Old Joe think about coming to say hello.

"I'm glad everything is okay, Al. I know you must be relieved."

"Yes, it's been a long twenty-four hours." I hold out my hand, but my cat just sits and cleans his front paws.

"So tell me about the truckers. That's crazy," Phillip says.

The truckers. I see them, their kind faces, three strangers giving me rides. "It was my friend's grandfather who set up the whole trip."

"Blossom."

"Yeah." I forgot that he knows about my teenage companion.

"He was driving from Arizona, heading east for a ways, so he picked me and my dog up from Grants and drove us to Oklahoma; then a second trucker got us to Arkansas, and a third dropped us off in Raleigh. I have to say I feel a little disoriented driving across the country in only a day."

"Yeah, I can see how that might confuse your biorhythms."

"It was good, though. A good trip."

"Did you bury Roger?"

"We scattered his ashes. I found out where he had lived and Blossom and I went out there and returned him to his place."

"That's nice," he replies.

I think again about the fine black dust as it lifted on the breeze and then settled on the ground around me. It *was* nice.

"I bet Oscar is glad you're home."

I think about my conversation with my dad, but decide against pulling Phillip into that little private drama. "I think he is. I'm glad I am, too."

"You know, you could have stopped in High Point."

"What?" I'm confused.

"On your way back. You could have stopped in Winston-Salem or High Point."

I guess I could have. I take a sip of wine.

"I would have brought you home."

Well, this is a surprise.

"I thought you weren't coming back to Clayton until the Fourth of July."

"I wasn't."

"So, it would have been a lot to ask you to come this afternoon."

"Actually, it wouldn't have. I'm already here."

I sit up at the table. "Here? In Clayton?"

"Here at your door."

Old Joe glances at me and then flips his tail and walks down the hall toward the back of the house. There will be no welcome as long as someone else has arrived.

I am still holding the phone to my ear when I see Phillip Blake through the curtain behind me. He waves and once again I am smiling.

Chapter Forty-nine

"Surprised?"

If I were writing an article about this, I'd probably use another word. *Shocked,* maybe. Or *astounded.*

"Hey, you," I say, suddenly mindful that I have been riding in trucks for twenty-four hours straight, and sitting in a hospital for six or seven more. I know I look rough. I try to figure out what to smooth down or straighten first, but it's all for naught. I just stand at the door staring at Phillip Blake, who looks so good I have to blink hard to make sure I'm not just making him up.

"Is it too late?" he asks.

"For what?" I reply, because I've been thinking about romance at my father's age.

He seems unsure of how to respond.

"I'm sorry. Not at all," I say, finally understanding his question and moving aside so that he can come in.

"I remember this place," he tells me as he glances around.

Right. There was that long-ago prom night with my sister. Of course, he stood at the front door, not the back; and I'm pretty sure he was never in my kitchen; but that certainly doesn't matter now.

"Yeah, not much has changed," I reply.

"Does it feel weird to still be in the same house you grew up in?"

I shrug. "No, not really."

And it doesn't, I don't think. *Wouldn't it feel even weirder to live in another house but still in the same town?* "Well, have a seat." I motion to the table. "Would you like a glass of wine?"

He nods. "Thanks."

Casserole finally makes an appearance. He gives me a look that says, *It is too late,* but I ignore him. He walks over to Phillip.

"Well, hey, there, buddy." And he leans over

and gives my dog a scratch. "Wow. He's only got three legs. How did that happen?"

I pour Phillip a glass of wine and walk back to the table. My hands are shaking. "Just showed up that way," I answer.

That's enough for Cass. He walks over to his water bowl, takes a few sips, and heads back to his bed.

"Well, here's to your dad being okay, and . . ."

He's staring at me and I go all wobbly inside.

". . . to old friends."

Maybe I was hoping for a little something different.

"To old friends," I repeat and take a sip, watching as he takes a sip, too.

"I guess you must be surprised to see me," he says after making his toast.

I nod.

"I don't know, Al, I think your trip out west inspired me or something."

I take my seat across the table from him, wondering what part of picking up teenage hitch-hikers or stopping at the homes of long-gone country singers has been so inspiring.

"I told you about me and Hillary."

I nod. Of course I remember the news about his divorce.

He puts down his glass of wine and runs his fingers through his curly brown hair. It's magnificent.

"I have just felt stuck for so long," he tells me.

"Ever since she left me. It's like I've been paralyzed or something." And then he hesitates and looks at me intently.

"I've been on antidepressants."

I shrug. "Aren't most folks?"

He drops his head. It seems that I've said the wrong thing.

"I'm sorry," I say.

He shakes his head. "It's just that I never thought I'd be one of those people."

I'm not sure I'm following.

"You know."

"No, not really. Do you mean a person who's depressed?"

"Right."

"Oh, well, I don't imagine anybody who takes antidepressants thinks of himself as one of those people, either. Depression just happens." *I sound like a commercial. I hope I can stop myself from saying "and it hurts."* I bite my lip.

"Do you take them?"

"No, but that doesn't mean I'm not one of those people. It could just mean I'm one of those people who doesn't have good pharmacy coverage."

Again, the long face.

"I'm sorry." This must be the third or fourth time that I've apologized to him.

"It's just that I don't think it's such a big deal. It's nothing to be ashamed of. Do they make you feel better?"

He shrugs and then nods.

"Well, if they make you feel better, help you get out of bed, go to work, function, then that's a good thing, right? You wouldn't think twice about taking an insulin pill if you had diabetes, would you?"

"No, I guess not."

"Of course, then you'd be one of *those* people." And I give a thumbs-up, realize how stupid that is, and then stick my hand in my lap.

"You're funny, Al. I don't remember you being this funny in school."

I give him the *well, what do you know* eyebrow lift. I would like to say something funny about growing into my humor or learning it in college, but I can't think of a good comeback line. I wasn't funny in high school because high school wasn't very funny. I was one of *those* people.

"So, what are you doing in Clayton?" I finally find the courage to ask.

"It's like I said, you inspired me with your trip and I just liked talking to you while you were traveling; so I thought I'd come home, see you, hear more about New Mexico, why you did it." He drinks the rest of his wine in one gulp.

I get up to fetch the bottle from the counter, and as I walk past him I feel his eyes on me. It's exhilarating.

"Why *did* you do it?" he asks.

I pour some more wine into his glass.

I shrug and take my seat again. "I don't know. I just decided it was something I should do."

"Like you were meant to find those ashes."

I hadn't really thought of it that way. "I guess."

"See, that's what I love. And that's what I'm missing. I need some purpose in my life. Something that calls to me." He finishes his second glass of wine.

I take a sip from my own glass, wondering if the rekindled call of my heart might finally be heard.

Chapter Fifty

"I want you to have the paper." Daddy has been released from the hospital and I am driving him home.

I look over at him. "What?"

"I don't want to do it anymore."

I turn back to face the road. I'm driving his Buick, and I'm not used to all the play in the steering. It takes both hands for me to keep it steady. "You're just wiped out from the surgery; that's normal. You can take some time off, get your energy back. We'll cover things for you while you're gone."

From the corner of my eye I can see him shaking his head.

"It's not about my heart, or maybe it is; I don't

know. I just know I don't want to do it anymore. I haven't wanted to do it for a long time."

I glance over at him again. He's holding out the seat belt so that it doesn't rub against the incision on his chest. He's lost weight, but he looks better than he did right after the surgery. He has good color and he doesn't appear anxious. "How can you say that?" I ask. "You love that paper. It's your life."

He keeps shaking his head. "I don't want that life anymore. I want something different. I'm ready for a change."

I watch the road ahead of me. It's suddenly very clear what my father is talking about.

"Dixie?"

"Yes, Dixie and her boys and . . ." He pauses. "I want to write."

I glance at him again. This part is not so clear.

"You do write," I reply. "Every day. You write articles and columns. You write the news. You've been writing the news all my life. You *are* the news. You get to write anything you want."

"That's not what I mean."

I wait.

"I want to write a novel."

My head is so full of trying to manage the surprises I've gotten since I arrived home from New Mexico, I don't think there's room for another one.

"A novel?" I ask.

"A novel," he repeats.

"You don't even read novels. You read nonfiction. You even said once that the only stories worth reading are the factual ones."

"I was wrong."

I blow out a breath. I'm tired. Since I've come home I've hardly slept. The first night, Phillip and I talked until well past midnight, finishing off two bottles of wine while he filled me in on his marriage and how hard the breakup has been for him. The second and third nights I was up until all hours trying to make sure the paper was ready to run. They called from the hospital before eight this morning and I'm hoping to get Dad home and settled, so that I can finally be able to get to bed early tonight. And I still haven't figured out how I'm going to get my car back from Texas.

"What do you want to write about?" I ask, deciding not to criticize my father's new passion.

"I've started it already. It's a mystery."

"Have you ever even read a mystery?"

"I have been reading more of them lately."

"Since when?"

And when he doesn't answer, I figure it out for myself. "Dixie." This, everything, it's all about Dixie.

"Al, she's opened my eyes to an entire genre. It's fantastic. And she thinks what I have already written is really good."

I nod, but inside I am shaking my head. "Well,

maybe you should give this more thought. You don't have to leave the paper completely. Maybe take some time off, see what it's like not having to be at the office every day; maybe you just need a vacation. Or maybe you can scale back, give Ben some extra duties. You don't need to walk away entirely."

"I've made my decision, Al. And Dixie is supportive."

"Dixie makes nine dollars an hour; I'm not sure how supportive that's really going to be for the both of you."

"I've saved some money," he says, sounding every bit like the child talking to the parent, explaining why he intends to quit college. "I'm ready to retire. I can draw social security soon. I've got a good IRA and it's enough for Dixie and her boys and me to live on. I've worked everything out except handing over the reins to the paper; and I'd like to hand them over to you."

"Well, what makes you think I want the paper?" And just like that, I landed my own surprise.

"You don't want it?" My father sounds a little dejected.

"I don't know, Dad. This is all really more than I can think about right now. You had a heart attack. You and Dixie are a couple. Now you want to quit work. It's a lot to take in, okay? Just give me a little time."

"I understand."

I slow down and take the exit toward Clayton.

"Dixie and I set a date."

"For what?" I merge onto the highway, heading east.

"The wedding."

Of course they have.

"Don't you think you're moving a bit too fast?"

"It's like you said. I just had open-heart surgery, Al. I think if anything, I've waited too long. But to answer your question, no, I don't think that. I love her. She loves me. We want to be together and I would really like it if you'd be happy for us."

"I am happy for you," I tell him. I glance over and see that he doesn't really believe me. I reach over and touch his arm. "I am. I'm really glad you found each other; I'm really glad, honestly."

"I'd like it if you stand with us."

I pull my hand away. "Where? At the wedding?"

He nods.

"Like a . . . a maid of honor?"

"Like family," he says, his voice softer. "I'd like you to stand with us, beside me, as my family."

"What about Sandra?"

"I will tell your sister about the wedding, ask her to join us; but I hardly think she will approve, or even show up."

I nod and give a slight laugh. "You are right about that."

I make the turn into our little town and point the car in the direction of Dad's apartment.

"I don't live there anymore," he tells me. "I moved out a week ago."

"When I left for New Mexico?"

He nods.

And I shake my head and drive toward Dixie's house on the other side of town. When I pull up in her driveway, she's standing on the front porch, her smallest boy, Tyler, riding low on her hip.

She seems skittish watching as Dad slowly exits the car. When she turns to see the expression on my face, I pause just for a second and get out. I see her nervousness and then I see my father's joy and I simply look at her and hold up my hand, in a wave of sorts, a display of my acceptance.

Chapter Fifty-one

"This is not acceptable."

Ah, the sweet voice of my sister.

"Hello, Sandra," I say, sticking my frozen dinner in the microwave.

Casserole glances up at me and I swear he shakes his head. He heads into the living room and I set the timer for my dinner.

"Did you know about this?"

"I assume you're talking about the wedding?"

I pour myself a glass of water and sit down at the table.

I know this isn't going to be a quick conversation. I anticipated a call from her at some point; but I was hoping for a bit more time. I look at the clock on the wall. Dad must have called her not long after he got up from his nap. I sat and talked to Dixie until lunchtime; played with her boys a little bit while she helped my father get settled for rest; and then worked all afternoon, trying to localize the national headlines. A Clayton family was vacationing near the site of the volcano that just erupted and I've been trying to get more information about them.

"Of course I am talking about the wedding. What else would I be upset about?"

I'm guessing he hasn't yet told her that he's already moved in with Dixie and that he's giving me the paper.

"What is wrong with him? Is he demented? Did something in his head come unhinged when they stopped his heart for the surgery?"

"Yes, I'm sure that's it. I bet that when they put him on the ventilator something in his brain circuit board blew out, causing him to fall in love with the first person he saw when he woke up from surgery. I guess we should be glad Ben or James William wasn't standing next to his bed."

"I am trying to be serious."

"I know you are."

"He's marrying Dixie Weston."

"Yes, it appears that is what is happening."

"Didn't you used to babysit her?"

"No, that was you."

"I never babysat Dixie; she's my age."

"I didn't, either; I'm saying I didn't babysit anybody else because I spent all my time baby-sitting you."

"Oh, not that again."

I close my eyes and rub my temples. "What do you want, Sandra?"

"What do I want? I want you to talk some sense into our father. I want you to tell him not to marry that teenager."

"You said it yourself; she's your age. And if I do my math correctly, your teens are way, way behind you."

I hear the Giant Sandra Exhale.

I wait.

"Are you saying you approve of this relationship?"

I sit back and think about that.

"Well, do you?"

"To tell you the truth, I don't know whether I do or not. But it doesn't really matter because he doesn't need my approval."

"Well, he's making a complete fool of himself and I can't believe you're just going to let him do it. Aren't you worried about our inheritance? Our family things? Don't you see that she's just doing this for his money?"

Finally, the truth.

"Sandra, Daddy doesn't have any money; he runs a small newspaper. He's lucky if he breaks even every month. Trust me, she is not marrying him for his money."

And then the timer on the microwave goes off. My dinner is ready. Just at that moment, I have a thought; and I sit up because it's a good one.

"Besides," I say to my sister, "don't you know that Dixie's the one who's loaded?"

I hear a sharp intake of air and I know the weight of my surprise hit her.

"What do you mean?"

"Well, I'm not sure I should say."

"Why? What do you know?"

"Well, just between us, Daddy is the one making out here. Dixie's first husband died, leaving a huge insurance policy for his sons. And he had just made a lot of money selling his software company; we're talking millions."

Casserole and Old Joe walk back into the kitchen together. They both know what I'm doing and Old Joe could care less, but I can tell that Cass is more than a little ashamed of me. He just gives me that look and walks back out; but I don't care because I'm not sure having a dog as your moral compass really means all that much anyway. Old Joe comes over and plops down at my feet. He has never disapproved of taking the lower road.

"I thought she was divorced."

"No, see, that's what everybody thinks; but they were only separated and when her husband died, he was in Costa Rica or somewhere. They were technically still married and she got more money than she knows what to do with."

Even with cellular phone service, I can hear the wheels turning in my sister's head.

"Well, it's still unorthodox. The two of them, I mean."

"Yes, but you know, Daddy's got a good head for business; so I think he can really help her manage her money." I pause for a long moment and give my cat a good scratch on his neck. "Wait, maybe J.T. might be able to advise her about her investments."

J.T. is Sandra's husband. He's a financial planner, always on the search for rich people.

She clears her throat. "Well, he's very busy already; but I can ask him."

"I am sure that he could be so helpful to the two of them."

"Well."

"Anyway, if you think I should say something to Daddy, try to talk him out of this relationship, I'll go over there tomorrow and let them both know how you feel and how you aren't planning to attend the wedding."

"I didn't say I wouldn't come to the wedding."

"Oh." And I say that perfectly, with just the

right amount of pleasant surprise attached to it.

"I'll check our calendars. I'm not sure the kids can come, but maybe J.T. and I can drive down for the day."

"Really, Sandra? Oh, that would mean so much to the both of them." I pretend to stick my finger down my throat.

"Well, you know, for him, I mean. We can come and support him."

"What a lovely thing. I will let them know you'll be there. Thank you, Sandra."

"You're welcome, Al. Okay, then, well, goodbye."

And as I put down my phone, Old Joe jumps into my lap, rewarding me for my shrewdness.

Chapter Fifty-two

I can't believe my eyes.

"Dude, this place is cool!"

Dillon and Blossom are standing at my front door.

"Hey, Al." Blossom steps forward and gives me a big hug. "We just decided to bring Faramond ourselves."

I can't believe they're here. The last time we talked, we made a plan to ship my car from Texas to North Carolina. I was going to call around and check on prices and then get back to Blossom.

But with the wedding coming up and me taking over the paper, I haven't had time to do any research, and since Dad's been restricted from driving for a while, I have just been using the Buick. I figured Faramond could wait in Amarillo until the summer was over.

Casserole hears the familiar voices and joins us at the door.

"Hey, buddy," Dillon drops down to give him a pat. "I missed you."

"You look good," Blossom says, and I'm not sure if she's talking about me or my dog; but I'm so happy to see her, it doesn't even matter. She looks exactly the same.

"So, this is your house," she says.

"This is it," I answer. "Well, come on in."

And they do.

"What made you drive all this way?" I ask, leading them to the living room.

"We missed the road, dude." Dillon is grinning. "Hey, a cat." And he heads over to Old Joe.

"I got a job," Blossom tells me as she takes a seat on the sofa and invites Casserole up to join her, which he does.

"Yeah?"

"At the Big Texan," she replies.

"The steak house?" I ask. The Big Texan is the name of the restaurant Phillip told me about over the phone, the place with the giant steak-eating challenge.

"Home of the seventy-two-ouncer," she answers enthusiastically, pulling her legs under her. "It's just temporary, though."

"You got something better on the horizon?" I ask. I've taken the seat across from her. I glance over at Dillon. He and Old Joe are getting to know each other.

"I signed up for a couple of classes at the community college." She smiles like she knows this will please me.

And it does. "That's great, Blossom, that's really great." I have to say, I feel a little proud of my young friend. "What are you planning to study?"

"It's just the basics for the first semester, English and math. I think I might like to go on for a bachelor's degree; but I'm not sure just yet. Dad says I can learn carpentry from him and if I like that I can just switch over to the more technical side at the college. So, I'm keeping my options open."

"Sounds great," I reply. I glance over at Dillon. "And what about you? Are you staying in Texas?"

"I'm training with Tony's friend in a couple of weeks," he says. "The one who drives the Jeeps."

"Clyde?"

"Yep, it's so cool," he replies as he leans back against the wall. Old Joe is walking across his legs. "I'll drive with him for a couple of loads, learn it some, and then take the class, get my license, and have my own work schedule by the fall."

"Tony worked it out for him," Blossom adds. "He's moving to Illinois."

"What? When?"

"I'm taking the train out of Raleigh tomorrow," he says. "It's crazy, right?" Old Joe has by now jumped off Dillon's legs and is walking around him.

"Wow." I'm trying to take all this in. Dillon is going to live in Illinois. Blossom is staying in Texas and starting school. And both of them are right now sitting in my house in North Carolina.

"We're hoping you can drive us to the station in the morning. He's going to Belvidere, and I'm heading back to Amarillo."

"Ah. Sure," I say.

"How's your dad?" Blossom asks.

"Better than you'd think," I answer. "He's getting married this weekend."

"No."

"Yes."

"I didn't know that he was seeing anybody."

"Neither did I," I say, shaking my head.

"Is it somebody you know?"

"A girl at work. She's younger than I am, has two little boys. I don't know what to think about it."

"Dixie?"

I forgot that Blossom has spent time on the phone with my father's fiancée.

"What's to think?" Blossom asks. "Do they love each other?"

"As far as I can tell."

Blossom shrugs. "Then who cares about how old they are?" She leans toward me. "Do you care how old they are?"

I think about it. I guess I did at first; but now, I don't know. Having seen them together now in a new light, it's clear to me that they care about each other. And it's clear that he loves the boys and that they love him. He's really happy with her.

I shake my head. "No, I really don't."

"That's cool," Dillon says. My cat is now lounging in his lap. "I hope when I get married to a younger babe the second time around that my daughter is like you."

I turn to him and he's petting Old Joe, not even looking at me. I turn to Blossom, who shrugs.

"Yeah, well. Me, too, Dillon," is all I can think to say.

"So, he's okay, then?" Blossom asks. "His heart is good?"

"His heart is better than mine," I answer, and I can see that she's waiting for an explanation. "Phillip is in town."

This raises her eyebrows.

"I inspire him," I add, repeating what he said when he was here.

"I get that," Blossom responds. "You seeing him?"

"I guess." I think about the night he was here,

our lunch the day after, how he's hanging around Clayton until after the weekend, after the holiday. It's been unbelievable really. I've not had anybody to talk to about it, which is why I'm so happy that Blossom is here. And then I think about how she's acting right now, how she acted before on our trip, when he called, when she knew I was texting him.

"Why don't you like him?" I ask.

"I never said I didn't like him," she answers, but her affect is off.

"This the dude from Facebook?" Dillon chimes in.

"That's the one," I say, waiting for him to tell me what Blossom will not. "What does she have against him?"

He pulls back his hair and rewinds the holder around his ponytail.

"It's not that she doesn't like him," he says. "She just thinks you can do better."

I turn my attention back to Blossom, who responds with a simple shrug.

Chapter Fifty-three

We slept late, ate lunch on the way to Raleigh; then Blossom and Dillon boarded their trains, one west, the other north. I was sad to see them go, hoping they might stay for the wedding; but I understand about new work schedules for them both and know they need to get on with their lives. I waited until I could no longer see the trains, hearing only their whistles in the distance, before I left.

Once again I am driving Faramond on the interstate and I have just merged onto Interstate 40 when my phone rings. It's Blossom.

"What's wrong?" I ask, wondering if something has happened, if she somehow boarded the wrong train, or left something at my house.

"I need to tell you the truth," she says; and this makes me feel a little weird. I didn't know she had lied.

"Okay," I respond. "Do I need to pull off the highway to hear this?"

She hesitates. "Maybe."

I take the first exit, drive to a convenience store, and stop the car. It's taken me only three minutes to manage this maneuver.

"Okay," I say. "I'm safely parked and all yours."

"He messaged me."

"What?" I don't follow.

"I don't like Phillip because he messaged me."

I don't quite know what to say.

"Dillon doesn't know, either. I haven't told anyone. But I need to tell you. You should know."

"When did he send you a message?"

"In West Memphis, right after he talked to you."

I'm having some trouble with her confession.

"You fell asleep and he messaged me. I erased it right after he sent it. I didn't reply."

"So, what was the message?"

"He had seen a picture of me."

"Yeah, I know—he saw all our photo albums. He knows who you are."

"It was the one of us at the bar in Nashville."

I recall that bar in Nashville. We took a lot of photos that night.

"He wrote that he thought I was hot and that I had legs like a dancer."

I admit that he's never really said anything like that to me, but this isn't the worst thing in the world.

"Well, Blossom, you're seventeen and you *are* hot. And you do have great legs."

"He shouldn't have messaged me."

It is a little unsettling that Phillip sent my young companion a flirty Facebook message, but I have lots of explanations for his bad behavior.

"He was just trying to be funny; he does that. He sounds like he's flirting, but he's just being friendly." I think about the waitress at the restaurant where we met for lunch the day before yesterday. He commented on her smile after he gave her his order, but I knew it didn't mean anything. And she seemed to brush it off.

"It just seems wrong," she adds. "He had just talked to you; you were just starting to get to know each other again."

Her kind confession and concern for me are touching. "Well, I agree, it was maybe a little inappropriate, but it's like you say, it was when we were just starting to talk. It was after one conversation. I don't really think he'd send the same message now. It's just that he didn't know you and he had only just spoken with me that one time."

"I'm just worried about how he'll treat you," she says. In the background, I can hear an announcement being made on her train. Tickets are to be out where the conductor can see them.

"He treats me really well," I tell her. "He is polite, opens doors for me, lets me enter a room first. He turns his phone off when we're together; and he's very gracious." I pause, trying to think of other examples. "He's staying in town all this week, so that he can be here for the wedding. How sweet is that?"

"I thought you said he was planning to be there anyway since it's the Fourth."

Well, I guess that's true. "Yeah, but he came early, and that was to see me. He wasn't supposed to come until Friday or Saturday."

She doesn't respond; I hear her talking to someone else. She must be handing over her ticket. Then I hear her say, "Amarillo," and then I hear a man's voice explaining to her when she will need to change trains.

"I even told him about Dad and Dixie. We went over there together a couple of days ago. He said the same thing you and Dillon said, that if they love each other, the age difference shouldn't matter."

"Well, that's nice of him."

"And you should have seen him with Dixie's boys. He wrestled with them and ran around the backyard, playing ball with them, while we were inside discussing wedding plans. It was sweet."

I consider telling her about our conversation on the way home that evening. How Phillip explained that he still hopes to have a family, that he wants three or four children, and how I replied that, when I was younger, I wanted two girls and two boys.

I think about telling Blossom that he then reached over and took my hand, and when we got to the stoplight a few seconds later, he leaned over and kissed me on the cheek. I think about telling her these things, but decide against it.

"He's a good man, Blossom," I continue. "And he's still really broken up about his marriage. He feels terrible about being divorced, embarrassed, really, since he always believed that a couple stays married forever, that those vows are meant to be taken very seriously."

"Well, that's good, I guess," she responds.

"And he really likes me, Blossom. He thinks I'm funny."

"You are funny."

"That's what he says. And he thinks I'm a good listener, and he really cares about me taking over the paper, thinks I need to get better insurance for myself. He's researched all kinds of things about the house, like whether or not it might be in a floodplain; he's really done a lot for me since he's been home these last few days."

"Okay," she responds.

"And he makes me happy. My stomach still does those baby flips when I see that he's calling or when I find him at my door." I pause because I realize I haven't said these things out loud to anyone. "I'm really happy being around him."

"I know," she says softly. "I just thought you should hear what he wrote to me. I thought I should tell you the truth."

"And it means so much that you did. Thank you for that. I knew something was bothering you and now I know it's nothing. It was just a silly Facebook post. We hadn't even gone out then; and shoot, he was probably drunk anyway and doesn't even remember sending it."

"You're probably right."

"Okay," I say, glad to have had this conversation, glad that it's out there, glad that it's over. "You feel better?"

"I feel better," she replies.

"All right, well, call me when you get home."

"All right."

"And thanks for bringing me Faramond."

"You're welcome."

"You're a good friend, Blossom Winters."

"So are you, Alissa Kate Wells."

And I hear the train whistle just as she turns off her phone.

Chapter Fifty-four

First there was the wedding and now there is the party. It is part retirement for Oscar Wells, part marriage celebration for Oscar and Dixie, and part congratulations to me for becoming the new publisher and editor in chief of the *Clayton Times and News*. All the employees of the paper are here, as well as everyone who has ever bought an ad, been interviewed, won public office, or been a source for a story.

It is, therefore, most of the town of Clayton who has shown up this evening at the community center. We've sprung for a catered meal from the White Swan, beer and wine from the Piggly Wiggly, champagne from the Costco in Raleigh, and a four-layer chocolate cake by Dolly Emerson, the owner of the ABC Cakeplace. The entertainment comes from the Lone Night Strings, a local bluegrass band that isn't charging us because the *Times and News* has always covered its events at no cost, and also because Ben sometimes plays bass when Lucas Browne, the regular bassist, is called out of town for his weekend duty in the Air National Guard.

It is a hot night in early July; but there are large fans blowing from the corners of the building and all of the windows and doors are propped open. I am sitting on the steps, watching the stars come out, thinking about the ceremony, how beautiful Dixie looked, how my dad cried, the youngest boy standing next to him, watching as his mother walked toward them arm in arm with her oldest son.

The service was perfect, even with Kimmie Johnson, James William's mother, missing her cue in "Ave Maria" and singing three bars behind the organist. Frankie Lowder, the musician, finally stopped and let her catch up and she finished on just the right note. Sandra and I stood with our father, and Dixie's sister and niece were the attendants for the bride.

Dixie chose red, white, and blue as her colors, fitting since it's the Fourth of July, and it was very easy to accommodate for such a large event in such a short period of time. We were fortunate that the paper came out four days before the celebration, so we could use the public forum as our community-wide invitation. And since the park had already been reserved for holiday festivities, we just bumped things up a couple of hours, offering a free dinner and giving everyone a bit more time for dancing and gathering before the fireworks. The mayor and city planner thought it was an excellent idea for such an important occasion.

The wedding itself took place at the First Presbyterian Church because it was within walking distance of the park and because we're giving them half a split page at no charge to advertise for their Vacation Bible School, which they scheduled for August. The pastor, a woman with a flair for the dramatic, spoke of Daddy's cardiac event as the wake-up call we should all heed as an opportunity to open our hearts and choose love over fear. Even Sandra seemed moved by the message. I saw her wipe away a tear just after Dixie placed the ring on our father's finger.

She's inside talking to the mayor, I suppose, trying to get in as many pictures as she can, and J.T. is working the crowd as well, trolling for potential clients, I imagine. Neither my sister nor her husband has yet to figure out that Dixie doesn't really have any money, and I'm sure one day I'll have to pay for my lie. For now, however, all I can say is that it was certainly a lie well worth whatever consequences it brings.

"You look a million miles away." It's Daddy, and he's sat down right beside me.

I'm surprised to see him. "Aren't you supposed to be cutting the cake or having a first dance or something important like that?"

"Dixie's changing Tyler's diapers so I have a few minutes to spare to be with my daughter."

"My diapers are fine," I say, leaning over and bumping him with my shoulder. I immediately think about his recent surgery and turn to him. "Oh, jeez, I didn't hurt you, did I?"

He shakes his head. "It's my chest that was sliced in two, not my shoulders."

"Right," I say.

"Thank you for today," he tells me.

"I didn't do anything. Dixie and her sister did all this." I point behind me at the decorations and the buffet line.

"I don't mean the barbecue," he responds. "I mean being here, being supportive, understanding how I feel."

"You're right to love her, Daddy. You've waited a long time. You deserve a little happiness."

"I still don't know how you talked Sandra into showing up; I owe you for that, too. She's been so nice to Dixie; it's uncanny."

"Yeah, well—" I mull it over for a second and decide not to say anything more.

"So, you and Phillip Blake?" He's watching me for my reaction.

"Maybe," I answer, turning behind me to try to find Phillip in the crowd. He looks very handsome tonight: blue blazer, white pants. I am still smitten. I don't see him, so I turn back around.

"You always had a thing for him, didn't you?"

I admit I'm surprised that my dad knows this.

"What, you think I wasn't paying attention?"

"I don't know what I think," I answer.

"Well, you look happy and I'm glad about that."

"Thank you. Me, too."

"Look, I don't want you to think I'm going to

abandon you." He takes my hand. "I'll write features for you if you need them. I can cover some of the local happenings, do the op-eds or any editing you need. I'm happy to help out."

"Thanks, Dad. We'll be okay," I tell him. "You should enjoy your time with Dixie and her boys. Spend your days with her, write your mystery. The *Clayton Times and News* will be just fine."

"I know it will."

"We need the groom." An announcement is made from the microphone in the main room. It sounds like Ben's voice.

"Oscar, it's too late to hide from her now!"

"I guess that's your cue," I say, leaning into him once again.

He puts his arm around me. "You think people will laugh at me? An old man trying to dance with such a young bride?"

I feel so close to him, so proud of him. "Not if they see what I see."

I pause for just a second.

"I see a man whose heart is opened. A man who loves a woman and wants to make her happy. Nobody will laugh at that. Not if they really see."

I feel him nod.

"And if they do laugh, I'll make up a terrible story about them and run it in next week's edition."

He kisses me on the top of my head. "That's my girl. Power in the pen, right?"

"Power in the pen," I repeat. And he stands up so that he can take his first dance with Dixie.

Chapter Fifty-five

"Have you seen Phillip?" The fireworks are about to start and I want to watch them with my date for this combination wedding and Fourth of July celebration. I wonder when we get married if I will speak of this as our fifth date or both the fifth and sixth.

Ben looks around the room. "I haven't seen him in a while," he answers. "I was filling in while Lucas took a break. Did you hear us do the Béla Fleck song?"

"I don't think I did, Ben."

" 'The Sinister Minister,' " he goes on. "It won a Grammy in 1997. We did it for the preacher. She was dancing. You didn't see it?"

I shake my head. "I think I was outside, Ben. Where did you see Phillip last?"

"Well, you missed it. It was a great moment."

"I am sorry. Phillip?" I ask again.

"Oh, right. He was here when they cut the cake."

"Well, I know that, Ben," I reply. "I was standing right beside him then."

"Oh, yeah, you were."

How Ben is ever able to get his facts together enough to write a story, I do not know.

"By the way, you look nice, Al," he says, causing me to shake aside my criticisms and doubts.

Ben is a friend. He always has been. He cares about Dad, about Dixie, about the paper, about me. He is always there when you need him. He's solid; I don't know how much more you really want from an employee.

"Are you going to fire me for sexual harassment if I tell you that dress fits you just right?"

"No, Ben, I won't."

"How about if I tell you exactly where the fit is best?"

"That would probably change things," I say, walking away, saving him from postwedding embarrassment.

It's clear to me now that we should have limited the amount of alcohol we served. I can see that Ben is not the only one who will need a ride home tonight. James William is hitting on Dixie's sister even while she's nursing her baby, and the mayor is trying to get those still in the building to join him in a verse of "God Bless America," even though he's singing the national anthem, which is confusing everyone. This is some night, for sure.

I am happy about my dress, however. It's the yellow one that Blossom bought me in Arkansas. It's perfect for the occasion, and I have to admit I feel pretty wearing it. Even Phillip gave a wolf whistle when he saw me, which made me blush and question whether or not it might be appropriate attire for the new publisher of the *Clayton Times and News*. After Ben's remark, I am second-guessing my decision to wear it after all.

I scan the room, but I don't see Phillip anywhere. I left the festivities after the cake cutting and the first dance to take a call from Blossom, who had just seen the pictures I had posted on Facebook from the wedding.

She kept saying how much she wished she had stayed when she brought me Faramond. She told me that she's working a double shift at the steak house, and that later, she and her dad are going to the town center to see Amarillo's fireworks.

"Lou says to tell you hello," she said, and I returned the greeting because that was the first I'd heard from her dad since I left Texas.

I head toward the restrooms. There's a line outside the ladies' but nobody near the men's.

"Hey, Al, are you going to write a feature about the wedding?"

It's Kimmie who wants to know. I knew she saw Ben snap a picture when she was singing; that was probably how she lost her place in the music, trying to make sure she was giving her best side to the photographer.

"Just the usual," I say and walk in the opposite direction.

"Did you like the song?" she is yelling.

"Beautiful, Kimmie," I yell back.

I'm sweating now. Even with a strapless dress, it is hot in eastern North Carolina on July fourth. I hope the fireworks don't last long; I'm ready to get home to the programmed sixty-eight-degree temperature that is the year-round setting for my air-conditioned house.

Where is he? I wonder, going from the main room, where I am congratulated for my new position (and ribbed a little about being a stepsister to a toddler), to the kitchen, where Dolly wants to know what to do with the top layer of the cake, which apparently the bride and groom usually save for their first anniversary.

"Ask Dixie," I tell her, since I'm the last person to ask about cake and protocol. I was going to take a bite out of it when I saw it on the counter next to the fridge. Little did I know you're supposed to save it for a year.

"Hey, Al." It's J.T.

"Hey, brother-in-law, how are you?"

How is it that I am running into everyone except my date?

He reaches for my hand, which I give to him, and he holds it to his chest. His shirt is unbuttoned at the top and his tie is loosened. He's had a few glasses of champagne himself.

"That was really a great wedding," he tells me.

"It is a nice affair," I agree and try to pull my hand away.

"Did I tell you thank you for hooking us up with Dixie?"

"You did not, but I was glad to do it."

"She's quite a catch for your old man, huh?"

"Uh-huh."

"Say, are Dixie's finances liquid?"

I have no idea what this means.

"I believe they are, J.T." And I finally get out from his clutches, but he's still talking to me as I try to walk away.

"Because if she's liquid, I have a couple of stocks that I think are burners, and if we could get her to throw some cash in my direction I'm confident that I could push her forward without even taking a peek at the whole portfolio."

"I will tell her that you're looking for her, J.T.; but maybe you should give her and Dad a little space to have a honeymoon first."

"Yeah, right, okay, the honeymoon. And then I'll slide down here and set up a meeting."

"That sounds great, J.T. You slide on down next month."

"A month? They're going to be gone a month?"

I keep trying to walk away, but he keeps following me.

"Sandra and I only had two weeks for our honeymoon—they're going for a month? Well, where are they going?"

I turn the corner. J.T.'s right behind me. And he literally collides with me when I stop short. And then we are right there. All of us. The four of us. At the same place. The same narrow hallway that appears to go nowhere. J.T. and I at one end and Phillip and Sandra at the other, standing in a corner, Phillip leaning closer to my sister than he's ever leaned near me. And he's saying something to her, his arm resting on the wall above her head, the other hand reaching out to touch her on the hip, and she's glancing down, but you can still see the biggest smile on her face.

"Sandra?"

J.T. stepped around me when he saw what I saw. And he was present enough to be able to speak. A name. His wife's name.

But I don't even wait to see what happens next because this is like a bad rerun for me. I turn around, run past the kitchen where Dolly is boxing up the cake layer, past the ladies' room where Kimmie is just now coming out and I don't even care that she has to step aside so I won't knock her over, out the side door, barely missing one of the large fans. I never even see my father when he looks in my direction; and I miss all of the fireworks, including, apparently, the ones in the back hallway between a member of my family and the boy I have loved since I was twelve.

Chapter Fifty-six

I hear ghosts. Muted voices, whispers from somewhere close by. Casserole is standing on the bed, unbalanced and tipping over. Old Joe is watching from the top of the dresser. I see light coming into my room; I assume the sun did rise and I feel like I may have swallowed one of the stuffed animals from my dog's collection. I feel fur in my mouth and throat.

When I try to sit up, the room starts to spin and I decide the supine position is best. I lie still and try to think about what happened and where I am, and I still hear the ghosts, so I'm also trying to figure out if I died and that's why dead people are talking to me.

"I think she's awake," I hear one of them say. I think this one is a male ghost. The whisper sounds like a deep voice.

"Is she dressed? Because if she's not dressed I think we should just call her." This is another male ghost.

"I can't see," says the first one. "And we've tried to call, but she won't answer. And she's moved her spare key."

Two male ghosts talking near me. Casserole is

whining and wagging his tail, looking out the window. He's going to fall on me or the floor if the ghosts don't leave.

"Knock so she can hear you."

There's a knock and my dog falls on top of me. I try to open my eyes, but they are stuck together, just like my tongue is stuck to the roof of my mouth. I move my arm, just to make sure my limbs are still intact.

"I think she's up."

I squint to see two men standing by my window, both of them staring at me with their hands cupped around their faces. I consider being anxious or afraid; but frankly, I don't have the energy, and besides, they don't really seem like dangerous ghosts. I slowly try to open my eyes until I finally get a clear view.

"Yep, she's up." And that one waves.

I see the bad comb-over and know right away the identity of one of the ghosts, who isn't actually a ghost but rather my employee.

"Is she naked?" There's the other; and now he waves as well.

James William and Ben are outside my bedroom window.

I turn to the clock. It's three. Must be three in the afternoon, not three in the morning, since my room is flooded in afternoon light.

I sit up again, trying to manage the spinning. This time I stay up too long, and I don't know how, but I am able to jump up from the bed and run to the bathroom and get my head in the toilet. I believe this is what is generally referred to as a hangover. Now that I am having one, I wish the two men at my window were actually ghosts because then I'd be dead. And death would be preferable to this.

I lie back down on the floor. The coolness of the tile is uncharacteristically soothing. I turn on my side so that I can rest my face on it and I think I may stay like this forever. Except that my cat is having none of it; it is past time for his first meal of the day. He walks over me and around me and down my arms and up my legs. I peek into the bedroom, noticing how much more polite my dog is being. Casserole even looks a little sorry for me.

I hear a voice from the front of the house.

"Al, are you okay?"

There are footsteps coming in my direction.

"Al, are you in here?"

I hope this isn't Ben.

I feel the presence of someone standing over me, but I can't see because Old Joe is flipping his tail across my eyes. The presence draws closer and my cat walks away.

"You look awful."

Daddy.

My head is in the toilet again; only this time there is a cold cloth on the back of my neck.

"My, oh, my," he says, but not like he's angry

or ashamed, more like he wishes he could take it all away, the same way he used to say it when I was little and scared or sad. "My, oh, my," he'd say and sweep me in his arms.

He sits down beside me and I fall against his chest until I remember his recent surgery and I yank myself away.

"It's okay," he says. "You're on the side that doesn't hurt."

And I carefully lean on him again, the toilet now supporting us both.

"You need some water?" he asks.

I shake my head, even though I know I could use something. I just don't want him to leave.

"Pretty bad?"

I nod, thinking, *This is as bad as it gets.*

"Headache?"

And then I think, *There's going to be a headache, too?*

"We'll get you some aspirin and tomato juice. You'll be okay."

I nod, even though I'm pretty certain I'm not drinking tomato juice.

"Where's Dixie?" I'm finally able to form words.

"She's at home with the boys."

"Honeymoon?"

"We're not leaving until next week. Her sister can't babysit until then, and I've got a doctor's appointment."

I nod, but only a very little.

"You want to talk about what happened?"

I close my eyes, thinking he's going to tell me, since I have no real memories I can count on at present.

There's no response. Maybe he doesn't know, either, and he's waiting for me to tell him.

"I think I drank two bottles of wine."

"I didn't really mean that part."

Oh.

"I mean do you want to talk about what happened to make you drink two bottles of wine. Phillip and Sandra?"

"Seems like I have a knack for walking in and surprising folks."

He sighs.

"J.T. punched him in the face and Sandra stayed the night with Dixie and me. She rented a car and headed back to Asheville this morning. She thinks she can work things out, that it was just a misunderstanding."

He pauses.

"Was it?"

I shake my head.

"Well, knowing your sister, she'll spin it however she can to get what she wants. Did you talk to Phillip?"

I shake my head again and just sit in the silence, rest in this safe place of my father's arms. Old Joe saunters back in, makes a lot of noise.

"Your cat's hungry."

I nod but still don't move. We sit like this for a while.

"Yesterday, in that dress, with your hair all fixed up, you were the spitting image of your mom, did you know that?"

I start to cry and I don't even know why.

"Do you realize that you are now older than she was when she died?"

I nod.

"Thirty-one. What person doesn't live past thirty-one?"

I shake my head.

"Dixie's thirty-two. What are the odds of that?"

I close my eyes.

"That I'd marry a woman one year older than your mom when she died. I guess some shrink would have a field day with that. I don't know that I was thinking about that when I fell for Dixie; but maybe there's some deep need to reclaim what I missed."

I feel him shrug.

"But you know what? It doesn't matter because I just feel lucky to have found her."

I nod.

And we just stay where we are for a few more minutes.

"Are you ready to get up?"

I shake my head.

"You want to talk about the news?"

I shake my head again.

"Okay, I've got a new question, then. Where did Sandra get the idea that Dixie has a lot of money?"

"I think I'm ready now," I say and the two of us, as wobbly as Casserole, lean on the toilet and then on each other until we are both upright.

Chapter Fifty-seven

It is Tuesday and I am sitting at my desk working on the makeup, cropping and adding cutlines to the pictures Ben took at the park. We're using most of the front page and the split to cover the fireworks as well as both the dinner and the dance. He took over a hundred photographs and we've already selected the ones that best cover the community-wide holiday event.

There's one of the mayor standing in front of the band (Town Mayor Leads Patriotic Song), one of a little boy sitting on the shoulders of a police officer (A Celebration of Local Heroes), and a couple of great shots of the fireworks, red and blue and white, streaming across the night sky (Clayton Lights Up the Fourth). Ben recorded and checked the spelling of all the names; and I have to say, especially considering that he was drinking pretty heavily the entire time, he did an outstanding job.

I add a few lines to the jumps, finish the cold

type, and get the edition ready for print. James William covered baseball, both a piece he wrote about the local farm team and several articles from the wire about the national pennant race. Jasper did a feature on the reenactment of the Civil War that is happening this weekend, as well as a story about the local fire station adding two new trucks. And Dad submitted a personal piece, thanking the people in town for all their support and announcing his retirement from the *Times and News*.

I wrote just a couple of pieces, one about the wedding and another about the Lone Night Strings, since the band just got a recording contract with a studio in Nashville. The rest of the paper is hard news from the Associated Press and includes all the local calendars. With the holiday photographs filling most of the space, it wasn't a hard edition to edit.

Since I've finished the layout and it's ready to roll, I look through some of the other pictures in Ben's photo files, the wedding shots as well as some from the reception. I see some really outstanding ones that I know Dixie and Dad will love. There are typical poses of a bride and groom—signing their license, serving each other cake—and some lovely ones of the entire family, including one of Dixie's two little boys clinging to my father's legs.

There are several shots of the ceremony itself,

with the wedding party standing around the altar and the pastor offering a blessing, as well as a beautiful one of Dad when he's putting the ring on Dixie's finger, the tears streaming down his face, and another of her walking down the aisle, wearing the widest smile I've ever seen.

There are a few of me; but none I am pleased with well enough to print, since I have never been photogenic. In fact, there are a few that I simply delete. And, of course, there are lots of shots of Sandra, since she has always known how to pose and where to locate the photographer, finding ways to offer up her best side.

My sister is a beautiful woman, much prettier than me; and I'm really honest when I say that this no longer bothers me. She always knows what dress to wear to accentuate her size 2 figure, the right colors to bring out her natural beauty, the most trendy hairstyle that keeps her looking young and stylish. Even years after the pageants, she is still a beauty queen; there's no doubt about that. And in the pictures where she stands next to her husband, it's easy to see why they would be attracted to each other, how perfect they look together, how well they fit. And seeing them, seeing their pictures from that night, actually makes me hope that they have worked things out, that they are back in Asheville, happy and secure, having already forgotten the entire holiday celebration and whatever it was that J.T.

and I walked in on right before the fireworks.

There are also a few pictures of Phillip in Ben's stash, a couple of the two of us standing side by side, him tall and comfortable in his own skin, me with my hunched shoulders and goofy smile. He is still just as handsome as I remember him to be, both from the wedding and from every day in high school so long ago.

He's as good on the other side of the camera as my sister and her husband, as easy with a goofy grin as he is looking serious and attentive. And as I study his face and remember how it was to be with him, how really nice it was to be beside him, I honestly hope he finds a new love and is able to settle down and have the four children he claims to want.

I hit the arrow and glance through the next page of photographs, without offering any description or headline of what I have just seen.

"You done?" Ben surprises me, since I thought he was at the hospital covering the ceremony for breaking ground on a new wing.

"Oh, hey." I click off his files. "You took some really nice shots," I tell him. "Daddy and Dixie will love them."

"Where did they go on their honeymoon anyway?"

"Wrightsville Beach," I reply. "The editor at the *News and Observer* let them use his beach house for the month."

"Well, that was generous, seeing how it's still the busy season and all."

"I know. I thought the same thing."

"Have you heard from them?"

I shake my head. "Not since they left."

Ben comes over and sits across from me.

"The ceremony over?"

He nods. "Too hot to stand out there for very long. The CEO of the hospital had to be taken to the emergency room for heatstroke. He was wearing a suit."

"In this weather?"

"He's from Oregon or Washington, somewhere out west. This is his first summer in North Carolina; he'll learn."

"I guess he'll have to."

"So, did you hear that story about the documentary they made about that guy in Maiden finding a human leg in the smoker he bought at a storage building auction?"

I did not. I shake my head.

"Yeah, it's crazy. They call it *Finders Keepers*. The guy who lost the leg wanted it back and the guy who found it didn't want to give it to him."

"Truth is stranger than fiction, I guess," I reply.

"I thought you might have heard about it since it sounds kind of like your story—you know, finding the ashes and everything."

I smile. "That's true."

"Only you gave yours back."

I nod. It's been only a few weeks since my trip and yet somehow it feels like months.

"Which, of course, is what Al Wells would do."

"What do you mean?"

"Nothing really, just that it seems like you have always done the right thing. Help your dad. Take care of your sister. Become the publisher of the *Clayton Times.*"

Hearing Ben say that gives me pause.

"All right, then." He stands. "I better get back to the news, tell everybody what they need to pay attention to and what they need to worry about, point them where they need to look." He's watching me, but he makes no comment about the lightbulb that has gone off above my head and that must surely be visible to anyone nearby.

"Well, I'm going to go check the police scanner, see if there have been any wrecks or high-speed chases." He grins at me. "Take it easy, Al."

"Yeah, Ben, you, too."

Chapter Fifty-eight

"Sign here and here." The attorney is pointing out the blank spaces where my signature is required.

This isn't completely brand-new to me, since I signed a similar stack of papers when Daddy gave me the newspaper. Only now I'm selling it to Ben.

"I know you and Oscar have spoken about this, Alissa, but are you sure this is what you want?"

I smile and put down the pen after signing and dating all the right spots. "I am."

"It's just you haven't even owned it a month yet. And I'm not sure about the asking price you've given to Mr. Vaughn. If you keep it a year, maybe you'd make more money, get more for it. And even though Oscar gave his blessing, it is still very early for you to be selling it."

"I know," I say. "But Dad agrees with my decision."

Mr. Creech is shaking his head. He wants to give me prudent counsel.

"I'm selling the paper because I realize that I don't want to be publisher and editor in chief of the *Clayton Times and News* anymore. I'm happy to write stories for Ben from time to time like Daddy does; but I don't want to run the paper. I don't want to be in charge of Clayton's headlines."

He pours out a long breath.

"You planning to write a novel like your father?" Joe Creech picks up the contract and taps the edges on the desk, straightening all the pages.

I shake my head. "No, I don't really have those ambitions, either."

"Going back to school?"

340

"Not sure about that. Maybe."

"Well, what are you going to do?"

"I'm going to build a boat."

He looks at me over his reading glasses. "You're going to do what?"

"Build a boat. Well, repair a boat, really; the frame of it is already built. I just need to add boards, hang the sails, make it water-ready."

"What do you know about boats?"

"Nothing really. That's actually the reason I want to do it—it's something I know absolutely nothing about."

I sit back in the chair at the conference table, clasp my hands behind my neck.

"Is it the boat you bought from that woman in New Mexico?"

He knows about it because Daddy called and asked him questions about a bill of sale for an impounded water vessel.

I nod. "Renee Lennon," I say. "Her father, Dusty, bought it but never got it fixed. He was building it to take a friend sailing. She sold it to me for next to nothing." I explain how I contacted her to arrange shipment of her father's things from my garage and how, out of the blue, I asked her about the boat and we reached an agreement for me to pick it up from a warehouse on the harbor in Wilmington where it was hanging, unclaimed, on a rafter.

"I remember that," he acknowledges. "And

you want to finish it, go sailing off into the sunset?" He glances over the papers, making sure I haven't missed anything.

"No."

He peers up at me.

I shrug. "I don't really know what I want to do except finish fixing it. After that, I'm not sure if I'll go sailing on it or not."

He stares at me, places his pen on the table. "I don't understand."

I shake my head. "I really don't either. I just realized that I don't want to report the news anymore. I don't want to fit life into vertical columns with margins on four sides and gutters in between. I don't want to tell people what's supposed to be important to them. I don't want to live my life like it's B copy, writing the story ahead of time even though I don't really know how it's going to end, just to make sure I don't miss a deadline."

He shakes his head, appearing every bit as lost as when I told him I was selling the *Times and News*.

"Mr. Creech, when my mom died, I felt like I was handed a script. I took on the role of caregiver for my sister and father; and I don't really have any regrets about that because it was the right thing to do and I was glad to do it. And then, when my sister was grown and that script was done, I took the next one handed to me, the one of helping my dad at the paper; and I don't regret that, either. I loved working for my dad; I loved covering the news with him. It was a good script to follow."

I realize I am trying to explain this change of direction for my life as much to myself as I am to the town attorney.

"I don't want to follow a script anymore. I don't want to report on other people's lives; and I don't want the burden of telling people what they should pay attention to, because I think people need to learn that for themselves. Everybody needs to listen to their own hearts, find out what's important to them, not just take what's handed to them. We should all decide on our own scripts."

He stares at me like I've grown a second head; but he's a lawyer—somebody probably handed him a script, too.

"I want to do something on my own, try something completely different. I want to write my own story, make mistakes, try things on that don't fit, and learn new lessons until I figure it out for myself, on my own."

I take a breath.

"I'm building a boat because nobody I know of has ever built a boat and I want to know what that feels like. I want to know what it is to sail across the water, to be loose, untethered. I want to know what it is to let go of everything that holds me back or down, let go of the script and the expec-tations and the heavy, heavy way I've been living. Mr. Creech, I want to know what it is to travel light."

The lawyer sits up in his chair and leans in my direction. He is nodding. "Alissa Kate Wells"—he hands me the contract—"per your wishes, you are no longer the owner, publisher, and editor in chief of the *Clayton Times and News*."

I smile and take the papers. "I know. I own a boat."

Chapter Fifty-nine

I kept the box. I scattered Roger's ashes near Grants, New Mexico; but I kept the wooden box with the butterfly carved on top. After Blossom and I had blessed his remains, we got back in her dad's truck and the box was still there. I stuck it in my suitcase and then when I got home I placed it on the shelf in my closet. Now it's in the cabin of my boat and in it I keep photographs and small toys, receipts for things I've bought for the restoration, my mother's wedding band. It's a dream box as well as a memory box; and I like having something of Roger's, something from that trip, close at hand.

I rented my house to Dixie's sister. She decided

to move to town after the wedding and is dating James William, who I think stays there as well. Her baby's daddy had left her, and when I found out she was staying with Daddy and Dixie, I offered her the house for not much rent. I didn't need it since I spend most of my time on the boat in Wilmington. Casserole came along with me, but Old Joe preferred things as they were; so we visit on the weekends, when I pick him up and take him over to Dixie's.

I've been here for a couple of months and so far I've learned the names for the front and the back of the boat, bow and stern, respectfully, and the difference between a jib and a mainsail. I had somebody else finish the hull so that I can stay on the water while I work. I have to say that part of what I like about this new project is learning the new vocabulary for sailors. The words are crisp and as unfamiliar to me as trying to figure out where to buy ring shank nails or deciding whether to use epoxy resin or polyester. I appreciate the words I pick up almost as much as I enjoy learning how to cut and measure, sand and fasten.

Today I'm working on the rigging, trying to decide what size ropes and chains I need to support the masts and sails. At the moment, I'm trying to learn to tie a solid sheet bend knot. I am reading Dusty's notes, which were found in his belongings, and following the diagrams drawn in a chapter in the book I bought that should help me navigate the entire project.

"Can I come aboard?"

I think I recognize that voice, but I stay where I am.

"If you can get through the mess," I answer and wait for the body attached to the familiar voice to step aboard.

Casserole stands. He's a little shaky on the water; but he seems pleased with his role as first mate.

"Wow. You aren't kidding. It really is a mess."

"Well, only a finish carpenter would say that."

Lou Winters stands on the other side of the boat. He is wearing jeans and cowboy boots, a long-sleeved Western shirt, and a Stetson hat, whereas I am in shorts and a sweatshirt, sneakers.

"Hey, Al."

"Hey, Lou."

And we are both smiling.

"I got your letter."

"Yeah, I could have texted or sent an e-mail, messaged you on Facebook; but what can I say? I like to communicate the old-fashioned way."

"It was a nice letter."

"Maybe your daughter explained that I'm good with words."

"She did."

"And did she come along with you?"

He shakes his head, looks out across the water.

"She's in school. Going to be a chef, if you can believe that."

"I can believe that."

"She's found a suitor."

"So I heard."

"Good Texas boy, wrangles and rides."

"A cowboy."

He nods. "You don't have anything against us, do you?"

I keep pulling the rope through my hand, trying to tie a good knot. "Not if they don't mind spending time on a boat."

"We adapt."

There is a pause.

"I hear the sky is as full and clear over the ocean as it is over the grand prairie."

"I've heard that, too," I reply.

"Dillon stops by on his cross-country drops, eats a meal. He loves trucking."

"Cool," I say, making Lou laugh.

He watches me. "You need help?"

"With the knot or with the whole thing?"

"Both, I guess. Maybe my daughter told you I was good with ropes."

"In fact, she did."

I put down the great knot experiment.

"It might take a while," I tell him, looking around my boat.

He shrugs, sticks his hands in his pockets. "I understood your invitation. I have time."

"I don't know how it's going to go. I'm pretty new at this."

"We'll learn as we go, how about that?"

"Perfect," I respond.

"Okay, then," he says.

"Okay."

And I stand as he walks toward me, the water around us crystal blue and the sun bright and full against his back.

Questions for Discussion

1. Al's life is changed by what she finds in a storage building. She decides to make this journey because of the discovery of the box of ashes. What do you think this box and these remains really mean to her?

2. This is a story of a great adventure, a long and life-changing road trip. Have you ever taken one of those? What was your trip like? What was the impetus for taking it, and how did it change you?

3. A truly good story takes the main character from one place to another in terms of development. Where did Al start at the beginning of this book? Where does she end up?

4. What does Blossom bring to Al's life? How does she help her to make the changes she makes? How does she become Al's teacher in learning to travel light?

5. What is the role of music in this story? What do you think it means to Al to start the trip listening to a song her mother used to sing? How does music define this trip? How does music define your life?

6. When the story begins, what is the relation-ship Al has with her sister? Does it change? If so, how?

7. Why do you think Al became a journalist? How has that profession served her prior to the point she makes this trip? What profes-sion do you think she might try next?

8. Why do you think Al is drawn to Roger Hart? Does she see herself in his story?

9. What role does Georgia, the hospice nurse, play in Al's development? What does she teach her about life and death?

10. What does traveling light mean to you? Does this story encourage or inspire you to let go of anything weighing you down? Was there a *script* handed down to you?

11. What does the boat mean to Al? Why do you think she is drawn to that kind of life?

12. Casserole, Blossom, and Dillon take this trip with Al. They are her traveling companions. Do you have traveling companions? How did they become your companions? What does traveling teach us about the choices we make in life?

About the Author

Lynne Branard is the author of *The Art of Arranging Flowers*. As Lynne Hinton, she is the *New York Times* bestselling author of more than a dozen books, including *Friendship Cake, Pie Town*, and *Welcome Back to Pie Town*. Visit her online at lynnebranard.com.

Center Point Large Print
600 Brooks Road / PO Box 1
Thorndike, ME 04986-0001 USA

(207) 568-3717

US & Canada:
1 800 929-9108
www.centerpointlargeprint.com